KU-468-476

FLIRTING WITH DESTINY

A First World War saga from a much-loved author

Summer, 1914. As the storm clouds gather over Europe, four privileged young women prepare to leave school and embark on adult life. But for Louise, Imogen, Cora and Miranda, the outbreak of war will change everything. Instead of foreign holidays and glamorous parties, leading to marriage and babies, they must learn to adjust to a new and very different world. The difficult years ahead test their characters to the full, and strain their once-strong friendship...

A Selection of Recent Titles by Sara Hylton
available from Severn House

THE LEGACY OF ANGER
TOO MANY YESTERDAYS

TELFORD & WREKIN LIBRARIES	
Bertrams	12/03/2012
HIS	£19.99

FLIRTING WITH DESTINY

Sara Hylton

Severn House Large Print
London & New York

This first large print edition published 2012
in Great Britain and the USA by
SEVERN HOUSE PUBLISHERS LTD of
9-15 High Street, Sutton, Surrey, SM1 1DF.
First world regular print edition published 2010 by
Severn House Publishers Ltd., London and New York.

Copyright © 2010 by Sara Hylton.

All rights reserved.
The moral right of the author has been asserted.

British Library Cataloguing in Publication Data

Hylton, Sara.
    Flirting with destiny.
    1. World War, 1914-1918--Social aspects--Fiction.
    2. World War, 1914-1918--Women--Fiction. 3. Historical
    fiction. 4. Large type books.
    I. Title
    823.9'2-dc23

    ISBN-13: 978-0-7278-9824-1

Except where actual historical events and characters are being
described for the storyline of this novel, all situations in this
publication are fictitious and any resemblance to living persons is
purely coincidental.

Severn House Publishers support The Forest Stewardship Council
[FSC], the leading international forest certification organisation. All
our titles that are printed on Greenpeace-approved FSC-certified
paper carry the FSC logo.

Printed and bound in Great Britain by the
MPG Books Group, Bodmin, Cornwall.

One

It should have been the happiest day in the school year, the end of the 1914 summer term with six weeks of sun and sea, lakes and mountains, and what passed as frivolity or culture, to follow.

Instead the clouds of war loomed over a fearful Europe and promised joy had become doubts and uncertainties.

Headmistress Miss Emily Nelson meticulously laid tissue paper in the folds of the skirt before placing it in her suitcase. It was the last one, and she stared down gloomily at the bulging contents.

She closed the suitcase quickly and placed it behind the cupboard in her study. She really hadn't intended to pack so many things, but then she'd packed for the holiday that might have been rather than the replacement forced upon her.

She and her sister Rose had planned it all so carefully: the peace and beauty of Tuscany, followed by Rome and the Bay of Naples. Six weeks of glorious sunshine and history. She'd promised herself that she would paint in Rome, sitting with other like-minded people in sunlit

5

piazzas overshadowed by towering campaniles. Instead was the prospect of the South Coast and Wales. Even though the weather could be unpredictable, their disappointment was inevitable, but there were sterner problems to be faced than the loss of a holiday in Italy.

From outside her window she could hear laughter and girls' voices, young girls who had looked forward to so much and were having to settle for something else. A sharp tap on her door announced the arrival of her maid, Edith, carrying a tray on which rested her usual afternoon cup of tea and a plate of biscuits.

Emily smiled, saying, 'I'm a bit cluttered up, Edith. Can you find room for the tray on that small table over there?'

'Oh yes, Miss Nelson. Shall I pour it for you?'

'Please, Edith.'

'It looks like we're in for some nice weather, miss. I do 'ope so.'

'Are you off on holiday soon, Edith?'

'Well, I'm goin' with my Mam to Brixham. We allus goes there, even when my dad was alive.'

'Then I might see you, Edith. My sister and I are spending a few weeks in Devon this year.'

'But don't ye allus go abroad, miss? I thought you allus went to Italy.'

'But not this year, Edith. The war news from Europe is very troubling.'

'But surely it can't be botherin' us, miss?'

'We'll have to wait and see, Edith. I hope not.'

Edith's face wore a look of utter confusion.

6

She was a nice country girl with little knowledge of the problems the war might bring, and Emily decided now was not the the time to burden her with them.

'Have you taken tea in to Miss Falshaw?' Emily asked her.

'Not yet, miss. I allus brings yours in first.'

'Then would you mind serving her tea in here with mine, and perhaps you'll ask her to call in to see me.'

'Oh yes, miss. Right away.'

Jane Falshaw was her deputy headmistress, and they'd been friends for a great many years. Jane was cheerful and down to earth; she felt she needed somebody like Jane to make her see that a lost holiday in Italy was not the end of the world. Indeed the first thing Jane said when she entered was, 'I see you're all packed, Emily, but nothing's quite the same, is it?'

'No. The news from abroad is terrible! I can't believe that last year it was all so wonderful. What will you do? At least you've got the horses.'

She looked at Jane in sudden consternation as the tears ran down her face, and Jane said sadly, 'They've taken our horses for the military, Emily, poor beautiful things bred for life on the fells, not the horrors of war.'

'Oh Jane, I'm so sorry. Somehow or other I thought it would never happen, that something sane and decent would make everybody and everything come to its senses and we'd wake up to hear that the world was back to normal. But

7

there isn't any normal, is there, Jane?'

'Not any more. I thought, like you did, that it was all a stupid ghastly mistake and it would never happen, then when I heard about the horses I knew it was already too late.'

They stood together, staring through the window at the green lawns and the groups of girls strolling across them. It was a perfect summer's day, warm sunlight and a gentle breeze, but somehow there was a difference from other years when there had been laughter and anticipated joy for the weeks ahead.

Three girls in particular demanded their attention, and Miss Nelson said, 'They should have been looking forward to it so very much – their last day here, and a future filled with promise. What changes will they expect, I wonder?'

'At least their families have money and position. They can still expect more than a great many young girls.'

'But will it be enough, Jane? With their brothers and fathers at war, and all those dashing suitors they'd promised themselves. They're suddenly not there any more.'

'Aren't they a little young to be thinking of marriage?'

'Oh my dear, I listen to their mothers when they bring them here, talking to each other and assessing the potential of each other's sons and already thinking which one of the girls might be right for them one day.'

'And now it can all be changed. Were you ever in love, Emily? You never talk about anybody.'

'I was in love with a boy when I was eighteen. He was our vicar's son; he was sweet and charming. I think he liked me, and I adored him, but then he went out to Africa to work with people who had nothing. He was happy, and he sent me long enthusiastic letters, but he died of malaria at just twenty-four.'

'Oh Emily, that's terrible. And there's been nobody else since him?'

'No. I wanted to teach, and my parents encouraged me. I was so happy to come here, and eventually to become the headmistress. It was a wonderful achievement; it took the place of so many other things.'

'You mean it's been enough?'

Emily's smile was sad before she said, 'And what about you, Jane? You seldom talk about yourself.'

'Well, there was no man who went out to Africa and died there! There's John McTavish, who's been in love with me for years, but I've never been in love with *him*. He's a good man, he'd have been a good husband, but I didn't want him, so we're just friends.'

'Will you see him during the holiday?'

'Oh yes, he doesn't give up. My parents despaired of me, said he was right for me. A landowner with a lovely old house and enough money to keep us in affluence. He's never looked at anybody else, and the entire village thinks I'm mad to keep him at arm's length.'

Emily laughed. 'Don't you really think it could be better than trying to install education

9

and a sense of decorum into young heads who don't always listen?'

Jane didn't answer, but after a few minute she said, 'What about those four? What is their future going to be?'

Four girls were running across the lawns, occasionally stopping to chatter, and then one of them would run off again, chased by the others.

Emily said dryly, 'I can only think that the next few months and years will be a great disappointment to them. Tomorrow their parents will be arriving to take them home. I doubt if their lives will be all they've longed for.'

'Or even their holidays.'

'No. And what of the right sort of suitors, with money, position and background? Most of those young men will be in uniform; what will the war do to them?'

'The war won't last forever, Emily.'

'And it isn't inconceivable that we could lose it. But even if we win, so many of those young men could die or be injured. So many changes are inevitable.'

'It seems so incongruous that the assassination of an Austrian Prince in a faraway country is dragging us into a war. So many of the girls have asked questions about things they don't understand, and it seems as though history has been suddenly thrust upon them,' Jane said. She stared dismally through the window at the four girls running towards the river bank. How could any of them think about war on a sunny afternoon at the end of July?

'I taught them for History, but none of them were what you'd call overbright. They were nice girls, intelligent, but hardly academic,' Jane added.

'They didn't need to be.'

'So what were they going to do?'

'I spoke to all their parents when they first came here; their lives were pretty well planned. What jobs are girls doing nowadays? Nursing, secretarial work, shop work ... This is still very much a man's world. The girls who come here are from monied families, though. They are not looking to work, only to marry well.'

Jane nodded. 'I suppose we were lucky to get into teaching. We never had a mountain of money, but we did have brains, Emily.'

Emily laughed. 'I hope that one day girls will aspire to greater things. Maybe the war will change things.'

'Don't tell me we need a *war* to change things!'

'Well, I do think that instead of the balls and garden parties those four were anticipating, something else will be found for them.'

'And what might that be?'

'I don't know, dear, but I wish I could hear their conversation.'

She would not have been surprised though, if she'd been an eavesdropper on that warm summer afternoon.

The four girls were now sitting on a bank overlooking the river, where younger girls were laughing and paddling in the water. They were

11

children from the nearby village, and Louise Maxton said, 'What are they doing here? I thought we'd have the bank to ourselves.'

'We can tell them to go,' Cora Hambleton said.

'And get bombarded with a lot of cheek? Miss Nelson said we must never tangle with the local children.'

Imogen Clarkson had walked on along the river bank, and Cora said, 'Why is she looking so miserable? It's the same for all of us.'

'It's worse for me,' Miranda Reed-Blyton said feelingly. 'My brother's had to go to join his regiment, and we should have been going to stay with Aunt Josie in Deauville.'

'Do you remember last year?' Cora said. 'We were all so envious of the girls who were leaving. We had another year to go, and now just think about it! There's a stupid unnecessary war, and we have nothing to look forward to.'

'Mother says half of our house will be turned into a nursing home, 'Cora said dismally. 'She says we'll probably spend all our time rolling bandages and knitting socks for wounded heroes. What sort of life is that going to be?'

'Our butler says it won't last long. By the time the summer is over, it'll be the end of the war,' Miranda said.

'What does he know about it?'

'Well, he was in the army. He was my father's batman. He was probably just trying to cheer us up though.'

'Imogen, come over here,' Cora called out.

12

'We're just as fed up with things as you are.'

Imogen strolled back to them and sat on the grass. She stared at the deeply worried faces round her, and Cora said, 'What's it going to be like in Derbyshire? Surely it's all country up there. You'll have your horses, and what about the boy you used to go riding with?'

'He's in the Territorials, and he's probably already been called up.'

'So have a great many more,' Cora said.

'I know, but he's only eighteen.'

'Like so many more,' Cora persisted. 'You're very quiet, Louise. What's going to change for you?'

Louise sat hugging her knees, an impish smile on her face, and the others waited in anticipation. Louise Maxton could always be relied upon to produce something provocative that none of the others had thought of. This time she didn't disappoint them.

'Well, I wasn't contemplating marriage to the *first* boy who asked me. I've no doubt my mother's lined up a few of them for my inspection.'

'Who, for instance?' Miranda demanded.

'Oh you know, boys with prospects. The right sort of background and lots of money. I've met a good many of them, and I wasn't impressed.'

'You're only seventeen,' Cora said.

'I know, but seventeen's when we begin looking, isn't it? Too soon to see disaster, too young to be in love with love. I'll be happy to wait until I'm thirty.'

'Thirty!' they cried in unison.

'I'll have got some sense by that time, and I'll have played the field.'

'And there probably won't be anybody left for you to marry,' Miranda said.

'So you agree that we all go to the right functions to meet the right sort of men, then we settle down to have children and live married life while *real* life escapes out of the window?'

'I can't believe that you're so shallow,' Cora said.

'Well, Imogen hasn't said anything. Perhaps she agrees with me? She's always the dark horse.'

'She's trying to shock you,' Imogen said. 'I think none of us can really know what's going to happen. Perhaps I'll go into nursing; the hospitals will need us. My father told us so many terrible stories about the Sudan, and this could be even worse.'

'But nursing, Imogen! Gracious, I could never be a nurse, all that blood and misery, and washing out bedpans, and what would any of us know about nursing, anyway?'

'Somebody's going to have to do it,' Imogen insisted.

'But not me,' Miranda said.

'If half of our house gets taken over, then I'll do what I can to help,' Cora said.

'Such as what?'

'I can chat to the officers, write letters for them, even read to them, but that's about it. What are you prepared to do, Louise?'

14

'Wait until they've recovered and then dance with them, flirt with them, make love to them. Far more beneficial than *reading* to them.'

'Your mother would be horrified if she could hear you going on about such things,' Miranda said. 'You're just trying to be funny.'

'And none of you really know my mother.'

'What do you mean by that?'

'My mother's pretty and flighty. She married at eighteen, and she's lived like a caged bird. I don't intend to live like her.'

'But she's a baronet's wife. She's awfully grand and very circumspect.'

Louise laughed. 'And my father's twenty-five years older than she is, and all he talks about is politics, money and horse racing. He's boring and pompous.'

'But surely your mother loves him,' Imogen said softly. Louise's expression was entirely cynical as she said, 'Maybe she's like me and doesn't know what love is. If she's in love with anybody, it's Martin Broughton.'

'Who is he?'

'Our Member of Parliament. He comes for dinner and they talk politics, then Father disappears into his study with a hot toddy and Martin and Mother are left together. They soon get rid of me when I'm there; when I'm not, it's no problem.'

'Don't you mind?'

'Of course not. But I'll tell you one thing! I'm not going to be married off to a man of thirty-something when I'm still only eighteen, and if

15

you've any sense you won't either.'

'I shall marry when I'm twenty,' Cora said firmly.

'And so shall I,' Miranda said. 'I'll probably marry Cora's brother, Cedric, and she'll marry my brother.'

Louise dissolved into laughter, and Cora said angrily, 'You needn't smirk. It's all perfectly sensible.'

'And terribly boring,' Louise said.

Imogen was quick to say, 'And none of us really know if the war is going to alter everything. There's nobody planned for me, I'm glad to say.'

'But isn't it far better than marrying some stranger and not really knowing his family or anything about him?'

'Perhaps not knowing could be an enjoyable challenge.'

'Well, it's not for us, is it, Cora? I know *you* don't agree with us, Louise.'

'Gracious no. By the time I'm thirty I'll have gone through the gamut of men and their life stories.'

'You're still just trying to shock us,' Miranda said testily. 'You'd shock my mother, but not us. What's everybody wearing for dinner this evening?'

'Oh heavens, yes. Do you remember last year when we were all envying the girls who were leaving for good? They were having a very formal dinner with the staff, while we had the usual in the dining room much earlier. Do you remember what they were wearing? All frills and flounces and high heels!'

'Well, I'm wearing the dress mother bought for me in Paris. She should have let *me* choose it. It's pink and I hate it,' Cora said.

'I'm wearing white,' Louise said. 'It's supposed to be pure and virginal, and I'm anything but that.'

'You're not virginal?' Miranda cried. 'Don't tell us it's happened already!'

Louise laughed, and Imogen said, 'She's trying to shock us again. I'm wearing my usual blue. It seems I never wear anything else, outside school garb.'

'Oh, I do wish those children would go away,' Cora complained. 'I wonder if they have any school functions? I don't suppose so.'

'My mother's going to make it her business to talk to Miss Nelson tomorrow, I know she is. I'd like to be a fly on the wall,' Imogen said.

'What will she talk to her about?' Louise asked.

'My progress, my expectations. She wanted to send me to some foreign place to finish me off. Now it won't be possible and I'm not sorry.'

'*I'm* sorry,' Miranda said. 'My sister Jean went to some place, near Interlaken. She said they had the most gorgeous men teaching them how to ski and how to dance. Frenchmen and Austrians and Germans.'

'And this year they'll all be shooting at one another,' Louise said feelingly.

'Oh Lord, yes. Here come the Mallondon

17

twins and Jenny Stafford. Why don't we all walk across the bridge before we go back to the school?'

Together with the three girls who had joined them, they sauntered towards the bridge, and the children playing near the river treated them to shrill screams of laughter.

Two

The farewell dinner party for the girls who were leaving the following day was going reasonably well, but there were subtle differences to the usual event. In other years the girls had had wonderful expectations, sureties they could rely on, but not this year. Looking round the room at the seventeen-year-old girls in their pretty dresses – girls on the verge of adult life with expectations of wonderful things – Emily thought that although they smiled and chattered, something was missing. So many of them were trying too hard to be carefree and joyous, while others were finding it difficult to hide the tension inside.

Emily looked into the eyes of Louise Maxton and was immediately aware of an amused cynicism.

There had been girls in this year group who she could instantly relate to – Imogen Clarkson had been one of them, with her pretty gentle confidence – but Louise had seemed too mature almost from the first day she had arrived, when her parents had handed her over with charming courtesy: her mother beautiful and vaguely aloof, her father distant and correct. Emily had done her best with all her pupils, but the uncertainty about Louise persisted. The girl returning to her parents in the morning was beautiful and frivolous, but did anybody really *know* Louise? Sitting next to Louise, Cora Hambleton was doing most of the talking, but Emily doubted if she was even listening. The smile on her face made her seem far away from the evening's event and those around her.

Emily gave her usual farewell speech, filled with advice and hopes for their future, but if and how the girls would respond was in the lap of the gods.

After the meal, the girls gathered together in little groups, and as Emily circulated amongst them she became dismally aware that behind the laughter and companionship there was fear, and a sad feeling that life had somehow let them down.

She joined Miranda Reed-Blyton, who stood alone looking through the window, and asked gently, 'Have you enjoyed the evening, Miranda?'

Miranda smiled. 'Oh yes, Miss Nelson, it's been very nice.'

So banal, so terribly trite, when there were so many things to be said.

19

'And are you looking forward to going home? What sort of holidays are planned for you?'

'I don't know. My mother is coming for me, but until I see her I have no idea what we're doing this year.'

'I know, it's very difficult.'

'But don't you go to Italy, Miss Nelson? You talked to us about Italy last year.'

'Yes. I was looking forward to it but we've had to cancel. It's all very uncertain this year.'

'Do you really think there'll be a war?'

'I don't see how we can avoid it. Twelve months ago I hoped it would never come to this, but now I think it's inevitable.'

'And all those boys will be called up. Instead of dancing with us, they'll be fighting the Germans.'

'It won't last forever, Miranda.'

'I know, but so many of them won't come back, will they?'

'Wasn't your father an army man?'

'A brigadier, and my two brothers are Territorials. Oh, I hate that this world can even *think* about wars.'

Emily patted her arm gently and thought it was time to move on.

Louise Maxton was entertaining a group of girls, and somehow their laughter seemed a little incongruous when so many of their thoughts were dismal. Emily joined them, saying, 'At least you seem happy enough, Louise. It's evident the war news hasn't made you too miserable. It's good of you to make an effort to cheer us all up.'

'We can't really do anything about things if we go on looking miserable, can we, Miss Nelson? I'm not going to let it get me down. Why should I?'

'Why indeed. And what are you promising yourself, Louise?'

'Oh, dancing and boys. Parties and boys. Hunting and boys! There might not be anything else left.'

'And the boys might be a little thin on the ground, dear.'

'Not all the time, I'm sure. Don't they get leave, and I'll be here to cheer them up. I only have one brother, but my friends have brothers, and I'm ready to play the field!'

Emily smiled and moved away. Louise was outrageous, but at least she had succeeeded in bringing smiles to a few faces.

Louise and her closest friends were the last to leave the party, and when they had done so Jane said feelingly, 'It's been better than I expected, Emily. Don't you think so too?'

'Perhaps. Some of them made an effort.'

'Particularly Louise.'

'Well yes. I'm not very sure about that girl.'

'Not the material you hoped to cultivate, dear, I know what you mean. I still have some packing to do, so I think I'll leave you to see everybody off to bed. See you in the morning.'

It was midnight when Emily finally put the light out in her bedroom and, pulling back the drapes from the window, she looked out at the

21

paths and grounds, shimmering under a full moon. There would be no Italy, but there was all this to come back to. In September the old girls would have gone and there would be a new contingent arriving. New girls with new expectations: new faces believing in a future, even when they were surrounded by uncertainties. She wouldn't let them down.

Imogen drew back the curtains in the room she shared with the three others, and Cora said sharply, 'Oh goodness, what time is it?'

'Almost eight o'clock. Time to get up,' Imogen answered.

They were all wide awake by now, but it was Louise who said, 'Oh gracious, I wonder who'll be coming for me? Not my father, I hope.'

'Why not your father?' Cora demanded.

'Because I never know what to talk to him about.'

'Tell him about the dinner last night. Surely he'll be interested in that.'

'Of course he won't. He only talks about politics and money. They're the only things he's interested in.'

'How terribly boring,' Miranda said.

'Didn't I just say so? Mother's not much better.'

'Does she talk about politics and money?'

Louise laughed. 'No, she talks about the latest shows in town and who she went with.'

'Well, that should interest you.'

'Not when she's been and I haven't.'

'I hate hearing you talk about your parents like that,' Imogen said softly.

'I know you do. That's why I do it.'

'We go on and on about *our* parents,' Cora said, 'but you hardly ever talk about yours, Imogen.'

Louise laughed. 'Was your father a highwayman and your mother a courtesan? Why don't you surprise us.'

'Well, since we're not likely to meet again, or at least in the foreseeable future, I can tell you that my father was an army officer serving in the Sudan, engaged to be married to a girl he'd known since they were children, a girl who his parents thought eminently suitable.'

'Your mother?' Cora said.

'No. Before he could come home he got malaria and was in hospital in Khartoum. My mother was his nurse. They fell in love, and when he came home it was to tell his fiancée that he was in love with somebody else.'

'Gracious me, how did the family take it?'

'They didn't. They never accepted my mother, and he never saw any of them again. They went to live in Derbyshire, and he worked on a farm doing things he'd once seen other people doing for a living, and mother continued with her nursing. The man he worked for was a bachelor, he took to my father, and when he died he left the farm and the land to him!'

'You mean they're still there?' Miranda asked.

'Yes. They've made a great success of it. They breed Herefords, and they're well respected in the village they live in. My mother's a magistrate, and I shall be happy to go back there until I know what life has for me.'

There was much doubt on the faces of her companions, and smiling, Imogen said, 'Well now you know all about me, isn't it time we went down for breakfast?'

'Heavens, I'm not ready,' Cora said quickly.

'I am,' Louise said. 'I'll come with you.'

'You put the cat among the pigeons,' Louise said, smiling, as they walked.

'Yes, I know! You can understand why I've said very little about my upbringing before.'

'Well, I think it's terribly romantic.'

They reached the dining hall where most of the pupils and staff had assembled, and it was somewhat later by the time Cora and Miranda arrived, to receive a look of admonishment from Miss Nelson, who was waiting to say morning prayers.

The hall was already filled with suitcases brought down by the porters and Cora said, 'What are we going to do until our parents arrive?'

Her question was answered by Miss Nelson, who advised them to wait downstairs, not to wander outside or go up to their rooms which were already being swept and dusted by the cleaning staff.

The four friends found a table in front of the window so that they could look down the long drive towards the gates, and they were soon rewarded by the sight of cars beginning to arrive.

Miss Nelson returned to her study for her first visitor, ready for the parents' usual questions on how their daughters had progressed, and doubting that her answers always produced the replies they waited for.

An hour later she was facing Mrs Reed-Blyton, a somewhat large lady wearing a large black straw hat and a short black and white jacket over a black skirt.

'This is all so terrible,' Mrs Reed-Blyton was saying. 'We were really looking forward to visiting my sister in France, and we've had such marvellous reports of the finishing school in Switzerland. Now it's all gone by the board.'

'I know, the disappointment is quite terrible. It will be a colder, crueller world for a time, but we shall survive it and perhaps even feel stronger when it's all over.'

'Stronger! Oh, I'm not sure about that. Those girls were looking forward to spending time on the ski slopes, to music and dancing, and then to return home to a galaxy of suitable young men. Those boys will be in the services now, and how can they be expected to tie themselves down when they may not even have a future?'

'It could well be that they will go to war as boys and return as men.'

'Really, Miss Nelson, I wish I had your confidence.'

'Did your husband bring you today, Mrs Reed-Blyton?'

'Heavens no, he's no time for anything at the

moment. He's a politician, tied up with war news in the House every day, so I seldom see him. No, my cousin brought me. He lives quite close to us. He's a bachelor, with too much money and time on this hands. He should be doing something for the war effort, but he's not army material.'

'Why is that?'

'Dodgy health, my dear. But it's never stopped him drinking or hunting, and he'll be out there trying to charm those young girls right now.'

Miss Nelson smiled and consulted her watch so that her companion said quickly, 'It is time to leave you, Miss Nelson. Thank you so much for all you've been able to achieve. I think Miranda's been very happy at this school. She's made friends, particulary with Cora Hambleton. I was at school with her mother, you know.'

'So you know the family quite well?'

'Very well. She has one very nice son, Cedric. Both his mother and I have great expectations that one day he and Miranda might see their future together.'

'Isn't she a little young to be thinking in that way? There are an awful lot of boys out there.'

'But are they suitable, Miss Nelson? I feel that Cedric would be. He's twenty. Oh, I wasn't thinking about tomorrow, or even next week. In about five years, I thought.' She smiled and got to her feet, then reaching out to grasp Miss Nelson's hand she said, 'Well, goodbye, Miss Nelson, I do wish the school continuing success.'

A few minutes later Emily's secretary announced that Baroness Maxton was waiting to see her, rather impatiently.

Isobel Maxton was as different from her last visitor as chalk and cheese. She was elegant and slender and wearing a dress that would have not looked out of place in the royal enclosure at Ascot. Blonde and pretty, she sat opposite Emily before taking off her hat and placing the pink confection on the corner of the desk.

'I thought Mrs Reed-Blyton was here for the rest of the day,' she said with a smile. 'I'm sorry to be a nuisance, but I have some friends in the area and promised to call on them, to show Louise off I thought.'

'Then we mustn't detain you, Lady Maxton. I think Louise will be all ready to leave with you.'

'And do you think my daughter merits the considerable sum we've spent on her education, Miss Nelson?'

It was a question Emily wasn't prepared for, and her initial thought was how to answer it. Louise was witty and intelligent, but she was not a keen learner. Louise liked the subjects that to some might have seemed frivolous, and even if she had been academic, it was unlikely they would have steered her into a profession. She would never have liked to be a teacher, or any of the few jobs open to women, and looking at the woman sitting opposite Emily could see Louise in ten years time: beautiful and amusing, married to some rich man, and possibly with a string of romances behind her.

Baroness Maxton read her thoughts well. 'My daughter resembles me, Miss Nelson. I hated school, but I made myself put up with it because it prepared me for what I wanted later: some rich man, money, a stately home and a lifestyle that lived up to it. Is my daughter like me, or has she suddenly become the bluestocking I never was?'

Emily liked this woman, but how could she answer her? Louise had been her pupil for twelve years. Girls like Louise had had their destinies planned for them almost from the cradle.

Picking up her hat, the Baroness rose to her feet, and with a sweet smile said, 'I feel I might have shocked you by my candour, Miss Nelson, but don't worry about Louise, you've done your best with her intellect. I've set her the sort of example I'm capable of, but only she will decide which path she wishes to follow. Most people will think yours is more admirable, but knowing Louise she'll probably opt for the more amusing one.'

Over an hour later, a tall silver-haired man was ushered into the study, and he introduced himself with an extended hand as John Clarkson, Imogen's father.

'I'm sorry my wife wasn't able to come,' he said. 'She is in court today, something she could not get out of.'

'She's a magistrate?'

'Yes, and very conscientious.'

'You've had quite a long journey, Mr Clarkson.'

28

'Yes, but on a very nice day.'

'Excellent for the start of the holidays, and I can tell you that we're very sorry to be losing Imogen. She's been an excellent pupil and is a delightful girl.'

'I'm so glad. But now what? We live in the country, surrounded by acres of green fields and cattle. Will she be happy to exchange this place for the simplicity of home?'

'The companionship of girls, do you mean, Mr Clarkson? Girls who had so many expectations and talked incessantly about them.'

'I know. Finishing school and balls, the theatres, and an endless stream of young men. I was brought up to that, Miss Nelson. Perhaps I'm unique, but I haven't missed it.'

'Have you thought what you will put in its place for Imogen?'

'Not yet, but we shall. I can promise you, Miss Nelson, that Imogen will discover the future she wants. No doubt in the months to come she will keep you informed; I will see that she does.'

'Oh yes, Mr Clarkson, I do hope so. Some of the girls don't bother – they finish with school and forget all about us.'

Mrs Hambleton was the last parent to arrive. She was accompanied by an elderly lady wearing deepest mourning, and Miss Nelson was immediately informed that she was Cora's Great Aunt, a recently bereaved widow.

Miss Nelson offered her condolences, which the old lady had difficulty in hearing, and Mrs Hambleton said quickly, 'My aunt is staying with me at the moment, Miss Nelson, so I felt I had to bring her.'

'Of course, Mrs Hambleton.'

'I was hoping to see Mrs Reed-Blyton. I suppose she came early.'

'Actually, she did, very early.'

'Oh well, no doubt we'll meet very soon at some function or other.'

'You meet quite often then?'

'Of course. Her son will be home on leave for a few days later in the month. He's been called into the army, you know, and I do want he and Cora to get really acquainted before he has to go back to his regiment.'

'The war news is very sad, Mrs Hambleton.'

'Indeed, but Peter was in an officer training unit. He expected to be called up. He will eventually receive a very good commission.'

'Yes, of course.'

'What commission?' the old lady mumbled.

'Nothing, Auntie, just something we were talking about.'

'I can't hear you!'

'No, dear. We're going to talk about Cora.'

'I thought we'd come to take her home.'

'We have, just as soon as we're ready.'

Thanks to the old lady's mutterings, talk about Cora was very brief, and Miss Nelson soon accompanied them into the school hall where Cora waited disconsolately near the large window, alone except for several staff members who were busily packing up.

Emily said her farewell to Cora, embracing

30

her gently and with every good wish for her future. She was surprised to find tears in the girl's eyes, and Cora said hastily, 'I'm sorry I'm leaving, Miss Nelson. I've loved being here.'

Emily stood at the window to watch them walk towards the large car where a driver stood to open the doors for them.

She wasn't sure how she believed Cora's last words. How many insincerities had been spoken, how many tears shed, and what joys and expectations were likely to be fulfilled?

Ah well, tomorrow on the south coast of England she would think about what might have been. The sunshine of Italy and the start of a new term, then with a degree of sadness she thought about the girls who would not be coming back.

Three

Conversation between Louise and her mother had never been easy, and today her mother sat back in the huge car taking them back to the city largely silent, her beautiful face thoughtful. Making an effort, at last she said, 'Your headmistress was very nice, Louise, there wasn't much for her to say.'

'Mother, we are going to Trouville, aren't we? You did promise.'

'It's impossible, darling, not with war being declared any day now.'

'But not in Trouville, surely? There won't be war in *Trouville*.'

Lady Maxton looked at her daughter impatiently. 'Louise, haven't you been told anything about what will happen when we go to war? France and England will be in it together. Trouville happens to be in France. What has that education taught you? Or weren't you paying attention.'

Louise bit her lip and shrank back in her corner. Of course she knew that Trouville was in France, but surely the war couldn't affect it so soon.

Her mother smiled gently. 'I'm sorry, darling, but there's so much to worry about at the moment; things far more important than the holiday we'd promised ourselves in France. What are your other friends doing?'

'Oh, Imogen's going home to her father's farm in Derbyshire, and the other two were talking about nursing.'

'Nursing?'

'Well, yes, they said much of their houses would be taken over as nursing homes for wounded soldiers.'

'And would nursing appeal to you, dear?'

'No, it would be horrible.'

Her mother didn't speak. Of course it would be horrible to beautiful pampered Louise whose thoughts had been miles away from the sordid effects of war. Louise had promised herself all the joys and excitement her father's money had led her to believe would be hers. She understood her disappointment – wasn't it reflected in her own?

They drove in silence for several miles, and it was only when the car left the main road that Louise said, 'Mother, where are we going? We've left the London Road.'

'I know, dear. I thought we'd call and see your aunts. I see them so seldom, and since we're so near I feel we should make the effort.'

Louise frowned. Why should they be bothering with aunts Pheobe and Beatrice? They were her fathers sisters, and they were sweet and charming, but they were also boring and too fussy. They always remembered her birthday with presents of expensive clothes that she found too boring to wear and were suitable for a woman twice her age.

Their small manor house nestled on the hillside, surrounded by a beech grove, and as soon as they arrived in front of the house the door was opened and the two ladies rushed out with smiling faces and excited words of welcome.

They were ushered into the house, where it was quickly evident they'd been expected, from the table laid out with plates of cakes and sandwiches.

'We've been staring through the window all morning,' Pheobe gushed. 'We were thrilled with your letter, darling, it's so nice of you to visit us, and Louise, you're so grown up and beautiful.'

Louise smiled. 'Thank you, Aunt Pheobe. My schooldays are over.'

'We know, dear, but don't worry about not going to finishing school in Switzerland. Maurice says the war will be over in weeks, and Switzerland will not go away.'

'Who is Maurice, Aunt Beatrice?'

'He drives us about all over the place. Not for us, those big smelly cars.'

'Do you still have that carriage then?'

'Well, of course, dear. We wouldn't part with it, or dear old Molly, our faithful horse. I believe the army are taking horses, but they won't want Molly, she's far too old.'

'Do come and sit at the table and have something to eat. You must have left London quite early, Isobel.'

'Well, yes, and I have to get back mid-afternoon. We have a function to go to this evening: something to do with the war effort.'

'Of course, dear. I expect Henry is terribly involved.'

'Yes he is.'

Throughout the meal the old ladies chatted and laughed; they talked about their garden and that instead of flowers they were growing vegetables, and they talked about the vicar and the meetings at the vicarage, where they knitted gloves and scarves and rolled bandages for when they were needed.

Neither Louise nor her mother contributed very much, but it was Isobel who said, ner-

34

vously and in some desperation, 'Henry and I have talked very seriously about this, and have to ask you both an enormous favour. Do please tell me if it isn't convenient, but we shall both understand. Could I possibly leave Louise here with you? So much is going on in London at the moment, and Henry is seldom at home, and I'm here, there and everywhere doing things for the war effort.'

The aunts looked at each other with smiling excited faces while Louise stared at them blankly, at first unable to believe that her mother was urging them to say she could live with them in this old house in a village miles from anywhere.

The aunts were saying they would love to have her, she'd be very happy with them, and her parents could visit as often as they liked. They said that Louise would love it, the gardens and the things to do with the church. She could join the choir and help with the war effort, another pair of hands would be so useful, and the bedroom overlooking the wood was beautiful, with beautiful views, and she could drive the trap and give Molly the excercise she wasn't getting.

Louise stared at her mother with wide incredulous eyes, but her mother was refusing to look at her. She was listening to the aunts enthusing over having Louise live with them. Finally, her mother rose to her feet, saying, 'I've brought some clothes for you, darling. You only have your school things with you, and I felt you should have the others.'

'You had it all planned, Mother.'

'It may not be very long, Louise, before you're back with us in London, but war can be very terrible and none of us really know how we'll be affected. Darling, please make the best of it until we're really sure things are going our way.'

At that moment Louise felt she hated her mother. Of course her mother wouldn't want her in London: she'd interfere too much with the galaxy of men she surrounded herself with, and her father would be so busy that he wouldn't be interested in her mother's activities. She'd be here with the aunts, safe from being a nuisance and secluded from seeing too much.

They all walked to the car with her mother, and if the driver was surprised to see Louise left behind, he did not show it.

The aunts waved enthusiastically, but Louise stood staring after the departing car with a frozen face, until Aunt Pheobe said, 'We know you're upset to see your mother go, darling, but we're so absolutely delighted to have you, dear, and Isobel is doing what she thinks is best for you.'

What was there to do in this house with two elderly ladies for companions? As if the old ladies had heard her misgivings, Beatrice said, 'We get up around nine in the morning, dear, and we go to bed around nine too, but there are books in the bookcase and there's the radio to listen to. You stay up as long as you like, dear. You'll soon get used to things around here.'

They had tea at four in the afternoon that day,

and then the aunts did their embroidery and Louise looked at the books in the bookcase. Hardly her choice, and at half past eight they had cocoa and after kissing her warmly went to bed.

Was this really what she had exchanged school for? The night before there had been four of them, and she had been the one who had entertained the others by her talk of a risky future she had imagined and which her companions had largely frowned upon.

What would they be doing now, those three friends? She had felt sorry for Imogen with her talk of farm animals and country living, but the other two had large homes close to London. Indeed, Cora had talked of the London House, and they both had brothers with men friends.

The news on the radio was all of war – war that was already raging in Eastern Europe, and all too soon the rest of Europe would be involved.

She felt that her mother had betrayed her, but where was her father in all this? Boring everybody at his club, unaware or uncaring that her mother was entertaining other men, and one of them married to Miranda Reed-Blyton's aunt! Cora's mother had once brought her to one of the concerts at the school, and Miranda had told them that her aunt was frightfully aristocratic, married to an Earl and with connections to the Royal family. It would have pleased Louise to have been able to tell her that the Earl was a constant visitor to her home, largely when her father was away, that he was not the sole recipient of her mother's favours and now she wished she had done so.

That first night in her aunts' house was a disaster. There was nothing to do, she hated their books, she was fed up with the radio, and sleep was a long time coming. Tomorrow, she thought, she'd find some way to liven up this sleepy old village and also find what there was on offer in the friendship stakes.

Indeed, it took over a week to familiarize herself with the church choir, the psalms and the hymns were hardly her taste, but it didn't take her long to discover that her aunts had a liking for operetta and kept a hoard of gramophone records of *The Merry Widow* and the like.

Not all the village girls were enthusiastic about church music, and in no time she had them dancing to waltz music and tunes from the London shows which their mothers knew nothing about.

She was quick to find an ally in the church organist, who was nothing loath to play for them in the village hall long after choir practice was over and the vicar had left for home.

Some of the village boys joined them, boys too young to have been called up for military service, but they added to the excitement, and they were indeed fortunate to have got away with it for so long.

It was one evening when she was walking home after a night in the village hall when a young man stepped beside her. He was good looking, but his smile was impudent. He looked vaguely familiar, and after a few moments she said, 'Don't I know you?'

'My father's your aunts' gardener.'

'Of course.'

'Haven't ye seen me in the garden?'

'I may have, I'm not sure.'

'Well, I've seen *you*. You're Miss Louise, aren't you?'

'Yes.'

'Some of the lads are enjoyin' themselves in the village hall. I thought I might go there one night.'

'Really.'

'Well, why not?'

'You're interested in joining the church choir then?'

'Not me. I helps out with the gardens on Sunday, but you're not singin' church music when the sexton and the vicar 'ave gone home.'

'You're very observant.'

'I like the music you're singin' and dancin' to.'

'We all enjoy it, and we don't want all and everybody to know about it. Are you good at keeping secrets?'

'Oh ay. It's all right if I join ye then?'

'What's your name?'

'James Kent, but you can call me Jimmy.'

'And you can call me Miss Louise.'

'Oh, I will, until we get to know each other better. You're the prettiest girl I've ever seen.'

She smiled, and turning away said, 'Goodnight, Jimmy, this is where I leave you.'

39

As she sat up in bed that night drinking her cocoa Louise reflected that life in the country had its compensations. After all, what would she be doing in London under the watchful eye of the housekeeper, with a mother too involved with one man after another and a father who was too occupied with other matters?

The girls she was with in the hall were village girls, most of them had left school at twelve or thirteen, but they had a raw sense of humour and they'd taken to dancing and singing the music she adored with enthusiasm.

She liked a good many of them. She could listen to their absurd stories about what they expected of life, about their innocent flirtations, or about the more exuberant rolls in the hay the bolder girls had experienced with the local lads. Few of them seemed concerned about the war, only that the men would be called up so they needed to take advantage of them before that occurred.

Some of them were seriously interested in some boy or other, but largely they all had parents who instilled in them some sense of decorum and a need to preserve their chastity.

They thought Louise to be somebody special, beautiful and clever, with a good education. Louise did not inform them that her father was a baronet: she preferred to be one of them, rather than some celestial being from another planet, and she found herself wondering how her old school friends might have viewed the situation.

Both Cora and Miranda would have been

quick to assert their superiority, and they would both have viewed Jimmy Kent with distaste as a potential boyfriend.

Was it boredom or resentment that brought out the rebellion in Louise's behaviour? In that community she was made to feel superior, but nothing in her new life obliterated the dreams and desires she had cherished for all too long – of balls and garden parties, of glamorous gowns and sparkling jewels, of handsome young men who would love her until she decided which one she would wish to marry. Now here she was in an old manor house with two elderly ladies, who were kind but hardly company for a young and vital girl. She was expected to be content to roam the fields searching for wild flowers, and her only entertainment singing in the church choir.

Jimmy Kent was hardly the type of young man she had envisaged, but he was young and virile, he thought she was wonderful, and her involvement with him would anger her mother if she ever became aware of him. That counted most, in her confused sense of anger. That her mother had left her with the aunts and disappeared out of her life to pursue her own dubious pleasures in London.

Jimmy Kent was no great lover, certainly not the sort of lover she had desired, but he was enthusiastic, and to lose her virginity to somebody like Jimmy was the only way she had of paying both her mother and the aunts back for agreeing together about how she must spend her life.

41

She had felt a certain pity for Imogen Clarkson, who was asking nothing of life beyond some old farm house in distant Derbyshire, but what about the other two? They would be near London, London and civilization. Even if there was going to be a war, they would be in the centre of things there.

Cora Hambleton stared with amazement at the activity surrounding her home as they approached it slowly to avoid the numerous vehicles parked along the drive. She looked at her mother curiously, and her mother smiled, saying quickly, 'I did tell you that this might happen, Cora. Part of the house is going to be turned into a hospital.'

'But that's horrible, Mother. Which part shall be ours? It'll be so small!'

'It's your father's idea, darling. He wants to be seen doing all he can to aid the war effort, and you have to admit he really can't do more than this.'

'But why are they changing things *now*? We don't even know if there will be war.'

'Oh there will be Cora, any day now. Your father says it's inevitable.'

'Oh, Mother, it's going to be absolutely terrible. I'll bet Louise isn't having to put up with anything like this. She went off with her mother early this morning, and when she came to say goodbye she was saying her mother had such wonderful plans for her.'

'What sort of plans?'

'Well, entertaining the men to balls and banquets.'

'Perhaps you're right, dear. Baroness Maxton can be relied upon to provide entertainment in many directions.'

'She's awfully pretty, Mother.'

'Yes, well, I think that what we're doing here will contrast very favourably with anything the Maxtons can provide.'

'But what about me, Mother? What shall I be expected to do?'

There'll be plenty for you to do, Cora. There will be young men here who have been wounded at the war. You can read to them, write for them, talk to them. I'm sure they'll be sadly in need of company while they're recuperating.'

As Cora followed her mother into the house her face was a mask of disappointment. It surely wasn't meant to be like this? She stared in dismay at the men working on the structural alterations. What were they doing to their beautiful house, cutting it in half?

Seeing her standing with a look of dismay on her face, a man nearby said, 'It'll look quite different when we've finished with it, miss. It's a fine thing you're doing at this time.'

'But our house will be so small!'

'Eh, lass, people have been living in houses ten times smaller than this one for years. This'll still be a very big house. You'll see, when it's all finished.'

'But there isn't a war yet, and we haven't any wounded soldiers.'

'Not yet we don't, but there will be.'

'And where will the nurses and doctors live?'

'Here, love. There'll be plenty of room for them, you'll see.'

'Oh, I wish it was all over and we were back to normal. When the war's over will the house be ours again, or will it always be like this?'

He smiled. How could this rich pampered young girl be expected to understand a world that was changing? So many expectations that needed to be forgotten. What kind of woman would she be when it was all over?

Four

Imogen jumped out of her father's car and ran towards the stables, looking with dismay at old Horace standing alone staring at her. She turned to see her father standing at the gate. His expression was sad, and running towards him she cried, 'Daddy, where's Julius? Where are the other horses?'

'Come into the house, love, we have a lot to tell you.'

'But where are they, Daddy. Why aren't they in the stables?'

'The army have commandeered them for the war. I had no choice, darling, I had to let them go.'

'But what have horses got to do with the war?'

'They are stronger than us, dear. They are needed to pull cannons, carry men, do all the things men cannot do. One day they'll be back: they haven't gone for good.'

'But they're needed here! You need them, and what good is Julius? He's not a shire horse, he's a hunter.'

'And strong, darling. Come inside the house. I hope your mother's arrived home, but if not I'm sure she'll be here presently.'

As she walked with her father towards the house, it seemed that things were much the same: cattle and sheep in the fields, men working there, some of whom waved their hands and raised their caps. Even the house seemed unchanged, and in minutes Nellie was there with a loaded tea tray and a warm smile saying, 'Welcome home, love. Ah, but it's strange to think you'll not be goin' back to school again.'

Nellie embraced her with a warm gentle hug, and her father said quickly, 'Mrs Clarkson not back yet, Nellie?'

'No, she said she'd be late.'

'Well, if she hasn't come back after we've had something to eat we'll go down to collect her. She said she'd get a taxi, but it isn't always convenient.'

Nellie poured tea for them, and they helped themselves to sandwiches and scones. They'd eaten lunch at an inn on their way back, and neither of them were hungry, much to Nellie's disappointment.

45

'Ye should be eatin' something,' she admonished them. 'Ye've had a long journey, and the mistress will have had tea at the court.'

'We'll do full justice to dinner later on,' Mr Clarkson said, and added quietly to Nellie, 'Imogen's upset that Julius has had to go, as well as the other horses. I've told her he's doing his bit for the war effort, something we'll be expected to do any day now.'

As they drove into Matlock to collect her mother, Imogen found herself looking at familiar villages and scenery. Nothing had changed, and yet she knew that things *had* changed; underneath the serenity things were happening that they were powerless to do anything about, and the tears rolled down her face at the thought of that dear beautiful horse she had loved being led away by strangers into a world he didn't know.

As she sat slumped in the seat beside him, her father knew the tortured thoughts she was experiencing, but he had no words to comfort her. How could he tell her that all would be well when none of them knew? When not even the men who were leading them into this war could be sure of its outcome?

But as she sat in the car, waiting until her parents joined her, it seemed to Imogen in those few moments that nothing in this small market town *would* ever change. They were surrounded by the dark Pennine hills she had known and loved all her life. The hills wouldn't change, how could they? When the men came home they would still be here, waiting, part of this land that had endured despite conflict and tragedies.

Her face lit up at the sight of her parents hurrying towards her across the square, and then she was rushing out of the car and into her mother's arms.

'Oh darling, I'm so sorry I couldn't go with your father to meet you, but I had to be in court this morning. Did you have a very wonderful leaving party?' her mother said.

'Yes, it was nice.'

'And are you going to keep in touch with your friends?'

'I hope so, Mother, but we live rather a long way away, don't we?'

'Yes, I suppose we do. And there'll be no Switzerland for them either at the moment?'

'No. I rather think Miranda and Cora were disappointed about that.'

'And Louise?'

'I'm not sure. We never really knew about Louise.'

'We'll have dinner early tonight and then we'll talk about the future, your future, darling, what you're expecting from it.'

'Mother they've taken Julius, I didn't care about Switzerland or all the things they were concerned about. I just wanted to be with Julius here in the Peak District, riding him, meeting people, helping out at the farm. It's never going to be the same without Julius.'

'I know, dear, but think what Julius is going to

do for England if war comes.'

'He could die, Mother.'

'They'll look after him very well, and when the war is over he'll come back like the hero he is. We'll be so proud of him and the other horses, Imogen.'

'Perhaps in the end there won't be a war and the horses will have to be brought back.'

'And that would solve everything, wouldn't it? We should pray for that, darling.'

This was how it had always been at the start of the school holidays, and even now, when there would be no going back, it was exactly the same. The three of them eating dinner in the cosy dining room overlooking the windswept hill leading down to the ravine.

All her favourite dishes were there, and her parents were jovial and light-hearted as always. She listened to them talking about friends and people at the church she knew well, all there was to look forward to at the usual agricultural shows, and then they talked about her school-days and what they had meant to her.

Her friends had gone back to a life that had once been her father's scene, even though it was one he had no regrets about losing, and as she talked about her friends and their matrimonial expectations she was suddenly aware of his cynical expression, and he reached out across the table to take her mother's hand into his own.

'You're going to miss your friends so much, Imogen,' her mother said sadly. 'It's quiet in the country. What can we possibly do in the place of

48

all you had at school?'

'We'll think of something, Mother. To begin with, perhaps I can find something to do at the farm. I'm sure you'll need all the help you can get.'

'Well, we'll think about that tomorrow. What are you thinking of doing tonight?'

'Unpacking my suitcase! It's up there in my bedroom, but what am I going to do with that school uniform? I can't even give it away.'

'I'm sure some good seamstress in the village can use those skirts and blouses to make something smaller for children to wear. I'll come and help you to unpack, dear, then you can challenge your father to a game of cribbage.'

Upstairs, Imogen gazed nostalgically at the pristine uniform laid out on the bed; black stockings and blue skirts, pale blue blouses, and the pretty white dress she had worn for her farewell dinner the evening before. She thought about Louise dancing around in her sparkling white dress, more dramatic than anything any of the other girls had worn, and even when her long silver earrings had been frowned upon she had defiantly worn them, and somehow the white party dresses of the other girls had paled into insignificance.

'And who is Louise intending to marry?' her mother asked gently.

'Oh mother, she used to say the silliest things.'

'Like what?'

'That she didn't intend to marry anybody for years and years.'

49

'And did she mean it, do you think?'

'Knowing Louise, I rather think she did.'

'Does she have brothers and sisters?'

'One brother. He's older than Louise, his name is Andrew. I've never met him.'

'A target for your other two friends, do you think?'

'Perhaps, although Cora and Miranda both have brothers. I rather think they were the targets.'

'But Andrew will be a baronet one day.'

'Yes, of course. Well, they all are in London. I'm sure they'll sort each other out.'

'Did it never worry you, Imogen, listening to their talk about how their lives would resolve? I never met your father's sisters, but just occasionally he's talked about them, cynically. If he hadn't met me, some girl or other had already been earmarked for him.'

'It sounds pretty dreadful, Mother.'

'Perhaps, but it does work in a great many cases, darling, even if it wouldn't have worked for your father.'

'Because he fell in love with you?'

'That amongst other things. He's too independent. He says he prefers to make his own destiny rather than have it planned for him.'

'Perhaps I'm like him. I hope so.'

'I didn't say too much in front of your father, dear, but do you really want to spend the next few years helping out on the farm? It's true a lot of the men will be serving in the forces, but I somehow don't think it's for you, dear. Have you had any thoughts at all about what you want to do with your life?'

'You were a nurse, Mummy. I rather thought that was what I'd like to be.'

'Imogen, I had a good, respectable family, but we didn't have money or great expectations. I had to find a job, and while there are not many things open to girls now, there was even less when I was a girl.'

'But you were happy being a nurse.'

'I had to make the best of it. There were times when I was happy. I had good friends; we had the feeling that we were doing our best, quite often against great adversity.'

'And then you met Daddy.'

'Yes. We loved each other, but I never thought it would last. He was a rich boy from a very upper-crust family, a family who expected great things of him, particularly the right sort of wife.'

'What had she got that you hadn't?'

'Money, the same sort of background.'

'And none of that mattered to Daddy?'

'No, he loved me and refused to conform. At first we were very poor; my family had little money, and your father's family didn't want to know us. You know the rest, darling.'

'But I've got to do *something*. Cora was talking about writing letters, reading books to wounded soldiers after their house has been turned into a hospital, but I want to do more than that. Poor old Julius had no choice, he was taken away, but I do have a choice and I want to be a nurse.'

51

'You'll have to start at the bottom, darling. Being a nurse takes time and learning; you'll need patience and plenty of it.'

'Then who can help me?'

'I can speak to the doctors at the local hospital, find out what openings there might be in Buxton or elsewhere in the area. Is that what you want?'

'No, Mother, if there's going to be a war, wouldn't there be more chance in London?'

'Oh my dear, you're thinking already about the glamour of nursing wounded heroes on the battlefield and failing to see the pitiful tragedy of it all. I have a very good friend in London, however, who is a matron in one of the hospitals there. I can only ask her advice, tell her I have a daughter who sees herself as Florence Nightingale. I served with Mary Stepson for years. She was a good friend, but she was stern and dedicated, not the sort of woman who would leave her career for love and settle down to domesticity in some rural area. Do you want me to contact Mary, Imogen? Or wouldn't you really like to think about it first.'

'No, I don't want to think about it, it's what I want to do. Besides, it's not as if I shan't know people in London. There's my old schoolfriends! I might even find a job in Cora's stately home.'

Her mother smiled. Inwardly she felt her daughter needed to face reality and readjust, but it was something she would have to find out for herself.

In the days that followed, Imogen felt more at peace with herself. She had arrived at a decision regarding her future, and only time would tell if it was the right one.

Several days later she heard from Cora that indeed her home was now largely given over to some sort of convalescent home, and the day after England declared war on Germany, together with France.

There was no going back.

Miranda Reed-Blyton sat on the edge of her sister's bed, watching her select a jacket out of her wardrobe. Jean was pristinely dressed in navy, with a cream silk blouse, and small navy-blue boater on her head. She was older than Miranda by three years, and seeing her sister's evident interest she said, 'Well, what do you think?'

'Not very glamorous. Looks sort of severe to me.'

'It has to be severe. I'm not going to a garden party, it's a suffragette meeting. We have to appear dedicated and certainly not frivolous.'

'Votes for women? You haven't got a chance.'

'How do you know? You've only just left school. You don't know anything about it.'

'I've been at school. I haven't been in Outer Mongolia.'

'Well, what did they teach you about it at school?'

'We heard about it. The teachers discussed it. What do Daddy and Peter think about it?'

'They're both away, but when Daddy was home we didn't discuss it. Mother said it was

53

anathema to him.'

'That's what I mean.'

'Well, I suggest we change the subject. Is that pal of yours still keeping her sights on our dear brother?'

'Of course.'

'And you're still expecting things from her brother. What's his name, by the way?'

'Cedric. He's handsome, charming and one day he'll be a baronet or something grander.' Miranda sighed. 'But he'll go to war, meet another girl and marry her, and where does that leave me?'

'You've read too many silly love stories.'

'It happened to Imogen Clarkson's parents. He didn't marry the girl his family wanted him to marry. In this new world men will be meeting all sorts of girls from all sorts of backgrounds.'

'Like I said, Miranda, you've been reading too many love stories. You could join our movement. We're looking for new recruits.'

'Not likely.'

'Then what *are* you going to do?'

'I'm not sure yet.'

'Well, I'll tell you what mother'll have you doing – knitting socks and rolling bandages. Can you think of anything more boring? What about Louise? What will she be doing?'

Miranda disolved into laughter. 'She's awful, Jean. She doesn't want to get married until she's at least thirty, and she wants to have affairs with a great many men who will all adore her and smother her with jewels.'

'She's in for a period of readjustment.'

'Oh, I don't know. She's very beautiful and she has great style. You should have seen her dress for the end of term party, and the long earrings.'

'Is she here with the family? I saw her mother on Bond Street yesterday, but she was alone.'

'I'm sure Louise is here in London. Her mother came for her very early.'

'Well I'm off, what are you doing with the rest of your day?'

'I'll think of something. Something more interesting than what you're going to do!'

Miranda followed her sister out of the room and watched her tripping lightly down the stairs. What was she going to do with the rest of her afternoon? What was the war going to do to London? Right now the sun was shining on a city where the parks were gay with flowers and children played happily on swings and ran cheerfully around.

It was so quiet in the house. Her mother was out, and she supposed that she too could wander outside and sit in the sunshine. Instead, however, she wandered into the kitchen, where cook was making scones and the housemaids were busy cleaning silver and brassware.

The girls looked up and smiled, and cook said, 'Why, Miss Miranda, it's too nice to be indoors. Why aren't you enjoying the sunshine?'

'I don't know where to go. Mother's out, do you know when she'll be back?'

'I don't rightly know. She's at a meeting of the

Red Cross; very important it is now there's war.'

'How long is it going to last, Cook? What's it all about, anyway?'

'Some trouble abroad. Why we had to be involved in it I really don't know, but we always are, aren't we?'

Miranda perched on a stool at the kitchen table, and Cook said, 'There's orange juice, Miss Miranda, and these scones will soon be cooked.'

'Just the fruit juice, Cook.'

'I can't think things'll be much different despite the war, though Polly here has a boyfriend who's been called up in the army.'

Polly dissolved into tears, and Cook said hastily, 'Now then, Polly, he's not come to any harm, and he's only like a lot of other lads. I suppose not going to Switzerland has upset you, Miss Miranda?'

'I was looking forward to it, we all were. But perhaps the war won't last long and I'll be able to go there later.'

'That's right, Miss Miranda, look on the bright side.'

Five

The church held its usual fair at the end of September, a warm glorious September, when all the village women wore their best dresses, and in spite of the war there were still young men busily helping out before they were called to sterner duties.

Two girls sat on the hillside watching a boy and girl walking up the hill in their direction. The boy had his arm around the girl's waist, and there was a frown of annoyance on the face of one of the girls watching.

The couple passed them and smiled, only to be met with an angry glare.

Louise said, 'She really doesn't like me, and I've tried to be nice to her.'

'Josie doesn't like you because she fancies me,' the boy said.

'You think all the girls fancy you, Jimmy.'

'Well, there's not many of us left, and I'll be gone soon.'

'Was she your girlfriend before you met me?'

'I suppose so. I took her out once or twice, but nothin' serious, not like you and me.'

She laughed. 'Oh Jimmy, we're not serious, we're friends. After the war, hopefully before it's over, I'll be back in London and you'll be back with Josie.'

He took his arm away and looked at her with an angry face. 'Why do you say that?' he demanded. 'We've been seeing each other for over a month now. I know your aunts don't know about us, but me mother knows and even she's told me not to expect too much.'

'Well, you'll be called up soon. None of us can expect much at this particular time.'

'Will you be livin' with your aunts when I get back?'

'I hope not.'

'What do you mean by that?'

'Well, this isn't my home, is it? I live in London. I want to go back there as soon as possible.'

'Then why aren't you there now? Why are you 'ere?'

Louise was getting tired of his questions. He was demanding and cocky, and she didn't have to stand it from a boy she wouldn't have looked at twice in normal circumstances.

Meanwhile, the two girls staring after them were busy speculating on what they seemed to be arguing about.

'They seem to be quarrelling,' Jenny said. 'You'd like that, wouldn't you, Josie?'

'What's she doing wi' Jimmy?' Josie demanded. 'Jimmy Kent's only an odd job man in the garden, so what's she doin' walkin' out with him?'

'It'll all fizzle out when 'e's gone into the

army. He'll be back with you then, Josie.'

'She's always off with 'im as soon as choir practice is over. The vicar doesn't know, nor the organist. They're gettin' away with murder.'

'I don't suppose the old ladies know what's goin' on or they'd 'ave put a stop to it. They'll not want 'er 'avin' anything to do with the likes of Jimmy Kent.'

That was the moment Josie decided something should be done about it, and who better to tell than her mother, who was a pillar of the church? Of course, so were the two old ladies, but only where money was concerned, not for doin' the menial jobs expected of them.

Her mother, however, wasn't at all sure that she should interfere. 'It's got nothin' to do with us, Josie,' she said tersely. 'They contribute a lot towards the church and other things in the village, and doesn't the vicar visit for tea an' to talk about other things? The vicar won't want to know anythin' about all this.'

'But Mother, it's wrong. Jimmy Kent was my boyfriend, and now he's off with 'er. Tonight it's the choir practice, and as soon as it's finished they'll be off to the woods together. Jimmy's a fool. She'll not want 'im, she's just using 'im.'

Even though her mother had said it was none of her business, Josie knew their talk would go further. She was the vicar's housekeeper, and she was a friend of Jimmy's aunt Mona. Give it a few weeks and it would all be over, in any case Jimmy's calling-up papers would soon be in evidence.

Louise herself was aware that some of the girls liked her, while others certainly didn't. She wanted to be liked, but the barriers of class were against her, and in this small village class mattered. But Josie lost no time in talking about the many differences between their own lifestyles, and that of this rich girl who had descended upon them, with her manor house life, her expensive clothes and her posh voice. It did not take very long to stir up bitter resentment, in a time when people were already suffering in so many different ways.

It was only a few days after Josie's conversation with her mother that Jimmy Kent received his calling-up papers, and after the choir practice they all sat in the village hall discussing it. Three other boys had also been called up, and even in the midst of the excitement there was suspense and sadness. The girls they had been fond of wept tears and tried to console each other; the boys, who had never been much further than the village, bragged a little and played the roles of heroes.

Louise and Jimmy disappeared into one of the barns because it was raining, and Josie's eyes followed them with a certain bitter satisfaction.

'I'll get leave, Louise,' Jimmy was promising her. 'You'll still be here, and nothin'll 'ave changed.'

She looked at him with a strange sort of pity that he would have been unable to understand. She liked him, but she didn't love him, and she had used him. Quietly, she asked, 'You're not afraid, Jimmy?'

'Course not. I'm only like all the rest.'

'My brother's in the army. He said he wasn't afraid.'

'What regiment is he in?'

'A cavalry regiment.'

She knew her brother's regiment, but she didn't want to tell Jimmy which it was. She didn't want to burden him at that time with another difference in their lives. Besides, her brother had a commission, and Jimmy was unlikely to get one. She was capable of antagonizing him with so many things, and although she could never love him, she would not hurt him.

Somehow that night she didn't want him to make love to her, and as his ardour increased she said, 'Jimmy, shouldn't you be going home? I'm sure your mother is worried. She'll want to spend all the time she can with you before you have to leave.'

'Don't you want to be with me?'

'She's your mother, Jimmy. She needs you at this time.'

'I don't see why. You don't see much of *your* mother. When does she ever come 'ere?'

'She's very busy. She writes to me, and she'll come whenever she's able to.'

'Funny sort of life you 'ave. Oh well, if ye wants to get back that's it.'

'Don't sulk, Jimmy. There'll be other times.'

'Ay, but when?'

He walked with her to the little gate leading into the shrubbery, and she was all too aware of his little-boy sulky face and the expression in his eyes when she left him. She was right to feel guilty about Jimmy. He loved her because she was different, because their affair gave him some sort of status in the small village community, but she suspected that in his heart he knew she didn't love him, that what they had had was all they would ever have.

It was dusk already, and the house was very quiet. She thought her aunts would probably be in the drawing room, reading or listening to the radio, so she went to the kitchen in the hope of chatting to Cook. Her aunts had little conversation, but at least Cook was humorous, and she invariably produced tea and home-made scones.

Cook was alone, and she looked up with none of her usual welcome. 'Your aunts have been asking about ye, Miss Louise. I told them you hadn't got in yet. The vicar's with them, so perhaps you'd better get in there.'

'I don't usually sit with the vicar, Cook. They don't usually want me there.'

'Perhaps not, miss, but this time it's different. You go in there and find out what's botherin' them.'

For the first time warning bells were ringing in her head. It had all been so easy: two sweet unworldly old ladies who were very fond of her, proud of her style and her beauty. Why was it suddenly so important that she join them in the company of the vicar?

Three pairs of eyes stared at her, the old ladies bearing pained expressions and heightened colour, while the vicar seemed unduly stern and accusing.

'Oh, Louise,' Aunt Beatrice said in a slightly trembling voice, 'we've been hearing such dreadful things from the vicar, we can hardly believe them.'

Louise joined them nearer the hearth rug, and the vicar said, 'I suggest you sit here, Louise. Your aunts are rather upset, and I feel very responsible by bringing them such problems.'

The two aunts wept, and Louise said quietly, 'What's wrong, Vicar?'

'I have had to tell your aunts about you, Louise, you and Jimmy Kent. It has come to my notice that you and he have been cavorting with each other for several weeks now, after choir practice, in the countryside or in the barn. The entire village is talking about it. I thought when you came here you were so very popular, Louise. You fitted in so well with choir practice, you danced in the village hall, and generally involved yourself with the life of the village. Now I am told you and young Kent have been missing from a great many things to go off on your own. Is this true, Louise?'

'I have been friendly with Jimmy, yes.'

'More than friendly from all accounts.'

Louise remained silent, and the sobbing from the aunts increased.

'What exactly is your association with Jimmy?' the vicar asked.

'We're friends. He helps out in my aunts' garden. He was the first boy I really met when I

63

came here.'

'But it's been more than that, hasn't it?'

Again Louise remained silent, and looking at the aunts the vicar said, 'Obviously, ladies, something has been going on between these two young people, and it's entirely up to you what you intend to do about it. Jimmy has received his calling-up papers so he'll be leaving the village within days, but Louise has made it difficult for her to be accepted in the village community. The younger people are resentful, particularly one of the girls who was friendly with Jimmy before Louise arrived here, and we do know that Louise and Jimmy's different stations in life make any long term association impossible.'

Suddenly, Louise jumped to her feet and with flashing eyes said, 'I liked Jimmy, I never looked down on him or intended to, we were friends, and nobody has the right to tell me who should be my friend. All right, we had something going, but it wasn't serious. How can anything be serious in this wretched world? I shouldn't have been here, I should be with my parents in London. On the morning I left school I thought that's where I was going, but my mother brought me here instead. Why, I don't know. I was resentful, angry, and Jimmy was just somebody who I used to pay my mother back. I'm sorry about that because I liked him, but I didn't love him, and it's all over now.'

'And don't you care that Jimmy might be very unhappy about it all?' the vicar asked.

64

'Yes, of course I care, but like I said it's over now. Jimmy's going into the army, and I want to go home. You've been so wonderfully kind, aunts, for putting up with me. I'm sure I haven't been easy, and I do love you both, but my life isn't here, I wasn't expecting this, and you'll both be relieved to be rid of me, I'm sure.'

'Well, ladies, there doesn't seem anything else to discuss. I think we've said it all.'

'But what shall we do, Vicar?' Miss Pheobe asked.

'I suggest you write to Baroness Maxton, but it's up to you how much you feel you need to tell her. At least you could suggest that Louise should be allowed to go home to London, because although you've tried, it hasn't worked out. She'll never truly settle down here, you've heard that for yourselves.'

'But we loved having you, Louise. You brought some laughter in our lives. Have you really been very unhappy?'

'I've been happy most of the time, honestly. I love you; I'm grateful to you for giving me a home. It's Mother who's been so wrong to even think that it would work. For years I've been conditioned into thinking that my life would be different. Even if war came, I never thought it would be here, in this quiet little village, surrounded by so many people I didn't really know.'

The vicar made his departure, shaking his head and smiling uncertainly, and then the old ladies drank their cocoa and decided to retire.

Disconsolately, Louise wandered around the empty rooms, and Cook decided to stay out of the turmoil that had gone on there. At nine o'clock, Mrs Watson the housekeeper entered the drawing room to ask if Miss Louise would like anything to eat or drink, and when she declined she wished her a frosty goodnight and left her to her own devices.

Louise decided to go to bed and for most of the night she lay sleepless until the first early light crept through the curtains. Normally at this early hour Jimmy would have made his appearance in the garden, but not this morning, and she could only assume that he would not be coming. She made her way down to the morning room, and already the two aunts were sitting at the breakfast table, their expressions dismal.

Aunt Pheobe said, 'Your mother is coming for you this morning, Louise. We're not sure what time, but I suggest you pack your case so that you'll be ready for her. She will want to get back to London quite quickly, I would think.'

Her mother came in time for lunch, which they ate in some degree of silence, interspersed with polite but meaningless conversations. Dutiful embraces were exchanged with the aunts, and then she was sitting with her mother in the back seat of the Bentley. The journey was taken largely in silence, and her mother's displeasure was very apparent, but when they reached the house, her mother only said, 'We'll talk later, Louise. In the meantime I suggest you get un-packed, change into something more suitable for staying indoors, and find yourself something to occupy your time.'

'Like what, Mother? Are you going out?'

'Yes, I *am* going out. I have a very important engagement to attend. I hadn't thought to be driving into the country, and I hope they will accept my apologies for being late.'

'I'm sorry, Mother.'

'Yes, you should be. Now go along and change, then find something to do. We'll meet at dinner this evening.'

'Will Father be home?'

'Yes, but I haven't told him anything about your indiscretions. You and I will talk in private.'

She hadn't been long in her room when one the housemaids entered to ask if she needed any help, but Louise was quick to inform her that she didn't.

'Which one are you?' Louise asked her. 'I don't recollect seeing you before.'

'I'm Kitty, miss. I've been 'ere six weeks.'

'Did somebody leave?'

'Yes, miss. Anna left to marry a policeman.'

'Are you happy here, Kitty?'

'Oh yes, miss, the mistress is very nice and I 'as no trouble with the gentlemen. I allus wanted to be a lady's maid, but I've had no trainin' so to speak.'

'Training, Kitty?'

'Why yes, miss. Dressin' ladies, doin' their hair and lookin' after them in all sorts of other ways.'

'You can be my lady's maid, Kitty.'

'But miss, Lady Maxton'll never let me be your maid. She'll want some other woman wi' training! I'm not fitted.'

'I'll talk to my mother, Kitty. I'll train you how to be a lady's maid, and you can train me how to be a lady.'

'But the Baroness won't want me lookin' after you, Miss Louise.'

'I rather think that my mother will be pleased that somebody *wants* to look after me.'

'But the butler and Mrs Astley are likely to say something, miss.'

'I'm sure they are, but I'm very good at getting my own way, Kitty. Leave things to me.'

They were interrupted by a knock on the door, and it opened to reveal a young man in army uniform smiling at them before Louise flew into his arms.

'Oh, Andrew, I thought you were in France! The aunts thought you were.'

'I'm going back there next week. In the meantime I've got four days to take you to the theatre and to some ball or other.'

'Don't tell me you haven't somebody more exciting to take.'

'Not at the moment. Now, what have you been doing to the dear old aunts?'

'Oh Andrew, it was so boring. They really were so kind and sweet, but I was so bored most of the time. I've been wrong and cruel with them, and others too, but I promise I'll be very circumspect from now on.'

'My little sister was never circumspect. Oh, perhaps outwardly, but in that head of hers? Never. Mother's furious with you.'

'She has no right to be! She was largely responsible.'

'Why?'

'For leaving me there.'

'I can't believe the aunts were unkind to you.'

'Of course not, but they were awfully dull. Daddy doesn't know about my disgrace. Mother said she hadn't told him.'

'What are you doing with the rest of the afternoon?'

'I don't know.'

'Then come for a stroll in the park and forget all about it. London's full of young men looking for excitement before sterner things block out frivolity.'

So she walked with Andrew in the park, and in the warm September sunshine she forgot briefly the last few weeks, seeing instead girls in summer dresses on the arms of young men in uniform. She listened to their laughter and tried not to think of the agonies of war. It seemed on that sunlit afternoon that the entire world was trying to forget the crueller, more real, world they were facing. She had always considered her brother Andrew to be the handsomest man she knew. She loved being with him, he was wise and funny, and if she ever found somebody like *him* she'd be happy to forget those silly things she'd trotted out simply to amuse her school-friends.

As they waited in the dining room that evening for her father to join them, her mother seemed able to respond to Andrew's good-humoured conversation, and then her father was there, raising her mother's hand to his lips and eyeing his daughter with a somewhat cynical smile, saying, 'So the aunts have had enough, Louise.'

Andrew laughed, and her mother said quietly, 'Well, they are getting on a bit. Perhaps it was a mistake to think Louise should stay with them.'

'Didn't I say so all along, my dear? Well, there's things to be done in London. There'll be something for you, my girl.'

Six

Mrs Hambleton viewed her daughter's face across the breakfast table with ill-disguised annoyance. Cora was unhappy and it showed.

'I wish you didn't look so sulky every day, Cora,' she admonished her. 'Nobody's happy with the situation, I know life isn't as you imagined it would be, but everybody has to put up with it. What do you intend to do for the rest of the day?'

'What is there to do? I could walk in the park, feed the swans. We haven't even got men in the wards that I could cheer up. Wasn't that what I was supposed to be doing?'

'With a face like that, Cora, I doubt if you could cheer anybody up. The war's only been on for several weeks, but I can assure you the men will be arriving very soon. This isn't a true hospital, Cora, it's a convalescent home. When the battle starts in earnest, we'll be overburdened with men recovering from their injuries and anxious to return to the war.'

'I'll believe it when it happens.'

'Doesn't it bother you that your brother is destined for France, that he will be among the first to go?'

'Yes, of course it does. I'm sorry, Mummy. I'm just sorry that everything seems so dull and empty.'

'Then I suggest you make the most of it while it lasts.'

'I haven't heard a word from Louise, and I've only seen Miranda twice.'

'I met Louise's mother at some Red Cross meeting or other. She said Louise was staying with her aunts in the country, didn't you know?'

'Oh surely not? Louise would hate it.'

'Her parents obviously feel she's better off with them than here in London.'

'Well, I know where I'd rather be, even when it is boring at the moment.'

'Why don't you telephone Miranda? Meet her for lunch, find out what she's doing with her time.'

'I suppose I could. I'll bet she doesn't know about Louise.'

'When did you last see Miranda's brother Peter?'

'Ages ago. We met him in the park, he was with some girl or other, but Miranda said it wasn't serious, just some girl he'd met in some club or other. She was pretty. He calls Miranda his kid sister and that's how he looked at me.'

'And I expect you and Miranda have been making all sorts of stories up about how you'd like it to be. It's too soon darling. He's twenty-five, you're seventeen. Time alters many things.'

'We heard you and Miranda's mother talking one day. You both were saying how wonderful it would be if Cedric married Miranda, and Peter married me.'

'Mothers do that sort of thing, dear. It's called wishful thinking, and it doesn't always work.'

'I'd like it to work. Peter's awfully handsome, and so is my brother.'

'It's all in the future, Cora. They need to come back safe, and you need to grow up a little more. Why *not* get in touch with Miranda? You'll both have so much to talk about.'

'You know, Mother, Imogen Clarkson told us her parents met in the Sudan where she was nursing and he'd been wounded in some skirmish or other. They fell in love, and his family didn't approve. Did you know anything about it?'

'Well, I did know the Clarkson family. His father is Viscount Clarkson, or rather he was. His elder brother is the Viscount now.'

72

'And it's true that they didn't like Imogen's mother?'

'She was hardly in his league, darling, although she was very pretty I believe. They have made something of their lives, though they got nothing from the Clarksons, nor will they.'

'I rather liked Imogen. She was quite clever really, a bit studious and very popular with the teachers, but she didn't talk about her family very much at all until recently. I don't suppose she expected to see us again, as she lives in Derbyshire, and that's why she opened up a little. If I'm bored in *London*, what's it like for Imogen in Derbyshire? Perhaps I will call Miranda, Mummy.

Mrs Hambleton's eyes followed Cora as she walked towards the door. She could understand her chagrin, feel her frustrations, but she could only hope they would be short lived. They'd been told that very soon now some of the wounded men would be brought home. The hospitals would be full of the more seriously wounded, but those less so would still need care and attention. In no time at all her spoilt daughter would be faced with the harsher reality of life.

Five minutes later, Cora's head appeared round the door to inform her mother that she was to meet Miranda in London, was invited to have tea with her, and suddenly the sulky little girl look had been replaced with cheerful smiles.

'Is Miranda's brother at home, or did he go off with his regiment?' her mother asked.

'I don't know, Mother, but she did say I was very welcome to stay the night if it was agreeable with you.'

'How kind, dear, of course I'm agreeable to it. Do give Miranda's mother my love, and tell her I hope to see her very soon.'

It always seemed natural that her mother mentioned Miranda's brother, and she knew full well that the Reed-Blytons would ask about her own brother. That was how it would be; one day they would be family – hadn't she always known it? – but not yet.

Her main thoughts were centred around Louise Maxton though. Was she really living with those two old aunts of hers? In all probability Miranda or her mother would know.

Mrs Reed-Blyton received her guest with graciousness and conviviality. Afternoon tea was a civilized, beautifully served, meal in the drawing room, and when Cora said how much she had enjoyed it, her hostess said gently, 'Well, for the time being, dear, we do our best, but we don't really know how long we shall be able to live as we do now.'

'No, that's what Mummy says. Our house is only half of what it was, but Mummy says we all have to do our best.'

'That's so, dear. I'm kept very busy with my Red Cross meetings and various other things, and I shall expect Miranda to help me with them as time goes by. We are having quite a huge function at the end of October; a ball for the Red Cross movement at the Dorchester. I shall make sure your family receive an invitation.'

'Thank you, Mrs Reed-Blyton, it will be so wonderful to be there.'

'And for your brother, too, dear. Indeed, for all the young men who are still in circulation.'

'Have you seen anything of Louise Maxton since we left school, Miranda? I haven't heard a thing.'

She did not miss the look exchanged between Miranda and her mother, but discreetly Mrs Reed-Blyton said, 'I do see Baroness Maxton at one or two of the meetings, but there's always so much to talk about, so we've never discussed Louise.'

'She would hate living with her aunts. Louise was always for the fun and good times,' Cora said.

'Then perhaps her mother thought it a wise thing to seclude her in the country for a while. We are not living in fun times now, girls.'

'But what will there be for her to do, living with those two old ladies?' Miranda asked.

'Well, we really don't know anything, do we? If I get a chance next time I see the Baroness I'll mention Louise to her, tell her you two girls have been asking about her. After all, you were all friends for a long time, so it will be a perfectly natural question to ask.'

It was later in the afternoon, when they strolled through St James's Park in the company of young men in new uniforms and girls in summer dresses, young people who were happy and in love, that Cora said feelingly, 'Mother says

75

that very soon our house will be filled with wounded soldiers, and already nurses are moving in. I don't want my brother to be wounded, nor yours either.'

'I know. Nor do I. Suppose one of them is killed, Cora, what'll it do to us?'

'I don't know. I daren't even think about it.'

They both looked miserably across the lake, but their anxieties were soon to be terminated when a laughing voice trilled, 'What are you two looking so glum about on such a beautiful day?'

They both turned quickly to see Louise bearing down on them, her face as alive as ever, fashionably beautiful, and anxious to embrace both of them as being her dearest friends.

Never the most tactful, Cora said, 'Louise, I thought you were living in the country.'

'The country?'

'Why yes, with those two old ladies who are aunts of yours. Mother said she'd heard you were there.'

'Oh darling, I was only there for a short while because mother was tied up with things here. They were awfully sweet, but I was never with them for keeps.'

'What are you doing here?'

'Well, right now I'm walking in the park! What are you two doing?'

'I'm only here until tomorrow,' Cora said, 'then I'm going back home. Half our house is a hospital.'

'Oh dear, and will you be nursing wounded

heroes?'

'No, but I shall have things to do for them.'

'And you, Miranda?'

'Mother's finding me things to do, she's awfully busy. How about you?'

'Well, I won't be any good at nursing, but I shall be willing to comfort and tease them, and surely you haven't forgotten what I said about my future? Nothing's changed. Not the war, not me, and certainly not the old aunts.'

'You know what people are going to say about you, Louise.'

'Of course, darling, I've already had a surfeit of jealousy.'

'Jealousy! Whoever from?'

'Oh, some girl or other near the aunts. Apparently I stole her boyfriend and she didn't like it.'

'Her boyfriend! Who was he?'

'Oh, some boy I got to know there. He was frightfully handsome and really very nice, but he's gone into the army so I don't expect we'll ever meet again. He'll probably go back there after the war and marry his previous sweetheart.'

'Were you in love with him?'

'Heavens, no. Like I said before, I don't intend to fall in love until I've played the field. I'll enjoy the young ones and marry an old one with a fortune, a man overwhelmed with gratitude at his good fortune in finding a woman young enough to tolerate his grumpiness.'

'It sounds awful.'

Louise laughed. 'Have either of you heard

from Imogen?'

'Not a word,' Cora said, 'but Mother told me she knew members of her father's family. They never approved of Imogen's mother and didn't keep in touch. Did you know her father's brother's a Viscount?'

'I knew,' Louise said. 'Mother told me. But Imogen's father didn't care, he married her mother because he loved her. If I met a man like that it might conceivably change my mind about a lot of things.'

'Will you be going to the Red Cross Ball at the Dorchester?' Miranda asked.

'I've heard about it, Mother mentioned it, but I don't really know.'

'We're going, aren't we, Cora?'

'Don't you think the men might be a little thin on the ground? After all, there is a war on.'

'Well, I must go now,' Louise said quickly. 'If I don't see you before, I might see you at the ball.'

They watched her walking quickly away, and Cora said, 'I really didn't think she could be staying with her aunts indefintely. I wonder who the boy was she talked about.'

'Oh, some upper-crust landowner's son from the area, I suppose. She didn't enlarge on him much.'

'That's what I thought.'

'I wonder if she'll ever fall in love.'

'I wonder if *we* shall?'

They stared at each other doubtfully, and then with a little laugh Miranda said, 'Perhaps we should go back now, Cora. I'm so glad you're staying this evening.'

Louise, meanwhile, was walking quickly in the opposite direction, and she had not gone far when a young man in officer's uniform joined her, and smiling toothily said, 'By George, it's Louise Maxton, isn't it? I thought it was you the other day walking in the park with your brother Andrew, but I wasn't exactly sure. I'm Algy Barrington, same unit as Andrew and a very old friend.'

'Old friend?'

'Actually, yes. We were at the same school and now the same regiment. Sometime next week we'll probably be moving out together.'

'Moving out?'

'To the war, darling. Not a very nice prospect, but the sooner we start things moving, the sooner it will be over.'

As they strolled around the lake, he talked incessantly about himself, his friends and family, his likes and dislikes, and it soon became obvious to Louise that he loved himself dearly. If he'd cared rather less about himself, he would have seen the cynicism in her eyes, particularly when he said, 'Why don't I take you home for tea to meet my mother? She's very friendly with your mother – the same interests, meetings and other activities, you know what I mean.'

'Actually, I don't. I see very little of my mother. I don't really know how she spends her time.'

'All the good works they're doing, I mean.

There's the big do on Friday. You'll be there, I hope?'

'I believe my brother Andrew is escorting me.'

'Really. Taking his little sister, is he? I'd have expected Andrew to have had some social butterfly lined up. But you'll save a dance for me, darling. The supper dance, perhaps.'

Ignoring his request, Louise said, 'Well, I must leave you Mr Barrington. It's nice to have met you.'

'Rather,' he said, taking her hand, 'and don't forget the do on Friday, and I really would like you to meet mother. She's not always sure I meet the right sort of girl, and she'd approve of you, I'm sure.'

Louise smiled and made her escape. Her conversation with Algy Barrington had made her strangely angry. Of course his mother would like to meet her! A baronet's daughter, her mother well known to her and with everything going in her favour – money, background – she was well able to take her place in a line of suitable would-be's.

The first person she met as she entered her home was her brother, who eyed her somewhat angry expression before he said, 'Something not right in the world? Why the expression of despair?'

'I met your friend Algy Barrington in the park. He invited me to meet his mother for tea. Apparently he thought she might approve of me.'

He laughed. 'And would that be a bad thing, Louise?'

'Yes, it would. Somebody to be trotted out for her inspection, either approved or disapproved of, and then what?'

'If you have the right sort of dowry, if the families approve, you know the strictures.'

'And love, what about love?'

'You mean you couldn't love Algy? There's plenty of blue blood in him, particularly on his mother's side, and although he isn't an eldest son, his grandmother favours him. She'll see to it that he's well taken care of.'

'You disgust me, Andrew. The more I mix with you lot, the more I appreciate that boy I knew in the country. At least he was honest. He loved me because I was me, not because I was some baronet's daughter.'

'But he loved you because you were Miss Louise from the Manor house, instead of some lassy he'd grown up with.'

'Do you like Algy Barrington?'

'I neither like him nor dislike him. Will he be at the dance on Friday?'

'Yes, and he's asked me to save the supper dance for him.'

'And will you?'

'No. Anybody but him. Is my mother in?'

'No, but expected, I think. At least, there's a Mr Martin Broughton waiting for her. He's been here some time.'

'You mean you didn't feel like keeping him company?'

'Actually, my father was talking to him. All rather civilized, don't you think.'

His laughter followed her across the hall and up the stairs. Louise couldn't decide what annoyed her the most: her brother's complacency, or the fact that her father could entertain Martin Broughton, who was here to see her mother – oh, palpably because he was their MP and her mother was one of his more ardent workers, but were they all blind to what was really going on?

She couldn't have said what made her change her dress and titivate her hair, but it was not until she was completely satisfied with her appearance that she went down to the drawing room on some pretext or other, but not, definitely not, to meet Mr Martin Broughton.

He rose with a smile, which faltered when he realized it was not her mother who had entered the room. Louise smiled and went forward to meet him, holding out her hand and saying, 'Mr Broughton, I'm sorry Mother isn't home yet. Can I get you anything? Tea, perhaps?'

'No, thank you, really. And you are?'

'I'm Louise. We've never actually met.'

'No, but I've heard about you.'

'I'm sure you have, and not all of it good, I'm afraid.'

He smiled. 'Your mother tells me you have now left school. Not exactly the best time to be facing a strange new world.'

'No, I was expecting there to be so much more.'

He smiled, and she was strangely entranced by it – the smile of a sincere mature man who had no wish to flatter her or impress her. That was the moment she felt agonizingly young and insecure, and that was the moment her mother joined them, taking Martin's outstretched hand and saying, 'I'm so sorry to have kept you waiting Martin. The meeting went on far too long, but I see Louise has been entertaining you.'

'Yes, we've met at last, just a few moments ago.'

'Then we must have tea. Will you see to it, Louise? Then Martin and I must get on with our problems. I'll try not to burden you with too many of them.'

Her mother's smile of dismissal said it all.

Seven

Mary Stepson read the letter through for the second time before putting it down and staring thoughtfully through the window. Of course she remembered Margaret Grant now Margaret Clarkson. They'd been friends and had served together in the Sudan and other trouble spots. Margaret had been a good nurse, but they'd gone their separate ways and hadn't been in touch for a long time.

So Margaret was living in Derbyshire now, married to a farmer, and with one daughter who was anxious to become a nurse in these troubled times. And now Margaret was hoping Mary would meet this daughter and offer some advice.

It was all so long ago. The Margaret she remembered had been pretty, popular with the nursing staff and those she nursed, a young woman who had been very much in love with a young army officer who'd been engaged to somebody else. She'd tried to warn Margaret that she was wasting her time, that nothing could come of it. He'd come from some aristocratic background, and she remembered the tears as Margaret, too, had seen the hopelessness of it all.

Well, apparently she'd found somebody else, hopefully a decent honest man and that other young man had been consigned to infinity. Wasn't that how so many of those so called romances ended? Thank heavens she'd not been susceptible to such foolishness.

Oh well, she'd meet the girl, see if she was nursing material. Heaven knows nurses would be in demand: the country wouldn't be able to get enough of them, soon enough.

Mary was proud of her profession. Now a matron in one of the largest hospitals in Essex, she was respected and dedicated, but how had the years since they'd last met treated Margaret Grant?

She settled down to answer her letter, agreeing to meet both Margaret and her daughter at the hospital and asking her to confirm the day and the time to ensure that she would be available.

* * *

Margaret read her letter from Mary with a smile. It was so like the Mary she remembered: terse, straightforward and uncomplicated. She wondered what she looked like now, for Mary hadn't been pretty. She'd been considered comely, always neat and tidy, but she'd never been the sort of girl the men had fancied. She'd been a good nurse, and Margaret hadn't been surprised that she'd elected to make nursing her life and forsake the joys of matrimony and motherhood.

She had many doubts about her involvement with Imogen, however. She was confident that Imogen would be accepted, though there would be no favouritism, and Imogen wouldn't want it in any case. But she was still faintly troubled, and her husband said calmly, 'She won't have an easy ride, darling. I remember Nurse Stepson. Bit of a tartar, wasn't she?'

'Dedicated. She's probably infinitely more so now.'

'Why is Imogen so anxious to be a nurse, Margaret? We could do with her here, and this is surely unknown territory she's wading into.'

'It's what she wants, darling. She won't change her mind.'

So she answered Mary's letter, and three days later she and her daughter took the early morning train to London, a train filled with khaki-clad soldiers, commanded by stern sergeants, with undefinable futures.

In the early afternoon, they both sat facing Mary Stepson. As Margaret looked into her eyes, the years dropped away, and they were together in Khartoum, in a ward filled with wounded soldiers, fighting heat, conflict and despair.

In spite of her matron's uniform, Mary had changed little. She was still the calm unruffled woman Margaret remembered. It was *Margaret* who was not as Mary expected. Mary was facing a beautiful sophisticated woman, who was elegant and not in the least like a traditional farmer's wife.

The girl too was beautiful, a girl who had greeted her with a charming smile, an adult composure and an upper-crust accent.

'Why are you so sure you want to be a nurse?' Mary asked shortly. 'Is it because your mother was one?'

'That does have something to do with it,' Imogen answered. 'I do want to do something in the war, and nursing will be so very important.'

'It's hard work, I'm sure your mother's told you that. You're seventeen years old. Haven't you worked at anything else?'

'I only left school a few weeks ago.'

'School! The girls working here left school years ago. which school did you go to?'

'St Clares in Hertfordshire.'

'Really. Rather a grand school, I think.'

'It was nice. I loved it there.'

'I'm sure you did, and now you are exchanging it for a very different life, mixing with girls who haven't had any of your advantages. Will you cope with all that, I wonder.'

'I hope so, Miss Stepson.'

86

'You will address me as Matron, and to me you will be Nurse Clarkson – a very junior nurse, you understand.'

'Yes, I have a lot to learn.'

'It will be hard work and long hours. Oh, I know some young girls come into nursing with romantic ideas of being Florence Nightingale and falling in love with young heroes. Your mother will tell you reality is a long way from fantasy.'

'I know, my mother has told me. I've listened to her very carefully.'

Mary's eyes moved over to where Margaret sat listening, and with a wry smile Mary said, 'You came to your senses, Margaret. You married a decent young farmer who has quite evidently done well for himself and given you and Imogen a good life. Emulate your mother, Imogen. You'll meet a great many young men here; just as long as you don't have aspirations that are unobtainable. Now, when are you joining us? Do you need to return to Derbyshire first, or are you intent on joining us right away?'

'I'm going home tomorrow,' Margaret said. 'So I would like to spend this evening with Imogen. Would that be possible?'

'Of course. Tomorrow then, promptly at eight o'clock. You will be rooming with another nurse, Jenny Fields. She's been here about six months. You may or may not get on, for she's had none of your advantages, and she's a type of girl you are certainly unused to. Concentrate on your nursing; your association with Nurse

87

Fields is relatively unimportant.'

Mary escorted them to the door and extended a firm hand to Margaret saying, 'Well, goodbye Margaret, it's been nice meeting you again. I'll do the best I can for your daughter, but there'll be no favouritism, you know. I have a job to do.'

As they walked across the grounds towards the gates Imogen said, 'Why didn't you tell her that Daddy was the young officer she was so sure you'd never marry?'

'I thought it was better for you, dear, that your father was Farmer Clarkson and not that young army captain she thought I should have had nothing to do with.'

'She didn't like me, Mother.'

'She doesn't know you, darling, and try not to worry whether she likes you or not. Mary was never easy; nursing was all she really cared about, I don't think she ever had a man friend, I never heard her speak of one, and although we were friends of a sort she did resent me in a great many ways.'

'How are we spending the rest of the day, Mother?'

'Do you want to visit the theatre, do some shopping or see one of your friends?'

'See one of my friends if they're at home. I'd really like to see Louise, but she'll be here there and everywhere. Perhaps I'll telephone Miranda or Cora.'

She was fortunate to find Miranda at home, and Miranda was quick to say she'd invite Cora to join them but it was doubtful if they could locate Louise.

While her mother was entertained to tea by Mrs Reed-Blyton in the drawing room, Imogen sat with Miranda and Cora on the terrace at the back of the house and their laughter could be heard throughtout the gardens leading down to the river.

That Imogen had decided to enter the nursing profession neither of them could fully understand, but it was Cora who seemed more dismayed. 'How can you even think of nursing?' she cried. 'We've had half of our house taken over, and the nurses are everywhere. They want a lot of waiting on, and they're terribly bossy. Mother says I'll have to help out when the wounded begin to arrive, but I'm certainly not nursing. I wouldn't know how to begin.'

'What about you, Miranda?' Imogen asked.

'Well, not nursing, but Daddy says he can probably get me some office work somewhere. I'll only be fit for making the tea and not very good at that.'

The others laughed, and it was Imogen who said, 'What about Louise? Do you see her at all?'

'We've seen her in the park, sometimes with her brother, he's awfully good looking. Do you know that for a few weeks after she left school she went to live with her two aunts in the countryside? I wonder why?'

'Well, you know what Mother said,' Miranda said with a giggle. 'Mother'd heard that she'd blotted her copybook in some way and her

89

mother had to bring her back to London.'

'I wonder what she'd done? Anyway, if it's something really dreadful, Louise will delight in telling us. She'll be at the ball on Friday, we'll ask her then.'

'Ball?' Imogen asked.

'Charity do, in aid of the Red Cross or something. Oh Imogen, why don't you come? You can stay here overnight, and you'll be a nurse and very welcome.'

'And Matron would be horrified if I even *ask* if I can go.'

'Well, of course you can! My mother and Cora's mother are on the committee, and Louise's mother is everybody's benefactor. I'll get mother to ring your matron and explain everything to her. She'll have to let you go.'

'And that'll only endorse what she thinks about me, some snobby girl whose been spoiled rotten. Besides, I'm being room-mate with a girl who's had none of my chances in life.'

'Well, that's not your fault.'

'I know, but will she see it like that, do you think?'

The afternoon was pleasant for both Imogen and her mother, and later in the evening Mrs Reed-Blyton spoke to Mrs Hambleton of their visit. 'She's a perfectly charming woman, quite a lady, but they've never been accepted into the family, you know. After all, he *was* engaged to Lord Barroclough's daughter.'

'Well yes, of course. Who did she marry, by the way?'

'Oh, she went off to America and married somebody over there. Somebody very affluent, I'm sure.'

'But hardly the same, dear,' Mrs Hambleton said.

'No, of course not.'

'I really am rather worried that this war is going to change so many things. After all, these boys are going to meet all sorts of girls from different backgrounds. There's the ball next Friday: Cedric's asked if he can invite some girl he's met recently, the sister of a brother officer, who I've never met.'

'Oh dear, I think that's dreadful, particularly as Cora will be there and expecting to spend some time with him.'

'I'm sure it's absolutely nothing, my dear, and she *is* very young. The world's topsy-turvy right now. It will all sort itself out.'

Sitting over dinner, Imogen told her mother about the ball. 'They wanted me to go with them, Mother, but of course I told them it was impossible.'

'There'll be other balls, darling. We'll all have much more to think about than balls in the years ahead.'

'Years, Mother?'

'Let's hope not, but we have been warned.'

Just before eight next morning, Imogen's taxi deposited her in the hospital grounds, where her mother embraced her with tears in her eyes and many misgivings in her heart.

Inside the hospital she was received by a

stony-faced nurse who said tersely, 'Your room is in the annex behind the hospital, number thirty-four. You're with Nurse Fields, who's from some way off. Follow the porter, he'll show you where it is.'

The porter grinned at her as he took her suitcase. 'Your first day, love?' he asked.

'Yes.'

'Oh well, don't let it worry ye, love. You'll soon get into the way of things. What part o' the country are ye from then?'

'Derbyshire.'

'What's made ye come down 'ere then?'

'The war, I want to be a nurse.'

'It'll not be easy, love. I knows some o' them nurses. They'll certainly make ye knuckle down! Just stand up to 'em.'

He was cheerful and chatty, and at that moment he was just what she needed, and as he opened the door of the annex for her he said, 'It's not much to look at, love, and the rooms are pokey, but it's been specially set up for the girls who live some way off. Ye'll get used to it.'

'I'm sure I shall.'

She was nice, he thought, but what would her room-mate make of her? Jenny Fields was quite the little madam.

The room was neat but tiny. There were two narrow beds and two dark wood wardrobes and two chairs. A large stuffed rabbit lay propped up on the bed nearest the window, and Imogen set her case on the other bed and started to unpack. It was only when she opened the wardrobe door that she found clothing hooked on the pegs there. She looked in the other wardrobe and found that also full of clothes and boxes, and the realization dawned on her that she was facing her first hurdle.

With some determination she took out the boxes and placed them on the bed to make room for her clothing, then she started to place her own things where the others had been. She was so engrossed with her task that she didn't hear the door open and was unaware of the girl staring at her until she said, 'What are all these boxes doin' on my bed?'

She turned to see a thin dark-haired girl staring at her with some animosity. 'I'm sorry, but there are two wardrobes, so I assumed that this one was mine.'

'So it is, but them boxes are mine.'

'But they were in my wardrobe.'

'There was nowhere else to put 'em.'

'Well, I'm sorry but we'll just have to find somewhere. I'm Imogen Clarkson, by the way. I take it you're Jenny Fields, my room-mate?'

The girl didn't answer, instead she strolled round the other side of her bed and opened her wardrobe door.

'It's crammed packed wi' things. There's no *room* for the boxes.'

'I'm sorry, Jenny, we don't appear to have got off to a good start. I do hope we can be friends.'

'Not at this rate, we can't.'

'There's probably room in my wardrobe for two of those boxes, but not for the rest of them.

Perhaps you can squeeze them into yours?'

With bad grace Jenny complied, finding room for the two smaller ones and leaving Imogen to take care of the others.

'Where'd ye come from then?' Jenny asked her.

'Derbyshire.'

'Are there no 'ospitals there ye could a gone to there?'

'There are, but I wanted to come to London.'

'Thought it were better than Derbyshire, did ye?'

'No. Just different.'

'I didn't expect to be sharin' a room with some stuck-up girl like you. I doubt if we'll get along.'

'I'm sorry you feel like that. Why do you say I'm stuck up?'

'The way ye talks.'

'Don't you think that's silly? I can't help the way I speak. It doesn't mean I'm snobbish or unkind. I'd like us to be friends. If we're not it's going to be unpleasant.'

Jenny laughed. Not happy cheerful laughter, but a cynical denial of everything she had heard.

'Unpleasant,' she said. 'That's a big word for what we'll 'ave to put up with. I take it ye 'ave to report to the 'ospital?'

'Yes. And you?'

'Nine o'clock, and I'm late, thanks to you.'

With that remark she gave Imogen a long hard look and rushed out of the room.

Imogen was five minutes late on her first

morning and received a look of admonishment from the sister greeting them. She knew that as long as she lived she would never forget that morning, and the knowledge that she was a very junior nurse indeed, with much to learn, and she would start at the bottom.

That the bottom was menial she was not left long in doubt, and the years that had gone before had not prepared her for what she was facing now. She saw nothing of the matron, but a succession of nurses instructed her on what to expect in the coming months. One nurse informed her that they were expecting a contingent of soldiers who had been wounded any day, and then they would really learn what nursing was all about.

It was nine o'clock that evening, after a hasty and largely uneatable meal, that she found her way to her room and gratefully sank down onto her bed, exhausted.

It was Jenny, several minutes later, who slammed the door with muttered cursing and collapsed on her bed. By this time Imogen was sitting up, expecting more.

'I hates them bossy nurses,' Jenny said angrily. 'I'm not stayin' 'ere! Nothin'll make me.'

'Then why did you want to come here in the first place?' Imogen asked.

'Because I were conscripted, weren't I? We didn't 'ave any money, and the men were goin' and the girls too. I thought nursin' would be all right.'

'It will be. It's only early days. It can only get

better.'

'Or worse. Well, I'm not stickin' it out. I'll go on the streets first.'

'You don't mean that, Jenny, how can you?'

'I can and I will. Me sister's on the streets, and she's makin' more money in a day than I'll earn in a year.'

'You don't mean it, Jenny. Tomorrow you'll think differently.'

'Oh you, with yer fancy school and yer different life, what do you know about it.'

What *did* she know about it? How would tomorrow and the future days and months make her feel? How could she even begin to understand this other girl, with her lifestyle so different from her own?

Eight

The early October night was mild after an Indian summer's day, and outside in the square crowds had gathered to watch the arrival of those attending the ball.

The ball was a function to be treasured in these spartan days, and the sight of women in silks and satins, wearing furs and feathers, lavishly adorned with jewels, was something to be wondered at. The younger women were wearing white, gowns originally destined for coming-out parties and debutant balls, while the older men either wore evening dress or dress uniforms. There was a shortage of young officers since already many of them were serving in France, and those attending the function would soon be joining them.

Miranda Reed-Blyton stood on the balcony watching her friend Cora dancing with a young Guards Officer, and when Cora eventually joined her she said, 'Who was that you were dancing with?'

'Tommy Jessop. he's a friend of Cedric's.'

'Who is that dancing with your brother?'

'She's some girl he met recently, nobody important.'

'Doesn't your mother mind?'

'Why would she?'

'He only said a few words to me. I don't suppose he'll even ask me to dance.'

'Oh Miranda, she's the present, you're the future. For now Cedric's my mother's blue-eyed boy who can do no wrong. He's off to France next week. If he was here with the daughter of Genghis Khan, Mother wouldn't say a word.'

'I don't know why I've come. There's so few men to dance with. They're all so old.'

'Oh, for heaven's sake, do cheer up, Miranda. You surely don't want my brother to remember you looking miserable.'

'That's if he ever thinks about me.'

'Well, I'm sure you'd rather he thought about you happy and smiling than looking miserable. Isn't that your sister dancing with that handsome man? Isn't she a suffragette or something?'

Miranda's sister appeared to be enjoying herself hugely. The young man was evidently capable of entertaining his pretty companion.

'Oh look, there's Louise. She's wearing blue! She would have to be different, wouldn't she? I do think her brother's awfully handsome. I wonder if he's got a girlfriend?' Miranda said.

'I'm sure her mother'll insist on it being somebody very special. That's Lady Maxton, dancing with that good-looking man who's our MP.'

'I expect her husband's in the Green Room talking war and politics, that's what my father does.'

'Don't you want to join the dancers?' Cora asked plaintively.

'We see so much more up here.'

'Well perhaps for a little while longer, but after the next dance...'

Miranda's eyes followed Cora's brother's progress around the room, and after a short while Cora said, 'Honestly, Miranda, forget about them for tonight. My brother is off to war next week, and your brother's been there for weeks. We have to live for today; tomorrow might never come.'

Reluctantly Cora took her hand and pulled her towards the stairs, where they encountered Cedric and his lady friend in the company of several other couples, and reaching his side Cora said, 'Cedric, this is my friend Miranda Reed-Blyton. You do remember meeting her at the Garveys? And our families are great friends.'

'Of course,' Cedric said, smiling. 'And weren't you at school together?'

'Yes.' Cora smiled at his girlfriend, and Cedric said, 'This is Julie Havers. Her cousin's in the same mob.'

Julie smiled, and they had to admit she was decidedly pretty, and Cora asked, 'Do you live in London?'

'At the moment, yes, I work here.'

'Work?'

'Yes, at the War Office. I'm a secretary.'

'How nice. I think we should be doing something like that.'

Cedric laughed. 'My sister only left school in July,' he said. 'Did you do any training for secretarial work, Cora?'

'Not really, but I'm intelligent enough to learn,' she said tersely.

'And what aspirations do you have, Miranda?' he asked her.

'I'm not sure. Our house has been largely taken over to accommodate Daddy and his political ambitions though.'

'Oh well, that really is something worthwhile.' Turning round he addressed the group of officers standing behind them. 'This is my sister Cora and her friend Miranda – beautiful, young and fresh out of boarding school. Why don't we all dance?'

Two smiling young men stepped forward, and if Cora liked the looks of her partner, Miranda felt a strange sense of anger and betrayal. *She* should have been the one dancing with Cedric Hambleton. From the age of ten, hadn't she believed that one day he would be her destiny?

Her partner was young and good looking. He informed her that he was expecting to leave for France within a few days, and he was brave, arrogant and excited, with no thoughts that this might be the last ball he would ever attend.

Their conversation was halted by a girl's voice saying, 'Miranda! I was hoping you'd be here.'

She looked round to see Louise in an azure blue gown, with the sparkle of diamonds round her neck and round her hair, and beside her was a tall elegant young man who smiled down at her charmingly and excused himself when another officer invited Louise to dance with him.

Louise had recognized him instantly as her companion in the park quite recently, and when she had finished speaking to Miranda he said, 'I was hoping you'd be here. I've been enthusing about you to my mother; she's wanting to meet you.'

'Is your mother here?'

'Of course. She's a keen worker on the committee. She's with the others, who are all doing their best to make a success of the occasion. Say you'll let me introduce you.'

Louise didn't see the necessity, but when the dance was over he escorted her determinedly into the banqueting hall where several ladies were officiating.

His mother was much of a pattern with many

of the others, a rather large lady in glistening brocade, gracious and smiling, informing Louise that her son had been enthusing about their meeting for days, wishing that his mother might meet her before his regiment left for France and telling her that he was more than confident that his mother would find her as beautiful and perfect as he did.

It was evident that his mother did. Here was this Baronet's daughter, beautiful and elegant, even though perhaps blue was a little too sophisticated for a girl fresh out of school.

In those first few minutes Louise felt that Mrs Barrington was welcoming her into her family as her son's chosen one, and she was introduced to his sister and several aunts, all of them gushing and welcoming.

Enthusiastically, Mrs Barrington was saying, 'It's such a relief, my dear, to see that Algy is interested in the right sort of girl. I'm so afraid that we're sailing into very uncharted water these days.'

'Uncharted waters, Mrs Barrington?'

'Well yes, my dear. Just look around you! Half the girls here are simply girls they've met around town, you know what I mean.'

'No, actually I don't.'

Mrs Barrington looked momentarily confused before she said, 'Didn't you come here with your parents?'

'Actually with my brother Andrew.'

'A friend of Algy's, such a handsome, charming young man.'

'I'm sure your description will please him enormously, but now if you'll excuse me I should be getting back to him. It's been so nice meeting you, Mrs Barrington.'

'Oh yes, dear, likewise, and do please come and have tea with me very soon. I shall look forward to it.'

Algy escorted her to where her brother stood chatting to Miranda and Cora, and after she introduced Algy to her friends she said, 'Aren't you going to ask Mother to dance, Andrew?'

'Thus providing you with the opportunity to dance with Broughton?' Andrew said quietly as he led her towards their mother's group.

'It never even entered my head.'

'Come now, little sister, this is Andrew you're talking to, don't think I haven't noticed your interest in Martin Broughton. Is it because you feel protective about father or for some more devious reason?'

'Don't be silly, he's hardly in my age group.'

'He's seven years younger than Mother, but I do agree, too old for you. They're over there, we'll join them.'

While Andrew and Martin chatted together and her mother was in conversation with another couple, Louise looked at Martin Broughton. He was handsome, tall and distinguished, and if he was seven years younger than her mother it didn't show. Her mother was beautiful, vivacious and they looked good together. What was her father thinking about to leave his wife in the company of this charming eligible man, while sitting in the company of men like himself and no doubt talking about the war and politics?

Andrew asked their mother to dance, and to her chagrin Martin invited the other woman to dance, while she had to be content to dance with the woman's husband, hardly a glamorous occasion.

After the dance was over her mother said, 'I suggest we go in to supper. Are you joing us, Andrew?'

To her annoyance the other couple decided to join them also, and when she met Martin's eyes he asked politely, 'Are you enjoying yourself, Louise?'

'Yes, thank you,' she replied tersely.

Her mother said, 'Have you spoken to your friends, Louise?'

'Yes, of course.'

'You should ask them to dance, Andrew. There does seem to be a shortage of young officers,' his mother said.

Taking his seat next to her, Andrew said, 'Too bad, you didn't even get to dance with him.'

'I didn't want to dance with him.'

'Oh but you did, little sister, be honest. You're not remotely interested in any of the younger chaps I've introduced you to tonight. Why Martin Broughton? Is it because he's with Mother?'

'Of course not. I simply don't know what they see in each other.'

The cynical expression in his eyes told her he didn't believe her, and she wished the dance was over and she could go home.

After they had eaten supper, Andrew went in search of Cora and Miranda. Another young officer came to their table to invite Louise to dance. He was nice, though he expressed the opinion that he'd be better employed in fighting the war than wasting his time on the dance floor, and Louise asked herself bitterly: what am I doing here? What can I do to bring the world back to normal?

Back in the ballroom her mother was invited to dance with the woman's husband, but his wife excused herself, saying that she felt rather tired and she would prefer to sit it out, leaving Martin to invite Louise.

They danced in silence, but she was aware of the restraint between them. Looking at her cold beautiful face, Martin couldn't be blamed for thinking that she disliked him, and she felt that he compared her to her mother, thinking her too young, too insecure and too unintelligent.

There were other men in the world, men as old as Martin Broughton, with money and titles, and younger men too, who would treasure her beauty and those other attributes Martin Broughton didn't like about her.

Cora was dancing with Andrew, laughing up into his face, enjoying the moment.

A while later, Louise's mother watched her daughter dancing by with a puzzled expression and mixed feelings, so much so that Martin said, 'Why do you worry about Louise, Isobel? I know that you do.'

'Because I don't understand her. One minute

she's sweet and normal, the next she's difficult. I think it's me she resents.'

'She seems perfectly normal now.'

'That's just it, with everybody else but me.'

'She's young. She won't always be like that.'

'I think she's still angry about having to live with her aunts. It should never have happened. I was wrong.'

'Don't you think *she* was wrong, too, Isobel? She didn't behave very well.'

'She was paying me back for leaving her there.'

'Oh, was that what it was?'

'You don't like her, Martin.'

'She doesn't like me.'

'Oh well, perhaps she'll find some young man who's right for her and we can all stop worrying.'

As they took to the dance floor their thoughts were largely different about the future and Louise, and after a few moments Isobel said, 'I wonder if Henry intends to spend the whole evening ensconced in there with his cronies. You're so very good to me, Martin. But for you, I'd be a very lonely wife.'

He smiled, and suddenly she said, 'You should marry, Martin. In your position you need a wife, somebody to boost your career. I feel I only detract from it.'

'Why do you feel that?'

'Because people talk, you know that they do.'

'They have to talk about *something*.'

'I'd rather it wasn't me.'

'Are you suggesting that our friendship must come to an end?'

'You know I'm not, but could you convince anybody in this room that that is all it is?'

'Does anybody care my dear?'

After the dance was finished, Andrew rejoined his sister and said, 'I've done my duty. I've danced with both your schoolfriends. Neither of them are exactly ecstatic about where they go from here.'

'Well, of course not. They thought of finishing school, every function under the sun, and then marriage. None of it's come true.'

'Marriage to whom?'

'Well, Miranda to that young man over there with the girl in primrose. He's Cora's brother Cedric and has apparently been earmarked for Miranda and shouldn't be here with somebody else.'

'So things might have to change.'

'Oh, it's ages away. He'll go to the war, no telling who they'll meet, but that's why she's looking so glum tonight.'

'And the other one?'

'Destined for Miranda's brother Peter, but he's already serving in France.'

'I haven't heard that you've been earmarked for anybody.'

'No. Have you?'

He laughed. 'So far I've managed to steer clear of the lottery, Louise. I'm twenty-five, and in a few days I'll be saying farewell to all this until who knows when. I'll probably end up like father, well into my forties and marrying some eighteen year old.'

Louise didn't speak. Somehow at that moment there didn't seem anything to say. She was thinking about her mother, the same age as herself and thrust into a marriage with a man old enough to be her father, a man with little warmth or imagination. If she was in love with Martin Broughton, who could blame her? So why did she mind so much?

'You're very quiet,' Andrew said.

'I was thinking about Mother. She was not much older than me when you were born.'

'Tricky, isn't it? And yet they've stayed together, if you can call it together.'

'She's more together with Martin Broughton.'

'Perhaps, perhaps not. They have learned to be discreet. Something *you* have to learn, my girl.'

'Oh I will, but I'm not going to be like her. I'm going to live a little before I find a man I want to marry.'

'And by that time you'll have gained such a glowing reputation, the man you want to marry might be afraid to marry you.'

'Oh I do hate this silly, stupid old world, where we have to conform all the time to outdated notions that worked for our parents but won't necessarily work for us! And there's Father. I see he finally decided to join the land of the living and is actually inviting Mother to dance.'

Andrew laughed. 'Leaving poor old Martin to dance with Lady Corbett, who's been chasing him for years without any effect.'

107

'Chasing Martin Broughton?'

'You're well behind in everyday scandal, Louise, but you'll catch up.'

After their dance, her father decided it was time they went home and her mother said quickly, 'You needn't come with us, Andrew. I really don't know why your father attends these functions at all. He's invariably ready to leave halfway through the evening.'

Appealing to Louise, Andrew said, 'Did you want to stay on? It may be the last ball for some considerable time.'

'He's right,' her father said tersely. 'I'd think about getting some sleep, Andrew. There'll not be much of that on the other side of the channel.'

It was Algy Barrington who pleaded with her to stay, and several girls watched Andrew's departure with sad speculation.

With Louise's mother out of the picture, Martin Broughton appeared to be having no difficulty in finding women anxious to dance with him. He had many of his constituents at the ball, most of them only too eager to chat and dance with him. Once, Louise met his eye across the ballroom and he favoured her with a cool remote smile, while she laughed merrily at Algy's rather less than amusing anecdotes.

Miranda had had a surfeit of watching Cora's brother obviously enjoying the company of Julie Havers.

As far as Miranda was concerned, the dance hadn't been a great success. Oh, there'd been young men to dance with, but the gaiety seemed enforced. It was as though they were all aware of a giant shadow looming over lives, making their laughter seem incongruous, their enjoyment false and unnecessary.

While Louise wished she had left with her parents, Miranda wished she hadn't attended at all.

Miranda was spending the night at Cora's house, and as they settled down to chat before going to sleep she said plaintively, 'I hope they don't have another ball. There'll be even fewer young officers at that one.'

'You really didn't enjoy it, did you, Miranda?'

'Not really.'

'It was seeing Cedric there with that girl, wasn't it?'

'No, of course not.'

'Honestly, Miranda, he's off to the war soon. This thing with Julie Havers won't last, how can it?'

'It all seemed so brittle somehow. Louise's brother left early, and that man she was dancing with wasn't really her type.'

'Who *is* her type?'

'Well, not him.'

'How can you possibly tell?'

'He was too ordinary, somehow, too pushy.'

'How can you possibly know? Anyway, I'm going to sleep. Mother wants me immediately after breakfast. Apparently there's to be a very busy day tomorrow.'

Nine

It was half past three in the morning, and as Imogen climbed the narrow steps up to her bedroom she felt she had never been so weary. The hospital was full, the wounded were coming in every day now, and there was never enough staff, neither nurses nor doctors. She had wanted to be a nurse, but those aspirations were still a long way from being fulfilled.

She was learning, but the menial jobs she was subjected to were far from those she had envisaged. Mary Stepford hardly acknowledged her presence whenever they met. Mary was the matron; that Imogen was an old friend's daughter had never been acknowledged.

Her room-mate was not in evidence. They were not on the same shifts and saw each other rarely. They were hardly friends; Jenny regarded her as somebody she would never have wanted to know, just some girl who had been thrust into her life.

It was now early November and the room felt cold and unwelcoming. The room was lit by a pale flickering moon, and not even troubling to draw the thin curtains she flung herself on the bed and closed her eyes. Although she was unutterably weary, sleep refused to come to her, and then the sudden opening of the door signified Jenny's appearance.

She heard her muttering under her breath, then the striking of a match as Jenny indulged in her favourite pursuit, smoking as many cigarettes as she could get her hands on.

The scent of cigarette smoke hung heavy on the air, and she opened her eyes to find Jenny standing at the window. She said quickly, 'Jenny, it's four in the morning! Must you stand around smoking now?'

'I've done me duty. Why shouldn't I smoke?'

'The room is full of it.'

'How long 'ave ye bin up 'ere? I've only just come off duty.'

'So have I, about half an hour ago.'

'There's a new lot come in. All the wards are full now.'

'I know. Are there some very bad cases?'

'I don't know, mostly shrapnel. I knows one of 'em though – a boy from near where I used to live.'

'Did you get to speak to him?'

'Not yet, and I'm not in that ward in the mornin'. You might be in that ward.'

'Is he badly injured?'

'I don't know. I just recognized 'im. Sometimes 'e'd come to something at the church, but he was goin' around with some girl 'e'd met when 'e was gardenin'.'

'He was a gardener then?'

'Somethin' like that. He was a good lookin'

lad, fancied 'imself. That girl 'e was with reminds me of you.'

'Really, why is that?'

'Talked like you, dressed like you when yer off duty. She lived with the two old ladies at the manor house, then suddenly she went off to London. We all guessed why.'

'Something unexpected?'

'Somethin' she shouldn't 'ave bin doin'. One of me friends fancied Jimmy Kent, but he 'ad no eyes for 'er once that girl came on the scene.'

'Who was she?'

'Oh, some fancy name. Lucy, or somethin' like it.'

'So you never really got to know her?'

'Not really. She got some dancin' goin' at the church hall, and we all enjoyed it. They said she'd bin at some school not far away and the old ladies were 'er aunts or somethin'.'

Bells were suddenly ringing in Imogen's head. She'd heard Louise speaking about her two old aunts, sisters of her father who lived not far away, but of course it couldn't possibly have been Louise! Surely her mother had been taking her to London, hardly to two old ladies living in the country?

'What was she like, this girl you speak of?' she asked.

'Blonde, some said pretty. They said her mother was some sort o' lady. Wait, I 'ave a magazine I pinched after some o' the visitors left. It's probably not true anyway, but some folk in the village said she was 'er mother.'

Imogen watched her leafing through a magazine before saying, ''Ere it is. Had somethin' to do with 'orses.'

It had to be Lady Maxton, looking beautiful in an exquisite gown and large white hat, enjoying Ladies' Day at Ascot and surrounded by elegant men and similarly dressed women, but could it *really* have been Louise, left to spend time with two old ladies and the somewhat dubious company of this man Jenny called Jimmy Kent?

Jenny stubbed her cigarette out, and putting the magazine away she said, 'If you get into that ward, will ye talk to 'im? I wants to know if 'e ever 'ears from 'er now.'

'How can I possible ask questions like that, Jenny? He doesn't know me. He won't talk to *me* about her.'

'Oh, but 'e will. He'll want to talk about 'er, particularly to you who looks so much like her. Oh, not just yer face, but the way ye are.'

It had been the longest conversation she'd ever had with Jenny, and Jenny was looking at her now with expectation in her eyes.

'You really are curious about all this, Jenny.'

'Yes I am. I 'ad a friend in the village who fancied 'im rotten. She were so upset when he ditched 'er to go out wi' that snooty girl. I'd like to be able to tell 'er it's all over and done with.'

'Well, I'm sure it is. He's in hospital and he's been wounded; she's probably with her family, whoever they are.'

'But ye will try to get to know, Imogen?'

'I'll do my best. I would like us to be friends,

Jenny. There's just the two of us in this place, and we don't really know for how long. Why don't we try?'

'What can we talk about? What 'ave we in common?'

'Well, now we have Jimmy Kent, and his future.'

Jenny stared at her for several minutes, then she laughed. 'Well, I reckon we can try. Ye can 'elp me to speak proper, and I can tell ye somethin' about what sort o' things we got up to in that tiny village. Did ye ever 'ave any fun, the way ye were brought up?'

'I think so, but evidently not your kind of fun! Why don't we have a cup of tea and get to know one another?'

'It's after four, and we 'ave to be on duty at seven.'

'I know. Perhaps we'd best forget the tea and try to get some sleep.'

She was two minutes late arriving in the ward for duty next morning and received a sharp look from the sister in charge, then as soon as she had turned to walk away she stole a quick glance at the young soldier sleeping in the bed across from the door. Jimmy Kent was not to know that he would soon be reliving a past he'd been trying to forget...

Imogen thought she would never forget the moans and cries of pain that were her everyday afflictions. Some of the men had missing limbs, incredibly dreadful wounds caused by shrapnel, and it was only much later in the day that she

114

had the opportunity to speak to Jimmy.

Jimmy lay back against his pillows, his eyes closed. but he knew that it was *her* voice saying, 'I've brought you a cup of tea. Can I help you to sit up to drink it?'

He *knew* that voice, and yet her face was not the one he expected to see. It was a pretty face, staring at him gently, and hoarsely he cried, 'Who are you? What's your name?'

'Imogen.'

'You're a nurse.'

'I'm hoping to be one day.'

'Where do ye come from?'

'From Derbyshire, near Bakewell.'

'You doesn't sound north country. Why's that?'

'Perhaps because I didn't go to school there.'

'Where then?'

'Why don't you drink your tea? We can talk some other time.'

'I'd rather talk now.'

'And I have to move on, there are other men to see to.'

His eyes followed her round the room. She didn't look like Louise and yet there was a graciousness about her, a strange similarity, something born of class, and when another nurse came to take away his tea mug he said, 'Who's that nurse over there? Does she 'ave folks around here?'

'I don't know, she's not been here long.'

'She talks different.'

'Don't get any ideas about the nurses, we 'ave

115

a job to do.'

He felt increasingly angry with the doctors and nurses who stood round his bed. All right he'd been wounded, his body was a mess, the war might even be over for him, but as he watched Imogen doing the more menial jobs on the ward he could only feel impatient that she didn't go back to him.

Indeed, it was only after the lamps had been lit that she came in with another nurse to serve the last drink of the day. He willed her to come to him soon, but it was later when they came to collect the cups that she came to his bed.

'Why didn't you come here sooner? I've been wantin' to talk to you all day.'

'I've been very busy, Jimmy. Let me settle you down for the night.'

'Never mind that. I *am* settled. I want to know about you: you remind me of somebody.'

'Really? I don't think we've ever met before.'

'We haven't, but I knew a girl who talked just like you. She'd been to some posh school, and she was livin' with her aunts in our village.'

'I don't know them.'

'Perhaps not, but I want to know where you went to school.'

'Why should that matter?'

'Please, I want to know.'

'It was a girls' school in Hertfordshire – St Clares, a very old school and I left nearly five months ago.'

'Then you knew Louise.'

'Louise?'

'Yeah, Louise Maxton. She went to that school, and she came to live with the two old ladies at the manor. Me uncle did gardenin' for 'em.'

'I knew Louise. I didn't think she was going to live with her aunts.'

'She wasn't there long. We got into trouble with the vicar and her aunts, so 'er mother came to take 'er away. Will ye be seeing 'er?'

'I'm not sure. They keep me very busy here.'

'But if ye do see 'er, you'll tell 'er I'm 'ere. Maybe she'll come to see me.'

'I don't know, Jimmy, I can't make any promises.'

Imogen was remembering Louise and the way she had entertained them with her talk of lovers, monied aristocratic men with titles, not this country boy with his smiling fresh young face and the pain in his eyes.

As the days passed, Imogen was not to know that the matron was becoming increasingly intrigued at seeing her constantly beside his bed, which brought back to her memories of Imogen's mother, desperately in love with that young officer years ago. She determined that she would make it her business to have a word with young Clarkson at the first opportunity.

Several days later the sister said to Imogen, 'Matron wants to see you in her office, Nurse Clarkson. She didn't look too pleased.'

Imogen stared at her, and the sister said, 'She doesn't often see the junior staff, so I suggest you get in there now.'

Timidly she knocked on the matron's door, and after receiving a curt response she entered the room and stood nervously in front of her.

The matron was in no hurry to start the conversation, and Imogen wondered anxiously what she could have done to have raised that stony frown on her face. At last she put down the pen in front of her and sharply closed the book she'd been writing in.

'I suppose you're wondering why I've sent for you,' she asked.

'Yes, Matron, I hope I haven't done anything wrong.'

'I've had no complaints about your work here, my nurses tell me you've settled in quite well, but I am rather more concerned with your behaviour where the young soldiers are concerned.'

'The soldiers, ma'am?'

'Yes, particularly that young soldier opposite the door with the shrapnel wounds.'

'Jimmy Kent!'

'*Private* Kent. What is he to you?'

'I've only known him since he was brought in here, Matron.'

'Yet you seem to be spending some time in his company. Why him in particular?'

'He knew a girl I was at school with.'

'And how did he come to know that?'

'He said I reminded him of her. He asked which school I'd been at, and I did know her there.'

'I see. I was reminded of your mother all those

years before when she was totally engrossed with that young officer. The tears when it ended! She was demoralized.'

'When it ended?'

'That's what I said. She was in love with him, and he went back to his family while I was left to instil some sense into her.'

Imogen stared at her in disbelief, then in a trembling voice she said, 'Matron, that was a long long time ago and I am not my mother. I really don't know Private Kent very well, and I am telling you the truth.'

'And I am very pleased to hear it, Clarkson. Your mother was a nice sensible girl who put it all behind her and has obviously married a decent hard working man. Wartime romances are more often than not doomed to failure. Now get back to your work, but remember all I have told you.'

As Imogen walked down the stairs towards the wards she could hardly believe what she had just been subjected to. Why did she mind so much about the things that had happened to her mother in another war, another land? She paused at the ward door and the sister said, 'You don't look very happy. Was it painful?' and suddenly, without answering, she ran back up the stairs and knocked sharply on the matron's door.

Without waiting for a reply she flung the door open, and the matron stared at her in some dismay. Imogen said, 'I'm sorry, Matron, but I need to speak to you.'

'I've said all I'm going to say, Clarkson, now

return to your duties.'

'I will, immediately, but I want you to know that my mother married Captain Clarkson, the young officer she was in love with. He's my father.'

The Matron stared at her incredulously before sitting down heavily behind her desk. 'Your mother said she had married a farmer,' she said. 'Wasn't that the truth?'

'My father *is* a farmer now. The farm was left to him by a man he went to work for – he wasn't married and when he died there were no children or relatives to take over his farm. He liked my father, they'd worked well together, and so everything was left to him.'

'But your father was some Lord's son. I had it on good authority. His family objected to his friendship with your mother.'

'That's true. My grandfather is dead and my father's elder brother is now His Lordship. It doesn't matter. I don't know any of them, I have no *wish* to know them.'

'Why didn't your mother tell me?'

'It didn't really matter. It's never mattered to my parents, so why should it concern anyone else?'

'So why are you telling me today?'

'Because you said I was like my mother and inferred that she'd been a foolish girl, paying too much attention to a soldier in need of her care, and said I was following in her footsteps.'

After a few minutes, and faced with Imogen's pale troubled face, she said, 'Then I'm sorry,

120

Nurse Clarkson. If your mother had been open with me, then obviously I would have been fairer in my judgement of you.'

For a long moment they looked at each other, before the matron said, 'You may return to your duties now. Thank you for being honest with me.'

After she had gone, Mary Stepson sat back in her chair to contemplate matters. Why had she been so wrong? It wasn't really because she hadn't known who the girl's father was. It was because it had all happened so long ago, and she too had been in love with that same young officer.

Her friend had been pretty, a happy, friendly girl, while she'd been undoubtedly plain, and while all the men had chatted to Imogen's mother and obviously found her nice and genial, she'd been distant and often morose.

How different their lives had been. Her nursing friend had married the man she loved and given him a daughter, while she'd soldiered on with her career. Surely she had to be congratulated on that? She'd done well, risen to matron, and what was love anyway? Even love didn't always fulfil the expectation of life.

She'd make amends – oh, very discreetly – but up to now the girl hadn't had an easy passage. From today she'd see to it that changes were made.

Back in the ward they were dispensing tea, and another nurse said, 'What did you want to see the matron for?'

'Oh, something and nothing.'

'Jimmy Kent's been asking after you. Said he hadn't seen you hardly. Reckon he's taken a shine to you!'

'Of course not.'

'He's not a bad looking lad. He'll allus have a limp ye know, that shrapnel's cruel. Just as bad as having a leg off.'

'There'll be so many more of them suffering from it.'

'There will. Here, take this tea over, make his day.'

Jimmy moaned as he tried to hoist himself up against his pillows, and she tried to help him. 'Is the pain worse today, Jimmy?' she asked him.

'It's worse every day. Some of the lads are going back there, and that's what I want to do too.'

When she didn't speak, he said quickly, 'You're not sayin' anythin'. Have ye heard something? Have ye heard 'em sayin' I'm back 'ome for good?'

'Jimmy, I haven't heard a thing, but you will hear in due course. Suppose you don't go back to fight again. Isn't there a life for you here?'

'Not back wi' the folk who were too old and too ill to fight, there won't be. I'll be a dodderin' old cripple. What girl'd ever look at me?'

'Oh Jimmy, that's a silly way to talk.'

'Would your friend Louise ever look at me? She didn't want me when I was well and strong, she certainly wouldn't want what's left of me.'

'If you're going to talk like that, I'm not going

to listen to any more of this nonsense.'

'You ask 'er when ye see 'er.'

'I doubt if I *will* see her, Jimmy. Louise Maxton and I live in separate worlds now. I don't know what she's doing with herself, but I hardly think it will be nursing.'

'Oh no, it won't be that. She's probably setting the world alight somewhere.'

Ten

There was deep consternation around the dining table at the Reed-Blyton's residence on the occasion of Miranda's eighteenth birthday. Her sister had delivered her bombshell by informing them that she had it on good authority that Cedric Hambleton intended to marry the girl he had escorted to the Red Cross Ball.

'But that's quite ridiculous,' her mother said sharply. 'Besides, how do you know? He's in France, and you don't know the girl.'

'I know her sister, she's one of our group, and she told me Cedric proposed after the ball and Julie accepted him.'

'And what do his parents think about it? Hasn't Cora told you any of this, Miranda?'

'I don't think she knows anything. At least, she hasn't said, although she does look pretty miserable at the moment.'

'Well, of course. Oh, this is quite ridiculous, who is this girl? She's quite out of his class, and haven't we always said Cedric and Miranda would be ideally suited?'

Miranda sat with a frozen face, and her sister wished she hadn't said a word.

'When is he proposing to marry this girl?' their mother was saying. 'After all, we don't know how long this war is going to last, or even if he'll escape from it unscathed.'

'Well obviously, Mother, nothing can happen until the war's over, but I heard the girl's sister talking at the meeting, and when I asked her about it she said it was all true. Cedric intends to marry her after the war.'

'You mean they're formally engaged?'

'It rather looks like that.'

Miranda jumped to her feet and ran weeping from the room, while her mother said, 'This is quite terrible. I intend to telephone Mrs Hambleton first thing tomorrow morning to find out what exactly is going on.'

'And if it's true, Mother, what can anybody do about it?'

For the first time her father entered the conversation by saying, 'His parents can object. The lad'll be out of the army with no money of his own and no career. Silly young fellas who think they're suddenly war heroes because they're wearing the King's uniform!'

'But if he loves her, Father?'

'Love, love! What has love got to do with it? He has a duty to his family. He'll have other things to think about, rather than this soppy idea of love.'

'Well, I'm in love with James. I was as soon as I met him at the ball. What's wrong with that?'

'Nothing. He's one of us, the right sort, I don't like this silly suffragette movement you're involved with, but where James is concerned you've shown a bit of common sense.'

Meeting her mother's eyes, her mother shook her head. Now was not the time to agree or disagree with her father, and he was already saying, 'Can't we get on with our meal without discussing this ludicruous talk of love and marriage? These next few years'll sort everything out. Get your sister back in here. I want no more drama-queen antics at the dining table.'

Miranda lay stretched out on her bed weeping copiously, and her sister was quick to encourage her to return downstairs. 'Father's furious,' she said. 'I wish I'd never said anything. Honestly, Miranda, why should you care so much? You hardly know Cedric Hambleton. It's only been you and Cora romanticizing about you for Cedric and Cora for Peter, there was never any substance to it.'

'Oh, but there was! Mother talked about it, *Cora's* mother talked about it. It was something ordained.'

'Oh Miranda, it's destiny that there'll be a tomorrow, that the sun and moon will appear. Anything else is wishful thinking.'

'Well I don't happen to think so.'

'Then you're going to have to face up to it,

Miranda. He's asked that girl to marry him, and even if it won't be tomorrow, it will be one day, if he comes back alive.'

'I don't want to come back to the dining room. I'm not hungry.'

'Don't be silly, Miranda. Father'll come and get you, and he's angry. What good will staying here do you?'

Reluctantly she returned to the dining room, where she encountered her father's stern frown and her mother's warning look, but all Miranda wanted to do was see Cora to find out if it was all true.

They couldn't all have been lies, those ecstatic dreams they had cherished of a perfect future with the perfect suitor in an ideal world. Now their ideal world was crumbling round their ears, and even the love they had promised themselves was fairy tale.

The meal was over. Her father left the table in grumpy silence, her mother stated her intention of attending some charitable meeting and her sister said she was meeting James.

'It's all right for you,' Miranda complained. 'Your James is at the War Office and likely to remain so. Everybody thinks he's perfect, and I'll be hearing about Cedric and this girl for months, years.'

'There are other men in the world. You surely don't want a man who wants somebody else.'

She received no reply, and there seemed no point in staying simply to look at Miranda's doleful, tearful face.

It was later in the afternoon when she heard her father leaving the house and she felt safe to use the telephone without being overheard. It did not need words. Cora's hesitant, doubtful voice said it all, and after a few minutes Cora said, 'I can't talk here, Miranda, there are so many people all over the place and it's difficult. I need to see you.'

'I know, but when?'

'It's all so busy here, and Mother's finding me all sorts of things to do. I'll try to get into London later this week, but I'm really not very sure.'

'But I have to see you, Cora!'

'I know. I'll try, honestly, some time this week.'

'Can't I come to see you?'

'Oh no, that wouldn't do at all.'

'Why not?'

'Because everything here is so upsetting. Daddy's away, and Mother is very sad and far too busy to think straight. All this has come as a terrible shock to us, Miranda.'

'So it's really true then?'

'It would seem so for now, but how do we know what's really going to happen? Cedric's fighting somewhere in France, we don't even know if he'll be safe or not, and nothing seems for real any more.'

'When shall we be able to meet?' Miranda asked forlornly.

'Soon. Aren't you doing anything at all? Aren't you bored simply going to charity meetings with your mother or collecting things for the war effort?'

'I'm not bored. These things need to be done.'

'Oh well, we will meet very soon, Miranda, and please don't go on being so upset about Cedric, it'll all sort itself out.'

Miranda had no such hope. Her mother had gone off to her meeting without inviting her to go with her. Miranda thought she knew why. All the talk at the meeting would be about Cedric and that girl. Her mother wouldn't want her to hear a word of it, but what could she do? The afternoon loomed ahead of her, dismal and empty, and then suddenly she decided to telephone Louise. Louise had answers for most things. Louise could be audacious about tragedy.

The telephone call came on a woefully empty afternoon when Louise was feeling despondent that there seemed to be little to do. Andrew had left with his regiment weeks before, and there'd been no news from him for ages. Her mother was at what she called a political meeting, which probably entailed nothing more adventurous than a meeting with Martin Broughton.

The voice of Miranda Reed-Blyton hardly merited a sense of adventure, however.

'Can't we meet somewhere?' Miranda was asking. 'I'm so fed up here on my own, and Cora can't get away.'

'You *sound* pretty fed up. Is something wrong?'

'Well, it's difficult to talk about it on the telephone. Can't we meet?'

'Where?'

'Couldn't we meet for tea at Julio's? Or we could walk in the park and have tea at the little cafe there.'

'Miranda, it's the middle of November and it's raining. Why don't you come round here? My mother's out, and I'll be glad of the company. Get a taxi, and you'll be here in a few minutes.'

Looking at Miranda's woeful face when she arrived, and listening to her string of miseries, Louise had a sudden urge to laugh.

How silly it all was. Lamenting about a boy she'd fantasized about for years without actually ever really knowing him! But when she said as much, Miranda looked at her with wide tear-filled eyes before saying, 'Oh Louise, how can you say that? Ever since I was very young I've heard Mother talking about Cedric as the boy I would marry, just as Cora's been destined for Peter. Now he's going to marry this girl and what's going to happen to me?'

'But you can't possibly want him now if he's engaged to her.'

'But who *is* she? Wouldn't it bother you if the man you were meant to marry found somebody else?'

'Well, I'm not meant to marry anybody that I know of. Oh, no doubt the parents would endeavour to make sure he was terribly upper crust and well endowed with money, but I'm not going to be pushed into anything.'

'I wasn't being pushed. I wanted it.'

'Don't you think you should be thanking your

lucky stars that you're out of it?'

Miranda wondered why she had thought she could ever talk to Louise – Louise, who with her cynicism was far too sophisticated for her age – while Louise herself was enjoying Miranda's feelings of betrayal, even though they were interlaced with so much stupidity.

As they walked across the hall, Miranda looked up at the portrait of Louise's mother. Isobel Maxton was a beautiful woman, even without the enhancement of jewels in her hair and round her throat, and Miranda said feelingly, 'She's very beautiful, Louise, and she was always so nice.'

'Nice!'

'Well, yes. Gracious and charming. What's your father like?'

'I don't see much of him. He's taciturn and grouchy, not in the least gracious or charming.'

'The man I see your mother with sometimes is nice, very handsome. Mother says he's a politician.'

'He is. Our MP.'

'Do you like him?'

'He intrigues me. He doesn't like *me*.'

'Really? Surely he hasn't said so!'

'He doesn't need to. I can tell.'

'Why doesn't he like you? How do you know?'

'He's distant and hardly friendly.'

'But surely your mother will want him to like you?'

'I rather think my mother's partly responsible

for the fact that he *doesn't* like me.'

'How can she be?'

'By regaling him with tales of my many misdeeds over the years. My high-handed likes and dislikes, and more recently my problems with Father's sisters. I've no doubt Mother's told him that I'm a temperamental little minx who is destined to cause mayhem wherever I go, and because she's gracious and charming he'll believe her.'

'Well, you always did set out to shock everybody.'

'I know, it was fun. You wanted me to shock you.'

'I'm so fed up with this war! Oh, I know it's only just got started, but life wasn't meant to be like this, learning to knit scarves and gloves, roll bandages and cram gift boxes for the men. Look at Cora, she's doing all sorts of silly jobs now they've turned their house over to a nursing home, and what about Imogen? She's nursing in Essex! I wrote to ask her if she could meet me in London one day, but she said she got very little time off.'

'Mother's on the Committee for a great many hospitals. I'll ask her if she can take me with her the next time she visits the one in Essex. I'd rather like to see Imogen again.'

'I suppose your brother is now at the front?'

'Yes, and it's so boring without him.'

'What do you do for the war effort then?'

'I smile and talk to the men I meet, and quite often one of their mothers invites me to tea. All terribly boring, Miranda, but it amuses me to see those mothers manoeuvring me into position for whenever the time is right.'

'Oh Louise, do you really think Cedric will marry that girl?'

'What if he does? There's other fish in the sea, and would you really want Mrs Hambleton as a mother-in-law?'

'Yes, of course, she's very nice. Our families are close.'

Louise looked at her in pitying silence. Her own future was a closed book, but she would never be like Miranda. There had to be something more to life than pining for a man who preferred somebody else.

Miranda summoned a taxi to collect her at three thirty, and after Louise had escorted her to the door and watched her driving away she looked gloomily across the gardens at a dull leaden sky and the gloom of a November day. It started to rain, and she quickly closed the door and went back into the house.

Miranda's visit had upset her strangely. She had listened so often to Miranda and Cora congratulating themselves on what they considered a serene, intricately planned future with a man ordained for them, marriage and children, prestige and wealth, and a continuance of their lives for their children in similar circumstances. She had never been able to picture it for herself, but perhaps she was the one who had no right to scoff at normality.

She glanced up at her mother's portrait, and

her lips curled in a cynical smile. Her mother was beautiful, and yes she was nice, so why wasn't it enough? Why did she look for more behind that beautiful, perfect face?

Conversation was minimal at the dinner table that night as she sat with her parents, her father as usual absorbed with his thoughts on other matters, her mother making polite conversation as to how she had spent her day.

Her mother had little to say about Miranda's visit until Louise asked, 'Mother, did you know that Cedric Hambleton had got engaged to that girl he took to the Red Cross Ball?'

'No. I only know the boy slightly and the girl not at all.'

'Miranda was upset. She had thought Cedric was for her.'

'Wasn't that a little previous?'

'It's what she was led to believe when their mothers got together.'

'Oh, well, the war could alter everything, even an engagement.'

'Mother, don't you go to the hospital in Essex? I believe Imogen Clarkson is working there as a nurse.'

'Really? Very commendable of her.'

'I would like to see her, Mother. Perhaps I could go with you when next you go?'

'Maybe Imogen could persuade you to do something similar. You seem so bored these days, Louise.'

'I am bored, Mother. I'm not sure that nursing would be the answer.'

'Does nothing else spring to mind?'

'I could join the suffragettes.'

'Oh, I don't think so. Martin thinks that is a lost cause, and he should know.'

For the first time she met her father's eyes across the table, and somewhat grimly he said, 'It does seem rather regrettable that girls with less education than you are earning a living. I've got girls working as secretaries, what's wrong with that?'

'Nothing, except that I haven't been trained for it.'

'What were you trained for then?'

'To speak nicely, to hold an intelligent conversation, and to know a little something about all manner of things, but none of the things that would have found me a job. I learned how to dance gracefully and speak a little French. Of course, if I'd gone to finishing school that would have put the gilt on the gingerbread.'

'Are you telling me we've wasted a great deal of money?'

'Not really, Father, but like Mother says, the war has altered a great many things.'

'And will alter a lot more things,' he snapped.

'So I can go with you to the hospital, Mother?'

'Of course. I rather liked Imogen, she seemed such a nice sensible girl.'

'Do you think I should telephone her first? If she's very busy she may not have time to speak with me.'

'Oh, I'll speak to the matron or one of the sisters. They'll arrange for her to see you.'

'Has Broughton said anything to you about that fracas at the House the other morning?' her father asked, fixing his wife with a penetrating stare.

'You know Martin doesn't discuss politics with me, particularly of that nature,' she answered him. 'In any case, he wasn't really involved.'

Did her father really not mind that Martin Broughton and her mother saw so much of each other? Had she really done all that was expected of her – produced a son and a daughter, graced his house and entertained his friends – so now it could all be forgotten and they could both go their separate ways?

Whenever they went out together it was a duty. They spent holidays apart and slept in separate rooms. Was that the sort of marriage she could look forward to? Either that or a marriage like Miranda and Cora had envisaged.

'Do you want coffee in the drawing room?' her mother asked them.

'Not for me,' her father said. 'I have a chap coming from the War Office. We'll have drinks in my study later on. I'm expecting Broughton too, didn't he tell you?'

'No.'

What did Martin Broughton and her mother talk about when they were together, Louise asked herself. For the first time in weeks she thought about Jimmy Kent. They'd talked about countless things, silly things perhaps, but there had been laughter and warmth, not this dried-up emptiness that meant nothing.

As she followed her mother out of the room she thought, we're like two wax dolls, well fed and pampered, waiting, always waiting, but for what?

Eleven

The two girls embraced each other warmly, and then Louise laughed, saying, 'Gracious me, Imogen, you really do look the part!'

Imogen smiled. 'Like a play, you mean? Dressed up like a nurse and waiting for the applause.'

'But you look so proper, darling. You're making me feel very superficial.'

'You look very elegant, just as I'd expected.'

'But Imogen, isn't it absolutely awful? There's nothing remotely glamorous about nursing, all those wounded heroes and bedpans, how can you cope with that?'

'It's what I wanted to do, what my mother did. How about you? I know what you said you'd do, but I can't think it's materialized.'

'Not yet, darling, but it will. One thing's for sure, I couldn't do *this*. Now, tell me about some of those young men you're nursing. Are they handsome? Are they in love with you? Is one of them destined to be the love of your life?'

'I don't even think about it, but one of them

was in love with *you*.'

'With me!'

'It is hard to believe, isn't it? But whenever I do speak to him he talks of nothing else: the dancing in the village hall, the saunters along the country lanes, the passion in the conservatory.'

'But who is he? I can't think of any boy who could know me. Really, Imogen, who in this place ever met me?'

'Not even Jimmy Kent?'

Louise stared at her incredulously, her face pink with embarrassment, then Imogen said, 'You do know him, don't you, Louise?'

'But why should he connect you with me?'

'He says we come from the same sort of background, we speak alike, then when he talked about you so much I knew you'd met, but I didn't know where.'

'At the aunts'. Mother dumped me there for a few months after she picked me up that last day at school. I was with them a few months, then they found out about Jimmy and me and I was sent home.'

'Did you love him, Louise? He loved you.'

'I liked him, and he was fun, but I'd have played around with a gypsy, *anybody* who could help me to get over being dumped at the aunts', and I needed to get at my mother.'

'Surely it can't have been all that bad. Why did she leave you with them?'

'Because I would interfere with her lifestyle too much, and because she didn't know what to do with me. No finishing school to get me out of London, no job to occupy me, nothing, and why should she spend time looking after me when she could be more gainfully employed being with Martin Broughton?'

'But you liked Jimmy. He's a nice boy. Were you unhappy to leave him?'

'Relieved, actually. I knew he loved me, but nothing could come of it, you know that, surely, and in the end it was for the best. Oh good heavens, is he badly injured? What is the matter with him?'

'They thought they would have to amputate one of his legs, but now they think it can be saved. He's terribly wounded with shrapnel, so I doubt if he'll be going back to fight. He'll probably be discharged.'

'He was good looking. Not his face, surely?'

'No, he's still good looking. A girl comes to see him with her mother, a girl he knew from the village where he lived. Did you know her?'

'I think I knew her, but not well. There was a girl who fancied him, but in those days he only had eyes for me.'

'I can arrange for you to see him, Louise. Is that what you want?'

'No, I can't see him.'

Imogen stared at her sadly, and Louise said quickly, 'Imogen, don't you see it would be terribly cruel to see him? I was cruel to Jimmy, I used him, I never loved him, and the best thing that can happen is for him to forget me, to go back to his home and try to love this girl who loves him. There's nothing for Jimmy Kent and me, there never was.'

'I suppose you're right.'

'Well, of course I am. But what about you? Are you here until the end of the war? We don't know how long it'll last.'

'No, we don't. I want to hear about you, Louise. How do you spend your time? What do you do for the war effort? There are so many ways you can help.'

'And you're beginning to sound like Florence Nightingale. I'll do something, never fear.'

'Do you see Miranda and Cora?'

'Occasionally. Cora's helping out in the nursing home they've created at her father's house, and Miranda's attending Red Cross meetings, rolling bandages and knitting socks. Can you see me doing that?'

'Then what? You could write letters to the men serving overseas, or you could do some sort of office work, perhaps.'

'Oh yes, my father could get me job with girls who know about reality, who've been educated to be secretaries, office workers, and all *I'll* be capable of is making the tea and running a few errands.'

'Oh Louise, you make yourself sound so worthless.'

'I *am* worthless in that department, but there are men who need cheering up out there, and I'm good at that. I can be the beautiful Louise Maxton who loves to dance and liven up parties, who women find fun with and men find irresistible. Don't you think that's a role that suits me better than what you're doing?'

'Your parents would never allow it. You're destined to behave yourself and marry well. I think it's time you faced reality.'

'My brother used to tell me I was obsessed with flights of fancy. I suppose he was right, but it's how I am. I say, can't we go out for lunch somewhere? We've exhausted the dull things in life, we could talk about something a little more adventurous.'

'And I have to get back to the ward. I was given an hour to chat with you and now I have work to do. I do want to see you again, Louise, out I'm not sure when I can.'

'Oh, I'll fix up something. I'll tell the girls we've met, but please, Imogen, can we let Jimmy Kent be a secret between us? Please don't tell him you've seen me. He'll think I should have wanted to see him, but it's better this way. I'm not a sweet, caring sort of person, but in this I intend to be.'

It was in the early evening that Imogen's room-mate accosted her on the corridor outside their room. 'I saw you talkin' to that posh woman just outside the boardroom this mornin'. I was sure I recognized 'er. She was that girl I knew back in the village, the girl who knew Jimmy Kent.'

'She was asking me directions as to where she could find her mother.'

'Ye mean ye didn't know 'er?'

'I'm telling you what we were talking about,

Jenny. Her mother was at a meeting with the powers that be.'

'I'm sure she was the same girl.'

'I wouldn't know, but hasn't Jimmy got a girlfriend? I'm sure he won't want reminding of another girl when he seems quite happy with this one.'

'Ye think I shouldn't mention it then?'

'Not really. I doubt it's the same girl anyway. Her mother's a baroness.'

'Oh, I doubt if she was *that* posh, but I just wondered, that's all.'

Talk of Jimmy had disturbed Louise strangely, and on the way back to London her thoughts dwelt on it, while her mother leafed through several documents she'd received at the hospital.

They had almost reached their destination when her mother said, 'How did you find Imogen? I'm sorry, I've been so engrossed with this paperwork that I hadn't got around to asking yet.'

'She was the same as always, Mother: sweet, very proper, and looking the part.'

'I wish you had something in mind, dear, some role to play in the country's troubles.'

'Not nursing, Mother!'

'No, I didn't think so, but I really do think we should have a word with your father. I'm sure he can find your some sort of role in his office at the House, something that you can later say has helped.'

They finished the rest of the journey in silence, and Louise dreaded the evening before them.

Her father was fractious. The war was not going well, there was too much disparity in the House and he had indigestion.

'The food's no good, too much sameness. No wonder everybody's grumbling about their stomachs. Look at this stuff! When did we last get decent lamb? And the vegetables are tasteless.'

'There is a war on,' his wife said calmly. 'We're lucky to be getting anything at all, I wonder what the boys at the front are getting, what is Andrew getting?'

'Andrew, Andrew, always Andrew.'

'He is your son.'

'I'm aware of it, but we have to live too. We're doing the best we can for the army, and we're endeavouring to do more. It doesn't alter the fact that we're suffering as well. I'm fed up with this sort of food. I'm going to my study. I'll do some work in there over a rum toddy.'

He stormed out of the room and, meeting her mother's resigned gaze, Louise said feelingly, 'There'll be no talking to Father about me tonight, Mother.'

'No, it would appear not. I'll have a chat to Martin about you, dear. I'm sure there's something he can do.'

'Why should he do anything for me? I'm not his daughter.'

'No dear, but he is our friend. He'll agree with

me that you should be doing something besides strolling in the park, giggling with your girl-friends and whatever young man is available. I think Martin disapproves of you, Louise.'

'I'm sure he does, Mother. It would be nice to reassure him that I am worthy of better things.' Why did she feel that Martin Broughton should be such a bone of contention between her moth-er and herself? 'But I don't want him to do any-thing for me, really. I intend to ask Father what he thinks. He's every bit as influential as Martin Broughton.'

'You've always inferred that your father shows little interest in what you want to do with your life. Now, suddenly, he becomes all caring?'

'Perhaps that's how I want him to be, Mother.'

'In that case, Louise, I hope you're not doom-ed to bitter disappointment. Speak to him, by all means. I'll await results.'

Her mother turned away with an impatient shrug, and at that moment Martin Broughton joined them in the hall.

Favouring him with a welcome smile her mother went forward to greet him, receiving a swift kiss on her cheek, while Louise received a somewhat absent smile, and her mother and Martin walked into the drawing room.

Of course she could interrupt their rendez-vous, join them for drinks, chatter about some-thing and nothing and receive her mother's impatient frown, but then her mother might actually ask Martin Broughton to find some-

143

thing useful for her to do.

A servant was approaching her father's study, carrying a tray containing his hot toddy, and impulsively she said, 'I'll take that, Charlton. I need to speak to my father anyway.'

He was sitting in his large easy chair in front of a blazing fire, an open newspaper on the table besides his chair. The room smelled of cigar smoke, and as she laid the tray down on the table he looked at her with a conspiratorial smile. This was the time of day he liked best, and she was aware that he hoped her visit would be brief.

'Your mother gone out?' he asked quickly.

'No, Father, she's entertaining Mr Broughton.'

'Oh well, they'll not be expecting me to join them. Shut the door as you go out, Louise.'

Instead Louise perched on the arm of a chair opposite and, receiving his doubtful stare, she smiled. 'I need to talk to you, Father, it's long overdue.'

'Talk to me? What about?'

'About me.'

'You?'

'Yes, Father. I am your daughter, and I'm eighteen, with no job, no prospects and no incentives.'

'Prospects! What do you mean by prospects? You've got a good home, sufficient money, clothes, jewellery, friends and a good education behind you, what more do you want?'

'Why did you bother to educate me if the results are so empty? England's at war, Father.

144

Girls are working at things that contribute some-thing to our winning it, and here am I taking afternoon tea with prospective mothers-in-law for sons I don't want, and watching my mother go off to her do-good meetings and having to listen to what she is advising other people to do. It isn't enough, Father!'

'What do you want me to do about it?'

'You're an influential man with irons in so many fires. Surely you must want more for me than this useless existence I'm living?'

'Get your mother to have a word with Brough-ton. He's an MP, likely to be far greater if what I've been hearing is correct, and he'll fix you up with something, I'm sure.'

'I don't want Martin Broughton to have anything to do with my future.'

'Why not?'

'He's well aware of my trouble at the aunts'. I'm sure Mother informed him that I was trouble she could do without, and he'll certainly not want this troubled girl to be foisted on *him*.'

'But what can I do?'

'You can't think of anything?'

'No. The girls who work in Whitehall are equipped for it. All you could do is make the tea, run errands, and talk on the telephone. We haven't educated you to do more than that.'

'If I can talk on the telephone, Father, I can talk to the sort of men you've brought here, men I've seen you with. I could entertain them once you're finished talking business. I know how socializing bores you. I'm intelligent, and

I've been told I'm pretty. It's a good start, surely?'

'You're talking about diplomats and ambassadors, girl, not some young lad like the one you cavorted with in the countryside.'

'I haven't got *designs* on these men, Father, at least not to marry them, but they could respect me as your daughter and admire me and wish to be seen with me.'

He stared at her long and doubtfully before saying, 'I hadn't expected to hear any of this from my own daughter. I wonder what your mother's going to think about it?'

'Why should my mother know anything about it?'

'Because she is your mother and expects better things from you than spending your time flirting.'

'Father what sort of things? My mother spends most of her time being charming and gracious to a man you know, a man you're always friendly with and appear to like. Isn't it within the realms of possibility that your daughter could learn to do the same, to be charming and gracious to some man who would appreciate your kindness and mine?'

'You've got a nerve young woman!'

'Father, I don't want a man to sleep with, to take away from his wife, to fall in love with. I could be as useful to this country providing comfort and support to great men as I would be nursing some wounded hero.'

She smiled, then looking at his empty glass

she said, 'Another, toddy, Father? I'll tell Charlton.'

She left the room without looking at him again, and encountering her mother in the corridor she smiled and her mother said, 'Is your father in his study, Louise?'

'Yes, Mother, I've just left him.'

'Mr Broughton and I are going to one of his constituency meetings, Louise. It's really very important. It'll probably be over around ten so I shan't be too late.'

'Very well, Mother.'

'Are you going out?'

'No, Mother. There doesn't seem very much to do in London at the moment. My friends are all over the place, and all the boys are somewhere in France.'

With a brief smile they parted, but in the Hall she met Martin, waiting for her mother near the door. 'Another meeting, Mr Broughton,' she greeted him.

'I'm afraid so. They are very frequent at the moment.'

'What does Mother do at the meetings?'

'She is one of my constituents, and I'm hoping there'll be a good contingent of them there.'

He smiled briefly before turning away towards the door.

Meanwhile in Henry Maxton's study, his wife said, 'You know I'm going out, Henry. It's a meeting Martin thinks we should attend. Why aren't you going?'

'Because I've got Rogerson and some Frenchman coming. Apparently it's something important.'

'What had Louise to say for herself?'

'Very little. She brought me a hot toddy.'

'And that was all?'

'What would we talk about? I don't know how she spends her time, and you can hardly expect her to be interested in the sort of things I'm doing.'

'She should be doing *something*. We met her friend Imogen at the hospital in Essex today. She's nursing, and the other two, Miranda and Cora, have more going for them than Louise.'

'Have you any suggestions?'

'I thought I might ask Martin if *he* had any suggestions.'

'I doubt if she'd go for that.'

'Why? Surely anything is better than nothing.'

'Aren't you going to be late for your meeting?'

'I'd better go. I won't be late back.'

Isobel closed the door quietly behind her and left him reflecting calmly about the sort of woman his wife had become. She'd been a beautiful, nice sort of girl. His parents had approved of her. She'd been a good wife. The right sort of woman to be with in the right sort of places. She'd given him a son he was very proud of and a daughter he had yet to discover.

He thought about his conversation with her, and making up his mind suddenly he rang the bell on the table near his chair. When Charlton appeared, he said, 'Another hot toddy, Charlton, and ask my daughter to come in here.'

Well, why not? The sooner they got started, the better for all concerned.

Twelve

The wedding of Jean Reed-Blyton had to be a very low-key affair. How could it be anything else after three years of war, with all the tragedies and trauma that went with it?

Miranda sat on her sister's bed thinking that her sister's dress was hardly one she would have chosen, but then there had been very little to choose from.

After a succession of twirls, Jean asked, 'Well, do I look bridal or could I be visiting one of our meetings?'

'It's alright, I suppose.'

'Is that all you can say?'

'Well, it's not one I would have liked. I always fancied myself in taffeta with lashings of embroidery and beading. That really is very plain, Jean.'

'I know. But there is a war on.'

'How long is it going to last, that's what I want to know.'

Just then the door opened, and their brother Peter walked into the room, holding on closely to his walking stick. He was pale, limping painfully, and Jean said, 'Come and sit down, Peter. How is the shoulder and the leg?'

'Not good.'

'Then why are you so insistent you want to go back there?'

'Because it's not over, because I still have a job to do.'

'Haven't you done your bit? You've spent weeks in hospital, and you're not fit to go back.'

'I don't want to talk about it. All ready for the wedding then?'

'As ready as I'll ever be. Miranda doesn't like the dress.'

'It looks all right to me. Anyway, it's in keeping with the state of things.'

'You really don't want to come to my wedding, do you, Peter?'

'Not if I can get out of it.'

'Look, Peter, everybody's looking forward to seeing you there. You're a hero, and you'll enjoy the feasting, such as it is. Can't you at least try to work up some enthusiasm for your sister's wedding?'

'Oh, I'll be there, I'll do my best.'

'You have to be there,' Miranda said. 'I've told Cora Hambleton, and she's dying to meet you again.'

'And who is Cora Hambleton?'

'You know very well who she is: my school-friend, and your intended. Surely you remember all that!'

'My dear girl, I haven't any intended. I'm fancy free and not looking for anyone. This war's going on, and until it's over there'll be no girls – intended or otherwise.'

'It didn't stop Cedric Hambleton from getting engaged before he went out there. If he could do it, why can't you?'

'And that bothered you, didn't it, little sister? Is the engagement still on?'

'Apparently,' Jean said, 'although mother doesn't talk about it, and neither do the Hambletons.'

'Don't they like the girl?'

'They don't really know her.'

'Why, doesn't she visit? Don't they ever see her?'

'They haven't seen each other for three years. Come on, Peter! The world's in a mess. Until it's over, how can we say what's going to happen to any of us?'

'Well, you'll be settled down with a man who doesn't have to face the conflict. You really did all right for yourself there, Jean.'

'Not intentionally.'

'Perhaps not, but very, very wisely.'

'Well, I think it's time we went downstairs to face the parents. I hope Mother's not wearing that awful beige dress she was intent on buying. I tried to discourage her, but you know what she's like.'

Indeed, Mrs Reed-Blyton was wearing the hated beige dress, in keeping with a large beige hat, adorned with feathers, that would have not been incongruous in the Royal Enclosure at Ascot.

The two sisters raised their eyebrows in sympathy, but quite unaware their mother said, 'What a time you've been taking. You and I are ready to go to the church, Peter, and we're late. You both look very nice, although I would have preferred Miranda to have worn primrose. Blue was never your colour, dear.'

'I don't see why not. I'm reasonably blonde.'

'With a touch of auburn, Miranda. Primrose or pale green suits you far better, even when you were a child.'

'I wonder what Louise and Cora will be wearing?' Miranda pondered when Peter and her mother had left. 'You can rely on Louise wearing something entirely flashy, but Cora will want to impress Peter, I'm sure of it.'

'And Peter has no intention of being impressed for some time to come,' Jean said. 'I suggest you give your friend a little bit of good advice: be nice, friendly, but leave everything else until much later, much *much* later.'

'I wonder if Louise has anybody in mind? She's never in the usual places, but somebody told Mother they'd seen her dining out with one or two different men, all of them very upmarket and evidently rich.'

'Probably friends of her parents. They would never allow Louise to consort with just anybody.'

'Louise would consort with any Lothario if she got a kick out of it. Perhaps she'll enlighten us about her men friends.'

'And I wouldn't be too curious, if I were you.'

Their father beckoned to them from the door, saying grumpily, 'The car's here, girls. Shouldn't you have gone with your mother, Miranda?'

'I should have, but I wanted to go with you and Jean. Peter had the utmost difficulty in getting into the car. Don't worry, Daddy, I'll try to remain in the background and not take too much of the limelight off Jean.'

They had known the church would be crowded. Society weddings were something to liven up the atmosphere in such depressing times, and from the array of flowered and feathered hats it was obvious the occasion had been one the guests had looked forward to.

Sitting beside his mother, Peter was favoured by smiles and whispered greetings from those sitting immediately behind them, particularly from a rather pretty dark-haired girl wearing gentle pink and a small flowered hat. She was Cora Hambleton, he thought, remembering her from Christmas parties and other functions before the world had gone mad.

Mrs Reed-Blyton wasn't at all sure that her daughter's choice of dress did anything for her. She was getting to be such an ordinary girl since she'd been involved with the suffragette movement. Votes for women indeed! When would women ever get the vote? Never, if men had anything to do with it. Neither Jean's father nor her prospective husband liked the idea.

Some day soon she *must* have a word with Anne Hambleton, for they really ought to know *something* about Cedric's association with that girl. They'd been engaged for three years, and absolutely nobody seemed to know where it was going.

After the ceremony, the bridal couple smiled and seemed entirely pleased with the day's events. Surrounded by their guests, who had collected to wish them well, they seemed happy enough, even when Miranda appeared slightly bored and Peter was evidently in some pain.

'Mother, I have to sit down somewhere,' he said urgently. 'Over there in the alcove. I'll be alright when I've rested awhile.'

'I hope you're going to eat something,' his mother said firmly.

'Oh I shall. Just go ahead and mingle with the rest of them.'

He tried to make himself comfortable, but was almost instantly joined by the girl in the flowered hat, who sat down besides him saying, 'Can I get you anything? You look dreadfully tired. We were awfully sorry to hear you'd been wounded, Peter, but you are recovering, I hope?'

'Yes, thank you. Rather slowly I'm afraid.'

'Then you don't have to think of going back to France, do you? I really don't think you should go back, you've done your bit.'

'But I want to go back, Cora. It is Cora, isn't it?'

She blushed. 'Yes, how nice to think you remembered me.'

'Well, we were all very much of a crowd in the old days. Who's the girl in bright blue with the

154

white hat? She seems familiar.'

'Louise Maxton. That's her mother she's with, Lady Maxton.'

'Do you know her well?'

'We were all at school together.'

'She's very attractive, don't you think?'

'Yes,' she replied tersely, 'and something of a flirt.'

'Really? Oh, well, it could relieve the monotony.'

'Well, if I can't get you anything, perhaps I should return to the rest of them. Nice to have met you again, Peter.'

It was evident that his admiration of Louise Maxton had annoyed her, and he smiled to himself cynically. It was all either too soon or too late. She was a nice girl, but there was a long way to go. He moaned a little as the pain in his leg increased, and he would have given anything to be able to excuse himself and go home.

Miranda, on the other hand, sat with her mother's friends rather than with the younger element. She was waiting avidly for the talk to turn to Cedric, and she did not have long to wait.

'How long since you heard from Cedric?' her mother asked.

'Months,' his mother said. 'It's absolutely terrible. We don't know where he is, and one battle after another simply means boatloads of soldiers being brought home either to get better or die.'

'Look at my Peter over there, in so much pain, yet all he can think about is going back there. I saw you talking to him, Cora. Did he say anything to you? It's all he can talk about these days.'

'Nothing really, Mrs Reed-Blyton.'

'But you did have a little chat with him.'

'Oh yes, he asked who Louise was, he thought her attractive.'

'Really. Well of course Louise is attractive, but we all know the sort of men she's interested in – foreign diplomats, men older than herself. I hope you enlightened him, dear.'

'No. It's really none of my business.'

The two mothers looked at each other anxiously, and Mrs Reed-Blyton said, 'Do you see anything of your son's fiancée, dear?'

'Nothing at all. Of course she's busy with her job, and quite honestly I've only met her about three times, once at the ball and once or twice since. Sometimes I think I might not even know her were I to meet her in the street!'

'Hardly something to make you feel hopeful, dear. About the marriage, I mean.'

'No, it isn't. I really want a daughter-in-law I can relate to, a girl I know and can feel comfortable with.'

'Perhaps when you really get to know her it will all fall into place,' another guest said feelingly.

'Oh I really do hope so. On the other hand, I think perhaps that this marriage will never take place. They haven't seen each other for three years, and even then they didn't really know each other all that well.'

Cora and Miranda left the group together, and

Cora said, 'That's what you wanted to hear, isn't it, Miranda? Mother doesn't want it to materialize, and it probably won't.'

'And what about you and Peter? You weren't exactly enthusiastic about that few minutes' chat.'

'And he wasn't enthusiastic about me. He preferred Louise.'

'Oh come on, he doesn't know Louise.'

'Who is that man she's with, anyway?'

'No idea. Do you think something could be going on between her mother and our MP? They're always together, and her father isn't here today.'

'Why don't we have a talk to Louise? She might introduce us to her man friend, and I can enlighten my brother as to who he is,' Miranda said.

Louise was thinking the wedding had gone very well, but was all a lot of fuss about nothing. This had been a relatively simple wedding, but she'd been to others where the bride's train had trailed down the central aisle of the church, where the bridesmaids had numbered five or six, and where the time taken up for photographs had seemed interminable. She liked Jean Reed-Blyton, but thank goodness that the wedding had been a simple affair and not one that had taken all day.

She greeted her two schoolfriends with a smile, and Cora was the first to say, 'You're looking very beautiful, Louise. I like the dress, frightfully sophisticated.'

'Yes, isn't it? Granny always said that blondes should wear blue.'

'We never seem to see you walking in the park these days. You must have something better to amuse you.'

'Actually yes, I do, some of the time. This is Monsieur Pierre Deviouze. He happens to be staying with us, and Mother got permission to invite him to the wedding.'

'Your father isn't here?'

'No. He's really very busy at the moment with matters to do with the war.'

Actually, her father had seen them depart with great relief. Functions of this sort were hardly his scene, and he was probably fast asleep in his study, after having partaken of several rum toddies and having got rid of both family and guest.

Louise knew what her friends were thinking: that he was far too old for her, and though he was decidedly attractive, there couldn't possibly be anything in it for either of them.

She'd wanted a job and she'd got one: being charming to her father's guests, the sweet, modest daughter of the house, and if any of them had liked her too well they knew their limitations. Only her mother was concerned. She considered it unnatural. Why couldn't Louise have taken to nursing, or something else that didn't open everybody's minds to crude speculation?

Her mother was mingling with other groups around the room, charming and gracious, and

Martin Broughton didn't lack for admirers. He was their well-liked and respected MP, and even if there was something not quite right about things, her Mother and Martin would know how to be discreet.

'Well, I suppose we'd better circulate,' Miranda said. 'Mother gets terribly worried about Peter, but he is improving. How goes it with your brother, Louise?'

'I don't know. It's months since we heard from him, and we're hoping no news is good news.'

'How long is this wretched war going to last?' Cora cried. 'We don't hear from Cedric either, and we don't even know if his fiancée hears anything!'

'Surely she would tell you?'

'We never see her. She's awfully busy, and so are we.'

Louise looked across the room to where Martin Broughton had rejoined her mother, and once again she became aware of his expression, coldly remote, the look of a man for a girl he disapproved of, and angrily she thought, he's not going to get away with it! How dare he treat me as though I was a loose, depraved woman when he's cavorting with my mother?

The reception limped on until the late afternoon, Jean and her new husband departed briefly for a short honeymoon in Brighton and the rest of the guests departed for their homes. The Reed-Blytons were the last to leave and, worried about her son, Mrs Reed-Blyton said anxiously, 'It's all been too much for Peter. We must get him home quickly.'

'He's been sitting down most of the day,' his father said sharply. 'he's hardly been cavorting about.'

'But there's been so much going on, the music and the chatter. He needs a rest.'

Mr Reed-Blyton shrugged his shoulders. How women went on, he thought. In a few weeks the boy would be back in France. That'd give them more to worry about!

As they walked out of the hotel, Miranda was thinking mainly about her last conversation with Cora about her brother's fiancée.

'I'm sure it'll never materialize,' Cora had said. 'Three years to be engaged and never see one another! What will they have in common? Not even so-called love can make up for that.'

The trauma of getting Peter into their car occupied some time, and even her thoughts on what might have been were obliterated until they reached home. She would miss having her sister around. Jean could always be relied on to provide light entertainment of some sort or another.

The Maxton house was a hive of activity when they returned from the wedding, and they stared around them with amazement at the numerous crates and bags until the butler explained that Mr Andrew had arrived home soon after they had left that morning.

'But we should have been informed,' his mother said sharply.

'Mr Andrew said not,' the butler explained. 'He went out immediately, My Lady, and said he would explain when he returned.'

'But where has he gone? Is he well? Has he been wounded?'

'No, My Lady. He appeared well, but very weary. I'm sure he will explain very soon.'

'How long is he home for?'

'My Lady, I don't know. It was all so quick: he went out immediately.'

'Does his father know?'

'I have informed him.'

'I must go to him. I suppose he's in his study.'

After muttered excuses, the Frenchman left with her, and Martin and Louise were left alone. Martin made his way into the drawing room, and Louise followed slowly, only to see him standing staring through the window and once more that day she felt angry. Did he have to treat her like a problem child standing before her headmaster?

Their eyes met, hers angry, his cold, and before thinking she snapped, 'Why are you always so angry with me? Why do you dislike me so much?'

Somewhat taken aback he said, 'I beg your pardon?'

'Why are you always so distant with me? I want to know why you dislike me.'

'Perhaps it's because you cause your mother so much worry. Since the day you left school, she's been very concerned about you. You probably think it's none of my business, but your mother does confide in me, Louise.'

'My mother has no right to discuss me with you.'

'She does so because she's worried. Have you no loyalty towards your mother?'

'I do. *And* to my father,' she snapped.

She stared at his cold implacable face, and he stared at her coldly angry one, but at that moment the door opened and her parents came into the room. Turning round swiftly, Louise fled out of the room.

Isobel looked at Martin curiously, but it was her husband who said, 'I didn't see Andrew. He was off as soon as he'd arrived. We'll have to wait for his explanation.'

'But it's so unlike him,' Isobel said. 'Something quite dreadful must have happened.'

'The war's happened,' Lord Maxton said. 'If there's bad news, we're expecting it. The only good news will be to tell us the blasted thing's over.'

'You'll stay for dinner?' Isobel asked Martin.

Martin shook his head. 'No, I must leave. There's a lot to do, and it's been a long day.'

'Ridiculous time to have a big wedding with a war on,' Lord Maxton said. 'The money could have been spent on better things.'

'It wasn't exactly a big wedding, dear. Besides, why shouldn't we try to act as normally as possible in these awful times? I'm sure you agree with me, Martin.'

Martin merely smiled and, kissing her hand and shaking Lord Maxton's, he made his departure.

As he walked quickly along the road outside he remembered Louise's anger, and he felt sure there was more to follow. Why should the conduct of a spoilt young girl concern him at all? Of course, he deplored the fact that some hare-brained scheme of her father's had her entertaining his numerous friends, instead of him finding the girl something proper to do like nursing or secretarial work. So what if she wasn't trained for it? She could learn, surely?

Her behaviour when she had resided with her aunts had been foolish and hardly that of a well brought up girl who had just left an expensive boarding school, and he had very little faith that Louise would improve her behaviour if she got the chance.

He felt irritable that he should be concerning himself about her at all, and what had she meant when she said she was loyal to her father, when she was so disloyal to her mother?

Thirteen

The hospital was bursting at the seams as yet another contingent had been brought in that morning – seriously wounded men who filled the wards with their moans of pain and the hearts of those who heard them with despair and pity.

Imogen had been up since five o'clock, and as she entered her ward she saw that every bed was occupied and another row had been placed down the centre. The room seemed to be crowded with khaki-clad figures, sitting and standing around with weary desolation.

Doctors and nurses were trying to organize some sort of order, and just then an officer who had been standing near one of the beds turned and walked towards the door. Like the rest of them his face was tired and strained, and addressing one of the doctors he said, 'That is my batman over there. He saved my life two days ago, but he's been very badly wounded. Do what you can for all of them.'

'We will, sir, you can count on that.'

'I shall be back sometime today to see him. If there's any change, please inform me. My name is Major Maxton, and this is my telephone number. I am going straight back there.'

Imogen watched his departure down the corridor outside. Of course, there could be a hundred and one men called Maxton, but there had been something about him that she felt she should know – perhaps from old photographs she had once seen in the room she had shared with Louise Maxton, or maybe it was simply wishful thinking. She knew Andrew Maxton had been in the army, but then so were millions of others.

She looked down with compassion at the grey face of the young man, and the doctor shook his head sadly, gently saying, 'We can only do our best, Nurse. Apparently it was one of the worst battles ever. What a bloody waste.'

Come seven o'clock in the evening, Imogen was still on the ward, tired and hungry, having survived the grim sequences of the day fortified by several cups of tea, but no food.

She looked across the room as she saw Major Maxton enter it and go to stand looking down at the man who had been his batman, and who lay seriously injured. His face was sad, and as he sat on the chair beside the bed he reached out and covered the man's hand with his own.

At that moment the sister said to her, 'Didn't you have dinner, Nurse Clarkson? If not, I'd get down there sharpish. You need something inside you, and there's no telling how long we'll be expected to stay on in here.'

She was halfway down the corridor when the matron came towards her, saying quickly, 'In my office, but I suggest you get something to eat. You can talk to your visitor in the dining hall.'

There was no other explanation as she walked quickly away, and Imogen hurried towards her office, confused as to who her visitor could be.

She stared across the room to where a tall fashionably dressed young woman stood staring out of the window, and Louise turned with a bright smile before she rushed across the room to embrace her.

'Gracious,' Louise explained with a laugh, 'you look as though you're carrying the world on your shoulders! I'm to go to some dining hall with you so that you can eat, and I'll join you in a cup of tea if that isn't forbidden.'

'Are you with your mother, Louise? It's very late. Or have you been here some time?'

'I'm with my brother. One of his men is here, actually several of his men, but this particular one is very important to him.'

'I must have seen your brother then. It was his name, Major Maxton. I've never actually met him.'

'Really, didn't you meet him at the Red Cross Ball years ago?'

'I wasn't at the Red Cross Ball.'

'No, of course you weren't. Miranda and Cora met him. I don't know how long he continues to stay here, but I'll introduce you when I get the chance.'

Food-wise there was very little to choose from, and Louise said dismally, 'How on earth do you survive on this? It's not enough to keep a sparrow alive.'

'It's much better than this normally. Today's been one of those terrible days, so we have to make the best of it. What will you have?'

'Oh, just a cup of tea. I wasn't expecting a glass of Madeira or anything remotely adventurous.'

'You're looking so well, Louise. What have they found for you to do during the war? Surprise me.'

'Oh, I can, my dear. I'm taking some of the workload off my father. It's the sort of job I hadn't envisaged, and neither will you have.'

'You're doing secretarial work? You did say you never wanted that.'

'And nor did I. My father's a politician, and he entertains politicians both from this country and from the continent. My father's lazy. When they've finished their discussions, he wants rid of them, and who better than his little daughter to pass them on to? I can amuse them, entertain them, but don't get any ideas that there's more to it. There isn't. Most of them are as old as my father, and if there are any younger ones, they know very well that amusing chit-chat is all there will ever be.'

Imogen stared at her curiously, and with a laugh Louise said, 'You're a bit shocked, Imogen, but really you don't need to be. It's all very circumspect, it has to be. Father's quite satisfied with the arrangement, but Mother deplores it, and I often wish that one or two of them were more like Jimmy Kent. At least he was warm and handsome.'

'Oh Louise, I don't know what to say.'

'Just don't say anything.'

'Doesn't anything about it worry you?'

'Like what?'

'Your reputation, for instance.'

Louise laughed, but the laugh was brittle, cynical, and she said dryly, 'I rather think my reputation had taken a downward turn before I embarked on this strange sort of service. *I* know it's perfectly respectable, and my father has convinced himself that it is, though my mother and her man friend are entirely dubious. I have no intention of enlightening anybody who thinks otherwise.'

'But Louise, it isn't right for them to question your morals when you know they're above suspicion! Why do you say your mother is unhappy about things?'

'I didn't say she was unhappy, only that she doubts my integrity and my morals.'

'But surely she talks to your father about it.'

'I don't know, she's never said so, nor has he. She talks to Martin Broughton, and the fact that he doesn't like me is evidence that she has nothing good to say about me.'

'But she's your mother, Louise. I can't think she has anything bad to say about you.'

'Perhaps we have nothing good to say about each other.'

Imogen looked at her helplessly, at her beautiful smiling face and the cynicism behind the confidence. She presented herself as a sophisticated confident woman of the world, but Imogen didn't believe that Louise's smiling face truly covered the doubts inside.

'Do you see anything of Cora or Miranda?' Imogen asked in an effort to change the subject.

'Well, we met at Miranda's sister's wedding, a rather quiet affair, but then it couldn't have been anything else at this particular time.'

'I liked Jean, I thought she was nice.'

'Yes, but most think she's misguided in carrying on with this suffragette movement. They say women haven't got a chance in parliament.'

'We'll have to wait and see.'

'I say, do you ever get away from this awful place? How long since you had any leave? How long since you managed to get home to Derbyshire?'

'Too long, but you see what it's like.'

'I'm going to invite you to come to us for a weekend and attend one of mother's terribly proper dinner parties in aid of some charity or war effort.'

'I really don't think it will be possible, Louise. There's too much going on here.'

'We'll make it possible. I'll ask mother to pull a few strings. You can meet the light of her life, meet my father who won't be happy at having to attend, and if Andrew's still with us you can do your best to charm him.'

'He's not going to be charmed by me. Besides, I've nothing to wear for such a function. I can't remember when I last bought a new dress.'

'Well, I didn't expect you to have anything sensational. As the men wear dinner jackets, and the women wear long sweeping dresses in order to vie with each other, I have too many for my own good, so you can wear one of mine. I'm not going to take no for an answer.'

Imogen laughed. 'You haven't changed, Louise, only this time you're not going to get away with it, times have changed for you. I've loved seeing you, Louise, but I do have to get back to the ward. I'll tell your brother where you are.'

Andrew was sitting where she had last seen him, and he got to his feet when a doctor approached him. They talked for several minutes, and when the doctor moved away Imogen went to speak to him.

'I've just left your sister, Major Maxton. She is waiting for you in the dining hall downstairs.'

'Thank you, Nurse. There's nothing I can do here, I'm afraid, so perhaps we should think about returning home. Good night.'

They smiled at each other. She did not tell him who she was or that she knew his sister. They would meet frequently during the next few days, she felt sure, but she said nothing of the weekend Louise happily envisaged.

Andrew was quiet on the journey home, and Louise too felt they had little to say to each other regarding their separate problems. It was only when they entered the house that Andrew said, 'Are we joining Mother in the drawing room,

Louise?'

'Do you want to?'

'Don't you?'

'Andrew, I don't know. Mother and I are very distant these days, and she may not be alone.'

'You think Martin might be here?'

'Could be.'

'Don't you like him?'

'He doesn't like me.'

'And why is that?'

'He thinks I'm a flibbertigibbet without a brain in her head and with an insatiable appetite for men.'

'Not father's friends or associates, surely. Aren't they a little old for you?'

'They're men, and after the aunts my reputation isn't exactly pristine.'

'Then you should put him right, and the sooner the better.'

Lady Maxton was sitting alone when they entered the drawing room, and immediately Andrew said, 'All alone, Mother? I thought Martin was here.'

'No, he's busy this evening. Every evening, come to that.'

'And Father?'

'Presumably at some meeting or other. I haven't seen him all day How is your friend, Andrew?'

'Not good, Mother. I doubt if he'll make it.'

'I'm so sorry. Did you see Imogen, Louise?'

'Yes, Mother, and she looks positively dreadful. I don't think she's ever got away from the hospital, and doesn't look like she eats or sleeps well. I've invited her here for a weekend, Friday until Sunday, but she doesn't think she'll be allowed to come. Can't you do something?'

'I don't suppose any of the other nurses get much leave.'

'But they do. They live near London, while her home is in Derbyshire. She's not been there for years.'

'And what do you propose to do for entertaining *here*, Louise? You're hardly ever in evidence, I am too busy, and Andrew will soon be returning to France.'

'Well, even one of your very proper dinner parties would be something, Mother. We could get dressed up, and at least she'd get a decent meal. Besides, I'd like her to come.'

'Who is this Imogen we're talking about?' Andrew asked curiously.

'We were at school together. She's one of the nurses looking after your batman. She told you where to find me.'

'I don't remember her.'

'You would have done if you'd met her four years ago. She was beautiful and intelligent. now she's like the proverbial mouse.'

'Then perhaps we should make the effort,' he said with a smile.

'The only young people there will be you and Andrew, Louise. We can hardly call that entertainment,' her mother said doubtfully.

Several days later, the matron sent for Imogen.

172

She did not like people pulling strings to accommodate any of her nurses, but she had to admit that in the years Imogen Clarkson had served, this was the first time it had happened.

The girl looked tired, and there was a weariness in her slender form that spoke of the trauma and turmoil she'd been subjected to.

'Sit down, Nurse Clarkson,' she said briefly.

Imogen complied, and after a few moments the matron said, 'I've had a request from Lady Maxton that you should spend a weekend at her London home. Apparently you were at school with her daughter.'

'Yes, Matron. I told Louise I did not think it would be possible for me to attend.'

'Why were you so sure?'

'We're too busy. I didn't think it would be possible.'

'How long since you had leave?'

'I haven't had leave. My mother's been up to London to see me once or twice, but leave to go home to Derbyshire didn't seem possible.'

'Then I think that for one weekend we can spare you, Nurse. Miss Maxton says she will be in touch with you very soon so that you can make your arrangements, and we shall expect you back here first thing on Monday morning.'

'Thank you, Matron. I appreciate your kindness.'

She was dismissed, and as she walked back to the ward she thought, I really don't want to go. What will I talk about, who shall I know, what shall I wear? And she wished avidly that something would happen to prevent the weekend taking place.

In the meantime, Louise was saying doubtfully to Andrew, 'Oh, I do wish Mother would invite some younger people along so that Imogen would enjoy things more.'

'Tell me about this Imogen,' Andrew asked. 'I've met the other two friends you had at college. Is this one very different?'

'Well, she was not nearly as stupid as the rest of us. The other two were always on about the boys they would marry, when they would marry, and what they expected their lives to be like. Imogen seemed a normal girl, but really she was the one with the secrets.'

'Secrets?'

'Well yes! Her mother fell in love with an officer in the Sudan, but his family wouldn't countenance him marrying her. When he did, they wanted nothing more to do with either of them.'

'So he married her all the same?'

'Yes.'

'And do we know this family?'

'Of course. Her uncle is now an earl, but the Clarksons managed very well without them. They have their own farm, and they gave Imogen the same sort of education I got.'

'I sincerely hope the other side of the family will not be invited to mother's function. That would be a bit difficult,' Andrew said dryly.

'If you're going to the hospital, perhaps you'll bring her here, Andrew? That way you can

174

introduce yourselves, and I do want the whole weekend to be a success.'

'It would appear that underneath the exterior of flighty sister I know dwells a kind heart. Why do you put on this couldn't care less attitude, Louise? It isn't for father, so it can only be for mother or Martin Broughton.'

'It's me, Andrew, it's always been me.'

'Well, it sounds like father's arrived home. I think I'll join him over his favourite tipple.'

Andrew had always been the best person in her life, Louise reflected. He'd teased her and laughed at her, but she'd always been able to confide in him. She'd never been jealous of him, even when she knew both her parents adored him. She only ever thought of him as her handsome, charming brother, whom they all had expectations of. Her mother particularly would want him to marry well, but Louise knew that her brother would decide that for himself.

Up in her bedroom she looked through her wardrobe, thinking about the dress that Imogen might want to wear. A dress to disguise her fragility. She could look pretty again in the right sort of gown – she, too, was blonde, if a little darker than Louise – but she wouldn't want a grand gown, like so many of Louise's were.

Louise had always liked flamboyant gowns, while Imogen had preferred something less colourful. She looked through her wardrobes with a frown on her face until she came to one she hadn't yet worn. Even her mother had approved of this one, a deep azure blue and without the usual trappings of sequins, feathers and flounces. Louise considered it plain. The slender bodice fell in long graceful flares, and and its only adornment was the circlet of silk roses at the neckline.

For the first time she realized that it was beautiful and elegant, perhaps not quite to her taste, but Imogen would love it and so she should wear it. Her mother would think she was being over-generous in letting her friend wear it before she had worn it herself, but she had plenty of others to choose from. Why not the black with the sable edging that her mother hadn't seen yet and which she would think far too old and sophisticated for her? Andrew would like Imogen in this gown, she thought mischievously, and a small secretive smile curled her lips. Well, why not? How simply delightful to be able to frustrate so many ambitious mothers, including her own, and a little matchmaking in these dismal, traumatic times wouldn't come amiss. Besides, Andrew would soon be back in the war. Nothing in these terrible times was ever meant to last.

It was several days later that Lady Maxton confided her misgivings about her forthcoming function to Martin Broughton as they left a political meeting together. 'I do want you to be there, Martin,' she urged him. 'It will be possible, I hope?'

'Yes, I promise. Why is this one so important?'

'Because Andrew's returning to France soon.

He's been so terribly unhappy. His batman died, you know, and several of the other boys, and now he can't get back quick enough. I've invited Louise's schoolfriends, Imogen, Cora and Miranda. Not Imogen's parents, of course, as they live in Derbyshire, but Mrs Hambleton and Mrs Reed-Blyton. A mixture of old and young, and my husband's sure to have some person he thinks should be there.'

'Are you and Louise getting on a little better?'

'Not so that you would notice, Martin. I'm just glad she isn't insisting on bringing a man to the evening.'

'You surely don't think any of your husband's acquaintances would mean anything to her? She behaved badly once, Isobel, almost four years ago. Hasn't she learned her lesson?'

'Are you trying to tell me you're taking her part, Martin?'

'I'm thinking that perhaps you should stop worrying about her, Isobel. She's not a child any more. She's a grown woman responsible for her own actions, and perhaps it's gone on too long.'

'She's my daughter and I want what's best for her.'

'And what *is* best for her?'

'Some nice young man with a good career, great expectations and a good family behind him. People we can relate to. But what young man is going to want Louise if she gets a reputation for being too free with her favours?'

'Isobel, these young men, or middle aged men Louise is meeting are known to your husband.

You surely don't think Henry would have sanctioned her meeting up with anybody dubious?'

'No, of course not, but after the problems we had with the aunts, we don't really know what she's capable of, do we? Why isn't she more like Andrew? I've never really been able to get close to Louise.'

'But this dinner you're organizing, isn't this something she has asked you to do?'

'Yes, but Henry will hate it, I don't really know her friend very well, and the others are not really in my circle. What do you think?'

Martin didn't know, it was one function he felt totally unsure about attending. Most of the guests were his constituents, but it was the thought of Louise that troubled him the most.

Fourteen

Imogen looked at the dress hanging outside her wardrobe and almost burst into tears. It was four years old. There'd been no occasion to wear party dresses, and she'd only kept this one out of a sense of loyalty towards the memories that now seemed so inappropriate.

Why had Louise been so insistent that she spent the weekend at her parents' house, and what would Miranda and Cora expect of her now?

She folded the dress and placed it in her suitcase quickly because she didn't want her room-mate to see it. It's age would not register with Jenny: all she would see was a long silk evening dress that would make her call Imogen snobbish and toffee-nosed.

It seemed so strange to be out of nurses' uniform and wearing high heels again. There was nothing new in her wardrobe because for three long years nothing new had been needed. Now, as she surveyed herself in the mirror, she was dismally aware of a too thin, pale-faced woman who was a complete contrast to the girl her friends would remember.

Andrew arrived for her just before lunch, and as he greeted her courteously she had the feeling that he didn't really remember her as one of the nurses who had cared for his friend.

On the journey into London he chatted spasmodically about the weather, the latest news in the morning papers and said that Louise was looking forward to meeting her and to the Saturday night function.

As for Louise, she sat on the bed watching Imogen take the dress out of her suitcsase before dissolving into laughter. 'Darling, you can't possibly wear that,' she cried. 'It's years old! You had it at school.'

'I know. When have I ever needed to wear anything like it?'

'Well, you can't wear it tomorrow. I've got just the thing and I won't take no for an answer.'

'I can't possibly borrow your dress, Louise.

It's beautiful, and new. Haven't you something older? Something you don't care about?'

'I'll show you what I've got – gowns that I should never have bought in these awful times, but I go to places where they're necessary, and none of them would suit you. They're extravagant and silly, and there's just this one that might be deemed satisfactory enough for Mother and Martin Broughton to approve of it.'

'Why are you always so caustic when you speak about your mother and Mr Broughton?'

'Because he doesn't like me and I don't like him. He thinks I'm a Jezebel, and I think he's too close to my mother.'

'Tell me about Cora and Miranda.'

'You're changing the subject.'

'I know. Tell me about those boys they were so sure they'd marry.'

'Peter and Cedric. Well, Peter was wounded, but he's back in harness now, somewhere in Flanders, and Cedric got engaged to some girl he met here in London.'

'But that's awful! What about Miranda?'

'Darling, it was never real, just a dream in their silly heads. Something their mothers wanted.'

'But he's going to marry her?'

'I don't know. How do we know anything about anything these days? I've seen her, she's quite pretty, but other than that none of us know much about her.'

'It seems to me I don't know very much about anything. I might as well have been in a nunnery these last few years.'

'Did you never fall in love with any of those wounded heroes?'

'Never, although I liked most of them.'

'Including Jimmy Kent.'

'Yes, I liked him too, but not as much as you did.'

'You know, Imogen, there really hasn't been anybody since Jimmy. I'm going to be a spinster until I find somebody older and wiser, somebody rich and sophisticated. Somebody who's not looking for a sweet young debutante.'

'Isn't that what Cora and Miranda aim to be?'

'Well, of course. I suppose it'll all come back after the war – curtseying to Their Majesties and parading their white pristine dresses to catch the eye of some ambitious mother. My mother'll be among them, but I don't intend to make it easy for her. Now what about this dress?'

'If you're sure, Louise, although I really do think I shouldn't wear it. I'll be terribly afraid I'll spill something on it and you'll never forgive me.'

'This afternoon we're going to walk in the park, and I'll lend you some something decent to wear in case we meet people, that thing you're wearing is years old too.'

'That's because I wear nurses' uniform most of the time.'

'Cora helps out in their so-called nursing home, but she manages to dress well.'

'The nursing home is not like a real hospital, Louise.'

'No, I suppose not. Come into my room and take a look at what I've got.'

Lady Maxton had greeted her guests graciously, and they were all of the opinion that Imogen looked beautiful in her borrowed plumes, except for the fact that she seemed incredibly frail, and rather unlike the girl they remembered from their schooldays.

Lord Maxton was fractious. He did not see the point of this gathering, even though his wife and daughter had suggested he tried to make an effort. So it was rather left to Andrew and Martin to gallantly charm the ladies.

They were halfway through their meal when Imogen started to feel unwell. The voices of the others seemed to be coming from miles away, and although the banquet was charming and entirely delicious the food tasted of nothing. She became aware that Andrew was looking at her anxiously from his place across the table, before she gave a little moan and slumped to the floor, drifting out of consciousness.

There was consternation all around Imogen, but it was Andrew who came to lift her up and carry her up to her room, followed by Louise and her mother.

'We must send for a doctor,' Lady Maxton said. 'The girl looks quite ill, I've thought so all evening. She's probably been working too hard. I'll ask the housekeeper and one of the maids to see to her, for we must join the others.'

'I'll telephone the doctor,' Andrew said

quickly. 'I'll join you all in a few minutes.'

As he'd carried the girl upstairs he'd been only too aware of her fragility, she'd seemed like a child in his arms, and speaking to his sister he said, 'Perhaps we should contact her parents?'

'Oh not yet, Andrew. Why don't we see what the doctor has to say?'

'Probably been working all hours,' Lord Maxton said grumpily. 'Instead of this do, she should have been enjoying a rest.'

Nobody either agreed or disagreed with him, and they all waited anxiously downstairs for the doctor's verdict.

By this time Imogen was awake and utterly miserable that she had caused such a problem in the midst of a lovely evening.

Louise sat on her bed, smiling. 'The doctor says you're simply very tired, Imogen. Mother thinks your parents should be told about it.'

'No, please, I'll be fine in the morning. It's simply that these last few days have been too hectic, not enough sleep or food probably. I'm young! I'll be fine in the morning.'

'Oh, well,' Louise said, 'at least you brought out the chivalry in my dear brother. I'll bet you're the first girl he's carried up to bed.'

Imogen blushed, and Lady Maxton said sharply, 'Really, Louise, you do say the most improper things. It's no wonder I despair of you.'

'No, Mother, I knew you did.'

'We should let Imogen go to sleep. The doctor's suggested she have a glass of warm milk and take one of these tablets. The maid will see to it. We really should get back to our guests. In the morning, Imogen, I'm sure you will be feeling much better.'

Louise retrieved the blue gown from the back of a chair, saying lightly, 'You won't be needing this any more, Imogen. You looked so pretty in it, but there'll be other times.'

Downstairs Mrs Hambleton was of the opinion that her mother should be sent for, but Lady Maxton didn't agree. 'The doctor says she'll be quite well after a good night's sleep, but I do intend to have a word with the matron at the hospital to suggest that she stays here for at least a week. I know that the men go to war and they die or get wounded, but the war affects women, too. So many of us are weary and exhausted.'

Lord Maxton permitted himself a cynical smirk, while the others were in agreement.

Three days later Imogen breakfasted with the others for the first time and all their thoughts were that she was a new Imogen. The colour had come back into her cheeks, and there was a new vitality about her.

'We should have gone somewhere together today,' Louise said. 'Unfortunately, I've got something else to do this morning. Do you mind, Imogen?'

'Of course not. I can walk in the park. It'll do me good.'

'And I can walk with you,' Andrew said. 'St James's, I think. Feeding the ducks was always a happy pastime of mine.'

So they walked in the park, laughed at the

antics of the ducks, and discovered in each other something warm and genuine. Imogen had gone from school into nursing, and nowhere along the way had she found a man's companionship. She'd found men to comfort and care for, but never really got to know any of them intimately. Now, for the first time, she was able to talk to a man and discover a human being she could relate to.

Andrew, on the other hand, had known a great many aspiring young women without having cared deeply for any one of them. And now, he reflected somewhat grimly, the time wasn't right to start anything.

He was going back to danger. He only knew that it was inconceivable that England could lose the war, but how long would it last? What calamities and trauma was there still to face?

They both only knew that this was a morning they would want to remember, a morning they would treasure when the present was bleak and frightening. Beyond that there was nothing more. It was too soon and things were too uncertain.

On the same day, Cora escaped from her numerous duties to an arranged meeting in London with her friend Miranda. The two girls hadn't seen each other since their evening at Louise's parents' house a few days ago and although they had invited Louise to join them on this occasion she had declined, saying she was busy.

They'd spent most of the morning in various

departmental stores. The stores were busy, even though there was little exciting to buy. Three years of war had taken its toll both on people's pockets and their enthusiasm for anything remotely adventurous, and at last the girls decided it was time to stop looking at things they didn't need, or even want, and eat lunch.

They were not too familiar with the small tearoom they chose, and Miranda said petulantly, 'Why did we come here? We've never been here before.'

'Because I'm fed up of looking around, and it's here.'

Most of the tables were occupied by shoppers and office workers on their midday break, and looking round Miranda said, 'I suppose they all work nearby. They probably come here every day.'

In spite of the unimaginative menu and the dullness of their surroundings, they found much to talk about. Imogen's fragility and Louise's extravagances, as well as Louise's brother's good looks and the fact that he and Imogen had quite evidently been taken with each other.

They were speculating busily as to whether it could ever come to anything, when suddenly Miranda said, 'There's a girl over there who keeps looking at you. There in that group near the window. Do you know her?'

Cora looked over at the group and at one girl who stared at them curiously. As their eyes met, the girl smiled.

'I don't know her,' she said. 'She's probably

some girl who's been to see a patient at the nursing home.'

'She seems very interested.'

'She was probably told I was the daughter of the house. I do help out in the wards, you know. That's probably where she saw me.'

'What do you really do in the wards?'

'I read to the soldiers, write letters for them. Quite a lot of them have eye problems. And sister's taught me how to roll bandages and do other jobs like that. Anyway, what do *you* do besides attend meetings with your mother?'

'I'm thinking of joining the suffragette movement. Jean says I'd enjoy it. She does an awful lot in the recruitment area. Mother says she should really ask for some sort of payment. It's so awfully tying, and she really does work long hours for them.'

'And are they giving her any money?'

'She's asked for two pounds a week. It isn't really very much, but she should have something.'

'And would they pay you?'

'Gracious, no, I'd be a new girl. I'd have to be a long-term member, doing something useful, to get money out of them.'

'Mother says it's useless, we'll never get the vote.'

'Well, my sister says they're all very determined, and I might just give it a try. That girl is still staring at us. I do think you should go across and ask her if she's met you.'

The girl smiled again, and Cora said, 'Why

doesn't she come here?'

'Perhaps she's shy. They're just office girls and shop girls on their lunch break. I'm curious, Cora.'

'Oh well, it'll do no harm I suppose.'

Miranda watched while her friend walked over to the table near the window, where the girl indicated that she pull up a chair from the next table and join them. Then after what she considered a very long time to be left sitting alone, Cora rejoined her.

'Well?' Miranda demanded.

'I feel so awful,' Cora said. 'That was Julie Havers, who is engaged to my brother, and I didn't even recognize her!'

'Well, how could you? She's never moved in our circle.'

'But she's going to be my sister-in-law! Oh, I know how you feel about it, but it's all so wrong, Miranda.'

'How? Why is it wrong?'

'It's all so class conscious. Just because we didn't go to the same school, mingle with the same people. My brother loves her. I should have gone over there and embraced her, just like I'd have embraced you if you'd been engaged to him.'

'It's not the same at all. You've always known me, I'm your friend.'

'I still think there's something terrible about it all. Cedric will want to marry her, and none of us will think he should. That's what it amounts to, surely?'

188

'If my brother had got engaged to some girl none of us knew *I* wouldn't like it. I want Peter for you, Cora. The family want him for you. And I thought that was how you all felt about me and Cedric.'

'Miranda, we did, but evidently Cedric didn't agree with us. He wanted Julie. She's really rather nice. We chatted quite normally together.'

'What are her friends like?'

'I didn't speak to any of them. I was just talking with Julie.'

For Miranda, the day was spoilt, and looking at her petulant, sulky face Cora said, 'We don't know what's going to happen, Miranda. Anything could stop them being together, and who knows who *we* might meet? We're young, we could fall in love. You were never in love with Cedric. You only wanted to marry him.'

'Love isn't everything.'

'Your sister thought so. She married the man she was in love with.'

'Oh, well, Jean never seems to think straight. Look at that suffragettte movement she's involved with! Votes for women, indeed.'

Suddenly, Cora wanted to go home. She had looked forward to spending the morning with her friend, but somehow or other it had all gone wrong. She needed to talk with her mother about Julie, and she wanted reassurance that one day it would all arrive, the good they had promised themselves in a world at peace.

'I think I should go home now, Miranda,' she said gently. 'I really do feel I ought to talk to mother. Meeting Julie like that has upset me, and I don't feel I'm very good company at the moment.'

'I've been looking forward to this morning.'

'So have I, but you do understand, don't you, Miranda?'

'I'm not sure that I do. When shall I see you again?'

'Oh soon. I'll telephone you. I get so busy at the house, but there'll be a time soon, I'm sure.'

Miranda had to be content with that, but she watched Cora climb into a taxi with ill-disguised annoyance. There was nothing to go home for. Her mother would be at one of her interminable meetings, and she hadn't seen her sister for weeks. She'd look at the shops instead, even though the shops had little to tempt her these days. She'd been looking forward to a gossipy morning, when they could talk about the evening they'd spent at the Maxtons, discussing Imogen and whether Andrew Maxton had appeared in the least captivated by her. Now that girl Julie had spoiled it all, and not just this morning, she told herself. Probably the rest of her life.

Her mood was not improved when she saw Imogen and Andrew Maxton walking in the park during the afternoon. They seemed deep in conversation – two young people who had come together briefly, enjoying what they had, their expectations of the future unsure.

Miranda hurried away. She didn't want to meet them, or indeed speak with any couple who seemed happy together when she felt so singularly alone.

As usual, Cora found her mother busy helping out in the laundry room. It wasn't really necessary that she should do anything at all, and the nursing sisters would have preferred it if she'd been conspicuous by her absence, but she deemed it necessary to make the effort.

Cora joined her and together they started to fold sheets, while her mother said, 'Did you enjoy meeting Miranda, dear?'

'Mother, I saw Julie Havers in the cafe where we had lunch. She was with a group of friends, but I went to speak to her.'

'Really, dear? That's nice.'

'I felt so awful, Mother, I didn't know what to say to her. I just felt that I really don't know her at all.'

'Well, no, dear. We don't really, do we?'

'She seemed very nice.'

'I'm sure she is, dear. Cedric wouldn't become involved with just anybody.'

'But don't you think we should get to know her better? Why doesn't she visit? Why don't we meet her family?'

'Because they live in Yorkshire, and because she's a working girl with very little time.'

'And because we don't consider her to be one of us.'

'That's a silly thing to say.'

'But it's true, Mother, isn't it? Before the war we'd never have met the sort of people we're meeting now, and don't you feel everything has to change?'

'Oh Cora, of course not. After the war it will all get back to normal. It has to.'

'Even when Cedric marries Julie?'

'Well, we're not really sure that he will, are we? I'm as confused as you are, Cora. Let us just wait and see, shall we?'

'And what about Miranda? It's difficult being with her these days. You know what you always said, Miranda for Cedric and me for Peter, and now I feel guilty if I even *think* of Peter.'

'That's a very silly thing to say. I like Miranda, I would have liked Cedric to like her, but he's met somebody else and that may come to nothing. Can't we just wait and see? Like I said, Rome wasn't built in a day.'

'I don't know how you can be so complacent, Mother, and I do think we should make an effort to entertain Julie.'

'And like I've said, Cora, she's in London with a job to go to and very little time. When I feel it's necessary to entertain her, I will do so.'

Fifteen

Imogen didn't meet anybody on her way up to her room at the hospital, although she knew that the wards themselves would be heaving with activity.

Laying her small suitcase on the bed she started to take things out, things that had looked decidedly old-fashioned beside the clothes she'd seen in Louise's wardrobe, but then Louise's lifestyle and her own were totally different.

She smiled a little as she thought about her friend. So many things and people had changed as a result of the times they were living in, but somehow or other Louise never changed. She was still the light and airy girl who had swept through their lives, beautiful and frivolous, and yet now and again she had sensed a Louise she had not yet discovered.

Only the day before she had watched Andrew leaving the house to go back to the battlefields of France, and after embracing his mother and sister he had merely taken her hand and held it for perhaps longer than was really necessary.

Would they ever meet again, she wondered. Perhaps at some function when the war was over, and perhaps he would be with somebody

else, and perhaps she too would have met some-
one.

The door opened and her room-mate stood
watching her before saying, 'So ye got back
then. Enjoy yourself?'

'Yes, thank you, Jenny, it was very nice.'

'Only very nice?'

'Well, I disgraced myself by fainting at dinner
on the first night, and I had to stay in bed all the
next day. The doctor said it was fatigue: I'd done
too much and worked too hard.'

'He could say that about all of us.'

'I know.'

'What about that 'andsome young man who
came for ye?'

'My friend's brother, Andrew. He went back to
France yesterday.'

'So there's no future in it?'

'I wasn't expecting one.'

'He was good lookin'.'

'Yes.'

'Well, *I've* got time off next weekend. I'm invited to a weddin'!'

'Oh that's lovely, Jenny. A relative?'

'No, just a girl I knew back 'ome. She's
marryin' that lad who knew that girl you knew.
Jimmy Kent.'

'Oh I'm so glad! I liked Jimmy. Is he well
now?'

'He's doin' a bit o' gardening with his uncle.
He's not up to scratch yet, but at least it's work
o' some sort.'

'I'm glad. Will it be a large wedding?'

'I wouldn't think so, not in these times. She's always fancied Jimmy Kent. He was convinced you knew that girl he was smitten with, that girl who lived with her aunts.'

'I don't really know how he got that idea.'

'Oh, *I* do. Anyway, he's over her. It wasn't meant to be.'

So many things weren't meant to be, but she hoped things would go well for Jimmy. He hadn't deserved Louise, but then she hadn't deserved him. They would never meet again, and she would never mention him to Louise.

During the next few days, life took up its usual pattern and in the months that followed she determined not to think about Andrew Maxton.

It was just before Christmas in 1917 when she was standing on a ladder to help decorate the Christmas tree that had been erected in the ward that she looked down to see a smiling Andrew looking up at her. In her confusion she almost dropped a box of baubles before he helped her down the steps.

'Are you on leave?' she asked him quickly.

'A very short leave I'm afraid. I brought a contingent of wounded men over, and I accompanied my mother here this morning. I was hoping I might see you, but now I can't even invite you for coffee.'

'I can – for something that passes for coffee, at any rate.'

So they sat in the canteen, and it didn't really matter that the coffee was inferior and the scones rock hard.

'No more fainting tricks?' Andrew asked, smiling.

'No. I'm still working very hard, but I make myself eat, even when the food is pretty dreadful.'

'Yes, you should.'

'Is it terrible over there, Andrew? Is there no hope that it's going to end?'

'Oh, it'll end, Imogen, and we've got to beat 'em, but we don't know when. So much is happening all over Europe: republics are going to be born. Who knows where it will all end?'

'But here, Andrew. Nothing terrible will happen here, surely?'

'There will be changes, it's inevitable, but whether they'll be for good or evil only time will tell.'

'I haven't seen Louise. Is she still busy entertaining your father's guests?'

'Up to a point. It's a strange sort of war effort, and I'm not entirely sure how she got into it, but it suits my father, and she's always been something of a rebel.'

'I wonder why she dislikes Martin Broughton so much, and why he doesn't like her?'

'Has she said he doesn't like her?'

'Yes, and when I asked her what she meant, she wouldn't say any more.'

'Some bee that she's got in her bonnet about his friendship with my mother. I don't know how deep it goes, and nor does she. She seems to mind too much.'

'Don't you mind, Andrew?'

'Perhaps it's to do with the way we marry – why we marry and who we marry. It's a pattern I don't intend to follow. But I'm keeping you from your duties,' he said, smiling.

'Perhaps. I'm certainly receiving very pointed glances from sister sitting over there!'

'Then I should let you go. The future is very uncertain, Imogen, but one day when the war is over and we get back to normality we shall meet again. There doesn't seem much use in making plans for anything at the moment. We'd be tempting providence, don't you think?'

'Perhaps.'

'I hope you keep in touch with my sister. I worry about her, you know.'

'But why? She always seems so self-assured and confident.'

'Maybe that's the trouble. She really doesn't know what she wants, and somewhere along the line she's getting it all wrong.'

For a long moment he held her hand before kissing her cheek gently, and she watched him walk away with a new strange ache in her heart. She would have been very surprised to have heard the conversation around the dinner table at the Maxton house the following day.

Louise was bored: bored with the middle-aged gentleman she'd had lunch with that day, and bored with the fact that Martin Broughton was dining with them. Her father was irritable, her mother slightly frivolous, and Martin Broughton strangely morose.

'Did Andrew tell you he saw Imogen at the

hospital, Mother?' Louise asked.

'No. That was nice of him, I suppose.'

'I think he liked her, Mother. More than liked her.'

'Oh no, dear. Andrew is always generous and charming. He was merely being nice to his sister's friend.'

'Imogen doesn't need him to be nice to her, Mother. I got the impression that he *really* liked her.'

'Louise, now isn't the time for liking, or anything deeper. When Andrew really wants a girl, he'll tell us. Don't you agree, Martin?'

'I really don't know Andrew that well, Isobel.'

'I think it's awfully silly to make any commitment at this time. I was speaking to Mrs Hambleton quite recently at some meeting or other, and she was *still* bemoaning the fact that her son has got engaged and they don't know anything about the girl in question.'

'And they really don't like it because he was earmarked for Miranda.'

'I don't think that has anything to do with it, Louise. While we're on the subject, I was at a meeting the other day, and Mrs Barrington was asking about you. She said she'd like you to take tea with her one afternoon.'

'I'm sure she did.'

'What is that supposed to mean?'

'Mother, she'd like me for Algy, and I don't fancy Algy in the slightest. Besides, he's in France.'

Her father suddenly came alive. 'Who is this

Algy Barrington you're talking about? Do we know him?'

'He's in the same unit as Andrew, Father. He's all right, I suppose, but not for me.'

'That young French fella was mighty taken with you the other day,' he chuckled. 'He made a nice change from the older fellas they send over.'

'He was fun, Father, and I do agree, he was a vast improvement on some of the others.'

'What do you talk about? Particularly as you don't really know him!' her mother demanded.

'We talk about restaurants and shows, we talk about the joys of Paris and Trouville, and Monte Carlo and Provence.'

'And has he suggested introducing you to those delights?' Martin asked dryly.

'Well, of course. The French can be awfully jolly, can't they?'

'Didn't you say Imogen had some connection with the Clarkson family? Lord and Lady Clarkson?'

'Yes, he's her uncle, her father's brother.'

'I didn't know he had a brother.'

'He hasn't for the last twenty years or so.'

'What do you mean by that?'

'They fell out when he married Imogen's mother, who was a nurse in the Sudan. It's all ancient history now, Mother. Imogen is a nice girl. I'd like Andrew to get to know her better.'

'And I don't think it would be a good idea, particularly when we know the Clarksons so very well.'

Louise's eyes met Martin's across the table, and she was surprised to see in them a cynicism she hadn't expected, but it was only later, when they went into the drawing room for coffee, that she managed to speak to him. Her father had retired to his study and his usual rum toddy, and her mother had been called away to the telephone. Martin sat in his favourite chair near the window, absorbed in the evening paper.

'You surprised me this evening,' Louise said softly.

'Did I? I can't think why.'

'By your cynicism about our way of life.'

'I'm not sure what you mean.'

'Oh, I think you do. Silly class distinctions that keep us all in little packages, making sure that we don't mingle with the wrong people.'

'Is that such a bad thing?'

'It is when it all ends up being predictable and boring. It doesn't have to be like that.'

'Oh, but it does, Louise. You should know that.'

'Why should I?'

'Didn't you try it once? Isn't that why your mother brought, you to London. You know it wouldn't have worked, either then or now.'

'You think you know everything about me, don't you? You listen to my mother, and you don't know *me* at all.'

'You're right, Louise, I don't know you. All I see is a young girl running around in circles without knowing where she's going. You're cry-ing for the moon, Louise, and the moon isn't being very accommodating.'

'And what about you? Does having an affair with my mother make you better than me?'

They glared at each other, their eyes filled with hostility, and then in a calm voice he said, 'You're surmising a great deal, Louise, without a shred of evidence to substantiate it. I admire your mother, although she is a product of that same package you find so demoralizing. I look around me and see so many people caught up in the same quagmire, but I don't know what the answer is.'

'You say you're *not* having an affair with my mother?'

'No, I am not. Grow up, Louise. Stop being the little girl who thinks she knows it all and start being the sort of woman you could be if you just admitted you don't.'

She glared at him in furious anger before she stormed to the door. 'You don't know everything, Martin,' she cried. 'I hated you when I thought you were in love with my mother, and now I hate you because you're self-opinionated and horrid.'

She slammed the door behind her and Martin sat back in his chair, a smile on his face. It would seem the next few months might prove to be anything but boring.

'All alone?' Isobel said as she entered the room and took her seat across from him. 'Where is Louise?'

'I haven't any idea.'

'Or Henry?'

'In his study, I feel sure.'

She sat staring into the fire, deep in thought, and he sensed in her the deep loneliness that had drawn him to her in the first place. Louise thought they were involved in some long-standing affair, and he wondered now how many people were of the same opinion.

Martin was ambitious. He had risen far in his chosen profession, and he would not allow any hint of scandal to prejudice it now. However, he sensed Isobel's need of him, the value she placed on their friendship. He needed to be sure that that was *all* it was.

'You're very thoughtful this evening, Isobel,' he said gently.

'Yes, I have a lot on my mind.'

'May I ask what it is?'

'My marriage, Louise, Andrew, and the war.'

'Your marriage troubles you?'

'It shouldn't, Martin, because surely I've always known what it would be like, but what is going to happen about Louise? She's flitting around with impossible men—'

'Who your husband has introduced her to,' he interrupted her.

'I know, because he's lazy and Louise saves him from entertaining them himself. Oh, I know there's nothing in it for Louise, but shouldn't she be with men her own age, men she could expect to marry?'

'Like you were expected to marry, you mean. I really don't think you need to worry on that

202

score, Isobel. She's got her head on her shoulders.'

'And *you* only *think* you know her, Martin. She could make a mess of her life!'

'Isobel, the world's in a mess, and one day when it's all behind us I think Louise will find what she should be looking for.'

'And Andrew?'

'Destiny will look after Andrew, my dear. We'll have to wait and see.'

'But is it ever going to end?'

'It will, my dear. We're limping to its conclusion now. Give it a few more months and hopefully the nightmare will be over.'

'I thought you had a meeting this evening.'

'And so I have, a very important one, which means I have to leave soon. Why don't you talk to Louise? Get to know each other, try to obliterate all those worries you have about her.'

'I will, Martin. I will talk to her, but not tonight.'

He sighed. The only person who had ever really talked to Louise had been her brother. But her happiness was not his responsibility, and even less so when she was so very sure that she hated him.

On the same day, Miranda Reed-Blyton strolled through the park with her sister, talking about their brother. 'He's so lifeless,' she said dolefully. 'He doesn't do anything but read the war news. There's no fun in him any more, even though it's nearly Christmas, and he says he

203

won't see Cora. That's awful when they were supposed to be for each other! It's almost as bad as Cedric and me.'

When Jean didn't speak, Miranda said feelingly, 'Oh, I know you think I'm stupid about Cedric Hambleton, but you know how Mother used to go on about us. Shall we have tea at that place in the park?'

'Why not? And we won't discuss either Peter or Cedric again for the rest of the afternoon. Considering it's Saturday, it's very quiet in the park,' Jean added. 'Where is everybody?'

There were several young couples walking along the path besides the lake and children feeding the ducks, despite the chill winter weather, and suddenly Miranda said, 'That couple there, I know the girl! She's engaged to Cedric Hambleton, I'm sure of it.'

'Who's the boy?'

'I don't know. Oh, that's awful. I must tell Cora. That girl is engaged to Cedric and she's out with somebody else!'

'He could be a relative or some man from her office. Keep out of it, Miranda, it's all perfectly innocent.'

'Not by the way they're walking hand in hand and looking at each other!'

'And you're not *wanting* it to be innocent, Miranda. We're not sitting here watching the way they're behaving. I'm going home, and you will too if you've any sense.'

'I'm thinking about Cora!'

'No, Miranda, you're thinking about yourself,

and whether you can stir anything up or put a stop to that engagement.'

Miranda watched her sister striding angrily away from her, then without a second thought she ordered another cup of tea.

Sixteen

It was all happening at once. Soon now the house would be their own again, but all Cora was aware of at the moment was the noise as the elegant rooms that had been turned into wards were disassembled and stacks of wood were being carried into the drive where huge lorries waited to take it away. She had watched the nurses and the few remaining patients leaving the day before, and although she had expressed regret at their leaving, today was the moment she had longed for for four long years.

The war was over. Victory had come at a price, a price barely reflected in the victory marches and extravagant expressions of relief that the trauma of the last terrible years had come to an end.

Cora had stood with her family and friends to watch the victory parade, glorying in the sight of her brother Cedric, proud and handsome, even though for days she had seen his face etched in pain and he had seemed totally unlike the brother she remembered.

'He's so different,' she confided to Miranda. 'He isn't fun any more. We still don't know what to think about *her*.'

'Is he going to marry her? Hasn't he said anything?' Miranda asked.

'Mother's afraid to ask. We don't even know if he's been seeing her. Father says we have to wait, that it's too soon to expect miracles. But Mother's determined to have those banquets she's been promising herself for months. The first is on Friday.'

'Surely Cedric will bring the girl if the engagement is still on?' Miranda said.

Cora shrugged her shoulders. It all still seemed too early for banquets.

Mrs Hambleton stood hesitantly outside her son's bedroom door on the same day, willing herself to go inside. She had to talk to her son. The banquet was only days away, and since the day he'd come home, there'd been nothing but constraint between Cedric and the rest of the family.

Her husband had said, 'Give the boy a chance, Sybil. He's still out there seeing his friends slaughtered, seeing all hell let loose. You can't expect him to be interested in parties yet.'

'But he has to pick up the pieces,' she'd argued. 'Besides, what about that girl?'

'Well then, ask him. You can't sit on the fence forever.'

So there she stood, biting her lip nervously, trembling with anxiety at the reception she might get. Her knock on his door was timid, and there was no answer, so she repeated it. When there was *still* no answer, she tentatively opened the door to find him staring through the window, oblivious to her presence.

'Cedric,' she murmured softly, 'we have to talk.'

He stared at her briefly, before saying 'Not now, mother.'

'But when, Cedric? You've been home for days, and we've hardly exchanged a word. It's the banquet on Friday, I can't put it off any longer.'

'Put what off, Mother? You're having your banquet, aren't you?'

'I hope so dear, but what about you? It's because you are home safely. It's a celebration, and we have so many guests. I want to know about your engagement, Cedric. Will you be bringing her? If so, perhaps we should meet her before.'

His smile was bitter. 'Mother, you've had three years in which to meet her. Did you ever make the effort?'

'Cedric, you saw what was happening here, and she *did* work in the city. Your engagement was all so fast. We only ever saw her at that one event, and then you were off to France. None of us realized it was serious between you and Julie, we didn't really know what to think. You are bringing her to the banquet on Friday, aren't you?'

'I've arranged to meet her tomorrow in the

park. She's asked for time off so that we can talk.'

'You haven't seen her for three years, Cedric. It will feel like meeting a stranger. Do you still feel the same way about her, Cedric?'

'Talk to me tomorrow, Mother.'

'Suppose she's met somebody else, Cedric.'

'That might solve a lot of your problems, Mother.'

'Oh darling, don't be like that. We'll really make an effort to get to know Julie if that's what you want.'

'Even when it's not what *you* want, Mother?'

'I've never said so.'

'You don't have to. I'll meet Julie tomorrow like we planned, and we'll take it from there.'

He turned away, and she knew nothing more could be said. Tomorrow he would meet up with a girl he might find to be very different from the girl he had thought himself in love with, and all she could do was wait.

Cora waited for her in the conservatory, and when she met her daughter's eye, shaking her head sadly, she said, 'He won't talk, Cora. He's meeting the girl tomorrow afternoon.'

'Is he bringing her to the banquet?'

'I don't know. He doesn't know until they've spoken together.'

'Oh Mother, I hope he realizes he's no longer in love with her. Miranda saw her with that man, and—'

'Cora, we don't know who that man was. Miranda would like it to be some sort of romance, I

208

don't doubt. I hope you don't expect too much from Peter either. We don't know how the war has changed him, or even who he met in France.'

'You think he might have met somebody in France, Mother?'

'I don't know. It's all too soon.'

'I wonder who Louise will bring to the banquet?'

'From the sort of men she's been seen with recently, it could be anyone – a foreigner, even.'

Indeed at that very moment Louise was wishing she was miles away from the American man who was talking about the war as though he had won it single-handedly. He was young, good looking and extremely full of himself, and she wasn't his sort of girl.

With his father, he had been a guest at the Maxton household, where he had met Louise, who he had found beautiful, charming, but obviously uninterested in his charms. He wasn't tempted by the daughter of the house. He would have preferred to meet up with his friends and the sort of girls they had bragged about spending time with the evening before.

They had been to the theatre, some sort of unexciting play he hadn't liked instead of some lively girlie show, and although she'd been polite, she hadn't exactly been over-interested in his adventures.

Now, he suggested going on to some night club but she said she felt rather tired and would prefer to go home, so – somewhat relieved – he dropped her off at home and directed the taxi to take him to some more exciting venue.

'Well,' Louise's father demanded of her. 'How did you get on with that young whipper-snapper?'

'He was all right, I suppose.'

'You don't sound very enthusiastic.'

'Is Mother out?'

'Some political meeting. One I should have been at.'

'Why weren't you?'

'Because they can do without me. Now the war's over, Martin Broughton's in for better things.'

'What sort of things?'

'Minister. He'll make a good one.'

'Then perhaps Mother won't see as much of him.'

'He's good for her, keeps her on her toes, stops her being bored by those silly women she surrounds herself with.'

'She wouldn't need to if you were around more.'

He grinned. 'You're an astute little madam, I'll say that for you, but your assistance to me is coming to an end. What are you going to do with yourself now, my girl?'

'I could still go to finishing school, Father. Put the gilt on the gingerbread, so to speak. Or can you think of anything else?'

'There'll be no finishing school for you, Louise, it'll cost too much. This *war*'s cost me too much. I've got to start thinking about cutting down on a great many things. What you want now my girl is a lucrative husband who can keep you in the manner you've become accustomed to. Like meals at the Savoy, riding in Hyde Park, the Royal Enclosure at Ascot, and first nights at Covent Garden. It's what your mother expected when she married me. Isn't it what we've brought you up to expect?'

'And suppose it isn't what I want now?'

'It had better be, my girl. I have strong reservations about your taste in fellas, and my finances are not a bottomless pit at the moment. Subsidizing my daughter till she makes up her mind what she wants out of life is not on the agenda.'

'And what about Andrew? Have you laid down similar laws for him?'

'He's got sense. He'll know what his obligations are.'

'He could surprise you, Father.'

'Well, here's your mother. We'll see what she has to say.'

'No, Father, not if Martin Broughton's with her. I don't want him having anything to do with my future.'

'I rather think he'd agree with me in this instance – keeping you on a tight rein, making sure you conform.'

Moments later Louise stared into Martin Broughton's eyes. It was still there: the cynicism, the doubts of a man strangely unsure of himself.

'Meeting go well?' her father asked her mother

211

when Martin had departed.

'I decided not to go until it was almost over. After all, dear, there was the parade, and Andrew was in it. I thought it far more important than some political meeting.'

'Shame on you, woman! This meeting was important, and there'll be other parades, too many of them.'

'He looked so wonderful on that beautiful horse, Henry, and you should have seen and heard the girls cheering them. It did so much for their morale, I'm sure. I hope you've remembered about the banquet the Hambletons are giving on Friday, Henry. I've promised we'll all be there.'

'Why, for heaven's sake? It only means we'll have to give one back, and then there'll be a succession of others we have to go to. I don't expect Andrew will want to go either.'

'Why wouldn't he? Do you have an escort in mind, Louise?'

'No, Mother. I asked Cora if they intended to invite Imogen. After all, we were all close friends at school.'

'Mrs Hambleton mentioned her to me. Apparently she's leaving the hospital in Essex, going home to Derbyshire and country living. Lord Clarkson and his wife will be at the banquet, so it could perhaps be a little embarrassing.'

'Meeting his brother's daughter do you mean, Mother?' Louise asked sarcastically.

'The Hambletons will want a banquet with no ruffles on the surface. Imogen's a delightful girl, we all thought so, but none of us want to be involved in family feuds, do we?'

'Tomorrow I thought I'd go to see Imogen before she goes north,' Louise said.' Perhaps I could persuade her to attend the banquet.'

'I should keep well out of it, if I were you,' her mother said adamantly. 'See Imogen by all means, but don't mention Friday evening.'

Mary Stepson sat facing Imogen in her office, reflecting that the girl sitting opposite her was vastly changed from the young girl she had interviewed three and a half years before.

That girl had been pretty and excited, a girl wanting so much of life and expecting it to deliver. The woman she looked at now was calmly beautiful. The traumas of the last few years were etched on her face, and there was a sense that growing up had not been easy.

'So, Nurse Clarkson, you have made up your mind to leave us. Has it been a hard decision?' she asked.

'Yes, indeed, Matron. In spite of everything I have been happy here. I shall never forget it, but my home is with my parents in Derbyshire, and I'm sure there will be much work for me there.'

'You intend to swap nursing for farm work then?'

'I haven't seen my parents for so long, and I love it there, particularly when they bring the horses back. It will take time, but hopefully life will sort itself out.'

'You've been a good nurse, Clarkson, I've

heard nothing but excellent reports about your work and I shall be very sorry to lose you. Remember me to your mother. I would like to see her again if it is possible.'

'Oh, I'm sure it will be, I will certainly pass on your good wishes.'

The matron rose to her feet and walked round her desk, where Imogen rose to meet her. Imogen held out her hand formally, then to her surprise Mary held out her arms and embraced her. 'God be with you,' she said gently, and there was no disguising the tears in her eyes.

Imogen's suitcase lay open on her bed; she had already started to pack her belongings when she had been summoned to the matron's room. Now back in her room, she felt the meeting had disturbed her strangely. She had had few encounters with Mary Stepson over the last few years, but now she felt that her presence at the hospital had been worthwhile.

There was a soft tap on the door, and to Imogen's surprise Louise was standing there, smiling. She came into the room, closing the door behind her, and sat on the edge of Jenny's bed. 'I asked for you in the office, but they said you were with the matron and told me to come up here. Heavens, but it's small! Have you really spent the last few years in this place?'

'Yes, with my room-mate Jenny.'

'And you're packing. When do you intend to leave?'

'Tomorrow. My father's coming to London, and we're leaving tomorrow evening.'

'So soon!'

'It's better so, Louise.'

'But you can't go tomorrow. There's the banquet on Friday, and Cora says you're definitely invited. It's to celebrate the end of the war, her brother's safe return home, and oh so many other things. Imogen, you simply *have* to be there!'

'It's not possible, Louise, but I'll think about you all. Perhaps soon I'll come up to London and we can all meet, just the four of us, to catch up on old times.'

'I really did want you to be there, Imogen. Cedric, Cora's brother, is home, and Peter, Miranda's brother.'

'And Andrew?'

'Yes, you should have seen him yesterday in all his pukka best, riding his charger in the parade, and all the girls falling in love with him!'

'I'm sure he looked splendid.'

'You'd have met him at the party, and who knows?'

The door opened to admit Jenny, who stared at Louise curiously before going over to her locker, and Louise said, 'I'm so sorry, am I sitting on your bed?'

'It doesn't matter. I only came up to wish Imogen good luck. What did matron have to say for herself?' Jenny said.

'She wished me well. She was very nice.'

'Oh, well, I reckon she has to be nice sometimes. Are you a nurse?' she asked Louise bluntly.

'I'm afraid not. I doubt if I ever could have been one. Are you leaving nursing too?' Louise asked.

'Oh, I'm leavin' all right. I'm not spendin' the rest of me life nursin'. I'll be looking for somethin' else.'

'Have you any idea what?'

'Shop work. There'll be plenty o' work in the city now the war's over, though I always fancied meself as a hairdresser.'

Louise was hoping that Jenny would not linger long, and as if Jenny guessed her feelings she said, 'Well, I'd best get back to the wards. I'll see you later, Imogen. Perhaps we'll meet in the canteen for the usual.' Then at the door she turned, and looking pointedly at Louise she asked, 'Did ye ever know a boy called Jimmy Kent?'

Louise stared at her in surprise, before saying, 'Why do you ask?'

'Because I think I met you around four years ago in a little village where Jimmy Kent helped in the garden o' two old ladies you lived with. I'm sure you're the same girl.'

'Yes, I did know Jimmy Kent.'

'Fancied you, didn't he?'

'We were friends. Do you see him? How is he?'

'He was hurt in the war, but he's better now and working doin' some sort o' gardening. He's married to a girl I used to know in the village.'

'Oh, I'm so glad, I do hope he's happy.'

216

'What's your name?'

'Louise.'

'I'll tell Jimmy I've seen you and that you've bin asking about him, that'll cheer him up I'm sure. Goodbye, nice to 'ave met ye.'

After she had left, Imogen and Louise stared at each other for several seconds before Louise said dryly, 'My past does seem in the habit of catching up with me, doesn't it? I'd rather she didn't mention me to Jimmy. What's the point?'

'I'll try to persuade her not to.'

'I doubt if you'd be able to stop her doing anything she'd set her mind on.'

'Is there no man in your life at the moment, Louise? No man who really means something.'

'You know what I used to say at school. Not until there's an old man who idolizes me, is content to smother me with jewels, and is unlikely to have a long lifespan.'

'You didn't mean it.'

'No, I wanted to shock you.'

'There's nobody you like a little more than you should?'

'Somebody I dislike. Well, we dislike each other.'

'It has to start somewhere.'

'But not there, Imogen. He's handsome and maddening, superior and in love with my mother. You met him during that weekend you spent with us.'

'Martin Broughton?'

'That's him.'

'I thought he was rather nice. He was certainly

handsome. Why the superior?'

'Because he is.'

'Are you *sure* he's in love with your mother?'

'Of course I am. They're together a lot, more than she's ever with my father, and my mother discusses me with him, tells him what a disappointment I am, and he believes her.'

'Has he said so?'

'He doesn't have to say so. It's in the way he looks at me, the disapproval I sense in him, his remoteness.'

'There'll be some man for you, Louise. Not an old man with too much money and not too long left to spend it.'

'I really wonder what's going to happen to the four of us and all the things we used to want for ourselves. Look at Cora, hoping Peter Reed-Blyton will notice her at last, and Miranda, hankering after a man who's engaged to somebody else.'

'And look at me, solitary, with no man on the horizon, soon to be home in distant Derbyshire, helping to bring the cows in, feeding the chicks and riding over the hills. Can you think of anything more boring.'

'What are the men like in Derbyshire?'

'Well, apart from the vicar, the local farmers and the choir boys, I haven't met many of them.'

'Well, I'll come to your wedding.'

'And I'll come to yours.'

'Imogen, are you absolutely *certain* you can't come to this party on Friday? I'd like you to meet Andrew again. I really did think he liked you. He did see you quite a few times, just the two of you.'

'And you're a romantic at heart, Louise. No, I really can't be there. I'll be on the way home with my father tomorrow, and in the months to come we'll be making up for lost time. I'd like to invite you to spend some time with us, Louise, but I'm not sure that country living would be exactly your thing.'

'It was once, when I met Jimmy Kent!'

Imogen laughed. 'Jimmy was something to fill in the time before something more exciting cropped up. Don't go down that way again, Louise. I liked Jimmy Kent. He was a nice boy, and you didn't deserve him.'

'I know, and before you criticize me further I'm going to go. I daren't risk Jenny coming back to ask too many questions, when I really don't have the answers.'

It was later in the evening, when Imogen met Jenny for their last cup of Horlicks together, that Jenny said, 'Perhaps I shouldn't have asked yer friend if she knew Jimmy Kent. After all, I never really knew her.'

'Why did you ask her? Why did it matter so much?'

'Because his wife was me friend, and I knew how much she liked him. Suppose he's never really gotten over her and simply married me friend as second best?'

'But you don't know that, Jenny. Louise has got over Jimmy; I'm sure he's over her.'

'No, he's not. He talked about her when he

was in here, just because you talked like her!'

'And that was years ago. Now he's got a wife and I hope he's happy. I'm really not very sure about Louise.'

Seventeen

Breakfast at the Hambleton household was hardly an uplifting event. Cedric sat grave and unsmiling, his sister glancing at him cautiously, while his mother found herself quite incapable of asking the questions she had agonized over for some considerable time.

Three days to go before the banquet she had promised herself to welcome home her son. Right now her husband was at the War Office, where he had gone too early that morning, decidedly out of countenance with the world in general.

She needed to talk to Cedric. What about this girl he was supposedly engaged to! Would he be bringing her to the banquet? Was the engagement still on? How would the girl fit in with others in the family, and guests of very long standing?

'Another parade this morning, Cedric?' she ventured.

'No, Mother, I'm hoping there will be an end to parades until Sunday morning.'

'Then how are you going to spend your day? You too, Cora?'

'I'm meeting Miranda.'

'That's nice, dear. Will you be seeing Peter?'

'I don't know, Mother. Miranda says he's awfully quiet these days, not really like himself. Perhaps it's too soon.'

Across the table she met her brother's eyes, eyes filled with a strange cynicism, and her mother said quickly, 'Yes, of course, dear, much too soon. I'm sure Cedric understands, don't you, dear?'

'I saw nothing of Peter in France, Mother, so obviously I know nothing of his problems, if he has any.'

'No, of course not. So how do you intend to spend your day?'

'I'm meeting Julie at some cafe near her office. She's very busy there, so we won't have much time together.'

'Haven't you managed to speak to her sooner? It seems so awful that you have to wait until she's free from office duties to speak with her.'

'And you know what *my* time's been like since I arrived home. We've spoken on the telephone. Today we'll have a little longer.'

'Will you be bringing her on Friday evening?'

'That is one of the things we need to talk about, Mother,'

How unsatisfactory it was. A girl engaged to her son who was practically a stranger, and the guilty feeling persisted. They could have done more to welcome the girl into the family, got to

221

know her, but then the girl had made no effort either. Still, what could she have done? It was an engagement that should never have taken place, and meeting his mother's eyes across the table, Cedric knew the thoughts passing through her mind.

'I've got that clapped out old car, Cora, so I can drive you to the Reed-Blytons. I might even have time to have a word with Peter,' Cedric said.

Mrs Hambleton was glad to see them go. She had never envisaged a time when she felt she couldn't talk to her son, but now she felt only relief to see them driving away.

At the Reed-Blyton house, Cedric was received charmingly. He remembered Mrs Reed-Blyton, but not the daughter. She was a pretty little thing who shook hands with him, blushing and shyly welcoming him. Then, for over an hour, he sat with Peter, while together they went over their experiences in France and discovered a new camaradarie, before it was time for him to go and meet Julie.

Some time later, Cedric sat at a table in the window from where he could look down the road, decidedly unsure as to what he expected to see. What did he really remember about Julie? A pretty girl in a dress bought for the occasion of the Red Cross Ball, a girl he hardly knew but was taking great pains to discover. A girl very unlike the usual sort of girls trotted out for his inspection.

Those girls had been well-briefed before

attending such functions: to appear gracious but shy, not overly intelligent but agreeable. Such girls had been to boarding school and finishing school in Switzerland. They knew how to ski and speak some French, they rode horses and did needlepoint, and they were all of a pattern, those girls, groomed and educated by ambitious mothers.

But not Julie. Julie knew how to laugh at jokes other girls might have found reprehensible. She was intelligent and bright without a finishing school education. She worked for her living, and she had a decent job in the Civil Service. She was independent and opinionated, and refreshingly able to argue with the best of them.

He had enjoyed the time he spent with Julie; he had felt liberated by the difference he sensed in her. They had laughed, and he had believed he was falling in love with her. Now he found difficulty in remembering what she had *really* been like.

Would he even recognize her when she walked down the street? London was full of pretty girls. Would he still appreciate her overloud laughter and the humour that had once amused him and which he was now unsure about?

He could not have known that Julie, too, was experiencing similar doubts. Once she had found it difficult to believe that she had captured a handsome upper-crust young officer, who she would never have met if it hadn't been for the war, thrusting everyone into an environment that was strangely different.

What would it really be like to marry a man who could give her a fine house and sufficient of the world's wealth? No more job-hunting if one job finished, no more wondering if she could afford the dress she'd seen in some shop window. No more joining the rest of them on their way to work on frost-laden mornings, hearing the moans of girls in similar situations, and then again at the end of the day, during the weary journey home.

Garth Thompson sat at the desk next to hers, and she'd known him for four years. He was nice and serious, but she wasn't sure how much she liked him, though she was certain that he more than liked *her*.

He had bad eyesight and consequently hadn't been suitable material for the forces, but he was intelligent and well thought of at the office. Most people thought he would do well, and he came from a decent, respectable family in Bermondsey. At night he went home to his mother's cooking, while she went home to a flat she shared with two other girls and whatever they could muster up between them.

But, there was Cedric. Cedric, with motor cars and horses. But, after four years, did he still love her, and how would she cope with his family, who had never tried to get to know her?

His sister had been nice on that one occasion they had spoken together, friendly, so much so that the girls she'd been with that day had thought she was rather nice, even though the girl Cedric's sister had been with had barely raised a smile.

What would his family be like? Suppose they'd scoff at the way she spoke? Suppose her sense of humour wasn't theirs? Suppose that girl who had been unfriendly was a girl he'd been expected to marry? That wouldn't have worried her unduly, but to be looked down on, that would be terrible.

She stood for a moment on the kerb, looking across the road at the cafe, and she even debated whether to turn tail and run, but then, shrugging her shoulders philosophically, she thought, oh well, if it's not going to work out, I've still got Garth.

Their eyes met across the room, and although she recognized him instantly, for a moment there was doubt. Then he smiled and came forward to meet her.

How could she not be impressed by his handsome face and officer's uniform? Others in the cafe were looking at them, seeing a pretty girl and a young man returned from the war. People smiled at them, and when they went to the table, those around them acknowledged their presence with words of welcome.

Julie felt strangely tongue-tied until Cedric asked, 'I hope you'll have lunch, Julie. I suppose this is your lunch-time.'

'Yes, we quite often come here. I'm not really very hungry.'

'But you must eat. Choose what you'd like.'

'How about you?'

'I'll have the same. What time do you have to

be back?'

'Around two o'clock. I asked for a little longer then usual.'

'Oh good. We do need to talk.'

Looking at her while she scanned the menu, Cedric thought, yes, she is pretty, I can understand why I liked her so much, but what do we really know about each other? And as if she knew what he was thinking she said, 'I was afraid of meeting you, Cedric. You're really a stranger, aren't you?'

'I suppose I am.'

'It's been so long.'

'Yes, four years, and we didn't really know each other then, did we? We had fun together, we laughed and liked each other. Julie, is it enough?'

'I'm not sure. What do you think?'

'I don't know what to think. It's certainly not enough to think we're ready for marriage. Isn't that what an engagement is all about?'

'I suppose so.'

'Julie, four years ago we thought loving each other was enough, but are we really sure it is? Shouldn't we start all over again? Or is there enough love left?'

'I don't know.'

She'd known they had to talk, but not quite so soon, perhaps. He was all that she remembered, all she'd aspired to, and yet apart from their pressing problems, what could they say to each other? On their last meeting they had found much to laugh at; she'd been gay and amusing, he'd been handsome and going away though for how long, neither of them knew. Now they were here together, like two young people meeting at some garden party, with nothing of the past to remember and an obscure future.

She'd watched girls running joyously into the arms of men they'd loved, and there'd been gratitude and ecstasy to be united with them, but now there was only uncertainty and the searching for words that should have been so easy to find.

Cedric, too, was miserably aware of the problems, and he said quickly, 'I believe you met my sister quite recently, Julie.'

'Yes, in some cafe across the way. She was with a friend.'

'Yes, an old school friend.'

'She seemed very nice.'

'You'll meet her again on Friday.'

'Friday?'

'Why yes, my mother's decided to have a banquet to welcome me home. I don't know whether it's a good idea or not, but she's set her heart on it.'

She stared at him doubtfully, and quickly he said, 'You're invited, Julie.'

'But I won't know anybody, Cedric. I don't know your mother and most of the other people who'll be there.'

'Perhaps it's time to get to know them.'

'I'm not sure ... Are you?'

'Julie, I don't know. We don't really know each other.'

And, of course, they didn't. Once, it wouldn't have mattered. They'd been sure of the moment, and the future hadn't mattered. Now it mattered all too much, and so Cedric said hesitantly, 'We did rather rush things, didn't we, Julie?'

'Yes.'

'Perhaps if we go to this banquet we'll rediscover the past, fall in love again, see if it's going to work out.'

'And perhaps we'll see how stupid we've been and we'll feel awful that everybody there will see it too.'

'We could just go and enjoy ourselves, forget about the rest.'

'We couldn't do that. Not when we're supposed to be engaged and so many people know about it. I don't think I want to go to your mother's banquet, Cedric. I don't think she'd want me to be there.'

'So you don't think we should continue with this engagement? Is there somebody else, Julie?'

'I'm not sure.'

'Then there *is* somebody?'

'Some man I met at the office. We like each other, we see each other every day, and I know he'd like there to be more. I know him a lot better than I know you, Cedric, and I know his family. They invite me to their home and make me very welcome. I know they'd be pleased if something materialized. I've never felt that with your family, Cedric.'

'I know, and I'm sorry. It's the world I grew up in, the sort of people we are in this class-conscious country we've created. It may not last, but it won't change immediately, and we may hate the waiting.'

There were tears in her eyes as she rose to her feet, and immediately he said, 'I'm sorry, Julie, does it really have to end like this?'

'Better that it does, I think. You'll probably marry some girl like your sister's friend, and I'll end up with Garth. You'll probably end up very important, and who knows? We might too. After all, there are different ways of getting to the top.'

Suddenly they were laughing together, and he was reminded of the old Julie and why he had once believed he loved her. With a little gasp, she said, 'Gracious, Cedric, I forgot about your ring. I'll never have one as beautiful as this, but it's not mine any more.'

She was struggling to remove it from her finger, and quickly he said, 'Keep it, Julie. I don't want it for anybody else, and I want you to have it, not as an engagement ring, but because you like it and it's something to remember me by.'

'I don't need the ring to remember you by, Cedric. I could even come to hate it.'

'Hate it?'

'Why yes. It could remind me of the good times I promised myself, a different world from the one I grew up in, money where I never had any, and perhaps more jewellery that now I'll never be able to afford.'

'But you will, Julie. You're going to the top,

remember? I'm more than confident that you'll get there.'

He watched her stepping out along the road, a slender pretty girl with her head held high, and he felt suddenly ashamed of the feeling of relief that the end of his engagement would please his mother and make her considerably more enthusiastic about the forthcoming banquet.

The house was a hive of activity, and although his mother looked at him searchingly he merely said, 'I'll see you at dinner, Mother. I have to go out this afternoon. I promised to meet some of the chaps for a bit of nostalgia.'

She could gather nothing from his expression, and after he had gone to his room Cora said, 'Why couldn't he say something now, Mother? Why didn't you insist on it?'

'Maybe I don't want to know just yet. Maybe I'd rather wait.'

'But why, when we're all on tenterhooks?'

'We'll hear it soon enough. Now, do get on with that list of names, Cora, and make sure nobody's been forgotten.'

Over dinner that evening Cedric and his father talked about the war, from its beginning to its ending, and his mother and sister wished the meal was over and both the men could find something else to discuss.

At last, Mrs Hambleton managed to say, 'Can't we talk about the banquet on Friday evening? Haven't we had enough war for one evening?'

'Isn't the war more important than your

230

banquet?' her husband said testily.

'But it's over, Arthur, and we're glad it's over,' she replied.

'Well, I hope we're not expected to dress up in glad rags for it. I intend to wear my uniform, and I do *not* intend to get my dress uniform out of moth balls.'

'I think you should. In fact, I'm expecting it.'

'And *I* think it's totally unnecessary. I ran into Henry Maxton this morning. I don't think he's looking forward to it either.'

'Did he say as much?'

'No, he had his daughter with him. Quite a stunner, she is. I'd take a good look at that filly if I were you, Cedric.'

'Really, Arthur. From what I've heard about that young lady, she doesn't lack for admirers.'

'Well, I'm going to the study, I've got letters to write. What about you, Cedric?'

Cedric smiled, and his mother said shortly, 'I want to talk to Cedric. I've seen little of him all day.'

Mr Hambleton went to his study, and Cora, after a knowing glance from her mother, disappeared also.

Mrs Hambleton smiled at her son, asking, 'More coffee, dear?'

'No thank you, Mother. Like you say, we need to talk.'

'Did you meet your fiancée then?'

'Yes, for a short while.'

'A short while, Cedric? When there's so much to talk about?'

'She has a job to go to, Mother. It was her lunch break.'

'Aren't you meeting her again this evening, or tomorrow?'

'No, Mother. Julie and I have said all we have to say.'

'What's that suppose to mean?'

'It means it's over, Mother. Our engagement, I mean. We've both thought about it. After all, we've had three and a half years to think about it. At first we thought it was the right thing we'd done, but then we realized we'd been impetuous and unsure. We fell in love with each other, but we didn't really *know* each other. She's a nice girl, but we're strangers, not so much boy and girl strangers, but two people living in different worlds. You have to admit it, Mother, neither you nor your friends have made an effort to get to know her or like her.'

'Oh darling, I know, and I'm sorry, but you're right, we do live in different worlds. I wanted to invited her here, but what would we have talked about? We didn't know Julie or her family, and we didn't know anything about her work. All I remember was that she was a pretty girl and seemed nice enough. It wasn't enough to base an engagement on, Cedric. Did Julie end it or did you?'

'It was entirely mutual, I think, Mother. We hadn't fallen out of love, it's doubtful if we'd ever *been* in love really, but there didn't seem very much left. She's met another man. She's not sure exactly where it's going, but apparently

232

they like each other.'

'Don't you mind?'

'No, Mother. If I minded then it would mean I was still in love with her, wouldn't it? The fact that I don't mind says it all, doesn't it?'

He got to his feet, and with a strangely sad smile he said, 'I'm having an early night, Mother. I've got to get ready for this terribly important function of yours, and right at this moment I'm not looking forward to it.'

'Oh but darling, it's for you, and for all the other friends who are coming. We'll be so disappointed if you don't enjoy it. There'll be several pretty girls who will help you to forget Julie, and like your father says, Louise Maxton is *very* fanciable.'

'No, no, Mother, not yet. Please don't start looking round for a replacement! I'm not ready for one. I know what you mothers are like. Concentrate on Cora! I'm sure you've somebody in mind for her.'

'Well, of course not. She's only just left school.'

'Four *years* ago, Mother. If there'd been no war she'd just have left finishing school, she'd be a deb, and all you mothers would have been lining up the right men in anticipation.'

'Well, of course we wouldn't.'

He smiled and shook his head, and his mother said swiftly, 'Cora's not going to finishing school, Cedric. It's a pity, but there'll be other things.'

'Of course there will, Mother. If she went off

233

now to Switzerland and finishing school, all the best young men would have been snapped up by the time she came home. We can't allow that to happen.'

'You're really very cynical.'

'I know, that's what war does to you. It will take some time before normality brings us down to earth. Goodnight, Mother, see you in the morning.'

Cora received the news of her brother's broken engagement philosophically, and was quick to agree with her mother that they hadn't tried to accept the girl, but it was just as well it had ended peaceably.

'Give it a little time,' her mother said, 'then he'll find somebody else. There'll be some nice girls here on Friday, and we'll just have to look around.'

'*We*, Mother?'

'Well, you know what I mean, dear. Men can be so hopeless about things like that. Look how silly this thing with Julie has been. They really do need some help.'

'You heard what Father said about Louise?'

'Yes, and I'm not sure at all. From what I've seen of that young lady, I rather think she's a little too worldly for Cedric at this moment.'

'She is, Mother. She's nice, and I like her, but I'm not really sure she'd be the right one. My friend Miranda on the other head, would be perfect.'

'Oh yes, dear, you're quite right. But Louise's

brother is handsome and charming. Be very nice to Andrew on Friday. Cora, he has great potential.'

Eighteen

Louise surveyed herself in the mirror and liked what she saw. The dress was unadorned by embroidery, frills or flounces, and yet it was elegant in its simplicity. Azure blue, the woman at her mother's favourite dress shop had called it, and she'd bought it, even when her mother had shown her evident disapproval.

'I can understand you choosing that colour if you were forty,' she'd said. 'It's a beautiful dress, but the girls of your age will be wearing white or pale pink or powder blue. You'll be looking for something quite colourful for your coming-out ball, I'm sure.'

'I don't want a coming-out ball, Mother.'

'I'm sure you will. Things will get back to normal, and you'll be presented at Court. It's tradition for all the girls to wear white then.'

Tradition, she thought savagely, who cared about tradition any more? Staring at her reflection disdainfully she said out loud, 'One day I'll wear black, beautiful sophisticated black, and I'll look like the Merry Widow, with a huge black hat decorated with white gardenias.' Then she thought about the gown her mother had chosen for the banquet. Beige, but her mother would look exquisite, as she always did.

There was a light tap on her door, and it opened to reveal Andrew smiling at her. She grinned at him, saying, 'You're not wearing your dress uniform, that won't suit Mother.'

'Apparently she's made enquiries and none of the men are.'

'You'll still be the handsomest man there, Andrew.'

'And you're my little sister and conditioned to think that way.'

'Do you like this dress? Do you think it suits me?'

'As always, you look very pretty.'

'But it's not really what I should be wearing, is it?'

'I'm not au fait with women's fashions, Louise. Will your friends be in evidence?'

'Cora and Miranda, of course.'

'And the other one, what was her name?'

'You know very well what her name was, Imogen, I thought you and she were getting along rather well.'

'It is some time since we met, Louise. She won't be there then?'

'No, she's left nursing and gone home to Derbyshire, back to horses and farming, feeding the chicks and herding the cattle. I doubt if it would have suited you, Andrew.'

'I'm an army man, Louise, even though the war's over. I think the parents are waiting for us downstairs, so do try to look a little enthusiastic, Louise.'

'Will Martin Broughton be there? Isn't he their MP?'

'I suppose so.'

'Why does mention of Martin always bring out the sulks in you?'

'Because we don't like each other, and I can't get away from him.'

'I should think there are quite a few girls in London who wouldn't be too keen to get away from him.'

'And I would think he's not into young girls, and is far more enthusiastic about older women.'

He raised his eyebrows maddeningly, and he smiled when she swept in front of him with lofty disdain.

To Mrs Hambleton's delight, all was going well. The female guests looked enchanting, as she had expected, even if Louise's gown did seem a little too sophisticated for her age. Shouldn't she have been wearing white or at least something paler?

Andrew, as always, looked handsome and charming, and she wished Cora didn't seem quite so obsessed with Peter Reed-Blyton when he appeared so strangely morose.

Peter was thinking the entire affair was incongruous so soon after the war had ended. They were celebrating victory, but there was no victory, only the aftermath of loss and desolation after four long years.

Cora Hambleton was staring at him from

across the room smiling, and although he didn't return her smile she walked across the room to join him.

'Are you feeling better, Peter?' she asked him. 'How is your leg?'

'I am feeling better. I'm simply suffering from the legacy of the war years. Not unusual, I think.'

'No. My brother, too, was in the war. I sense it in him as well. We're all laughing and chatting about nothing, and then I find him staring into space, remembering.'

'Give us time, Cora. One day we'll have to get back to normality.'

'Oh yes. I think we're going in for dinner now. Mother took charge of the seating arrangements. Perhaps I'll see you later?'

'Of course.'

It was a start, she thought.

Across the room, her brother Cedric was chatting to Louise and her brother and they were moving with the rest of them into the dining room.

To her chagrin, Louise found herself sitting next to Martin Broughton, and although he acknowledged her presence with a brief smile, she gave her full attention to the man sitting next to her, a young man who was quick to inform her that he worked in the Foreign Office and was 'going places'. Indeed, during the next half hour he talked incessantly of the dizzy heights his chosen profession was taking him to.

It was with something approaching relief that

she heard Martin ask, 'Are you finding life very dull now that the war is over, Louise? It can't be much fun being back to more mundane activities.'

'Why are you so sure that they're mundane?' she snapped.

'Surmising, that's all.'

'Perhaps I'll surprise everybody and become a missionary.'

'I doubt if it would suit you.'

'Perhaps you'd like to tell me what would suit me.'

'How can I possibly know what might suit a girl I'm supposed to dislike? I'd be sure to get it wrong.'

'Yes, you would, just like you've got me wrong.'

'Wouldn't that be mutual? *You* think I'm a cynical, self-opinionated man who is totally satisifed with his life and everything in it.'

'And you think *I'm* a spoilt silly woman with not too many morals and hardly any brains.'

'Really? Did I say that?'

'You didn't *have* to. You made it very obvious from the start.'

'This is neither the time nor the place to say whether either of us have been right or wrong, I think. Let's discuss it another day.'

'One day, when I can please myself about what I do, what I say, and and who I want to be. One day, when I can wear black and huge hats and towering heels. One day, when I don't have to explain to anybody what I'm really like.'

He stared at her in some dismay, before saying, 'What's all this about wearing black and enormous hats? I don't think this ever came into my assessment of you!'

'Perhaps not, but it's all tied up with how I should look, how I should feel, how I should act. Why must I be like everybody else? Why can't I simply be me?'

'Your mother doesn't like your dress?'

'No. I should be in pristine white, with gardenias instead of jewels. I'm told I must look like everybody else in white at the debs ball, and I mustn't give an opinion unless it's asked for, and there's to be nothing controversial in case it's frowned upon by so-called adults.'

To her amazement he threw back his head and laughed.

Sitting next to Cedric, further down the table, Miranda ventured, 'You're here alone, Cedric?'

'With my parents and my sister, of course.'

'Not your fiancée?'

'Ah. So you knew my fiancée?'

'No, I didn't. I met her once at the Red Cross Ball, but I heard you'd become engaged.'

She was embarrassed, she wished she hadn't been so personal, and quick to change the subject, she said, 'This is a lovely party, isn't it?'

'Yes, my mother enjoys giving her lovely parties.'

'I've been looking forward to it.'

'That's nice.' He sensed her embarrassment, and his mind went back over the years to the birthday parties and functions they'd both attended, while their respective mothers had looked on.

'You mentioned my engagement, Miranda,' he said gently.

'Oh, I shouldn't have. I'm sorry.'

'It doesn't matter. I'm no longer engaged, Miranda. Julie and I decided that perhaps we'd been a little hasty. We hadn't got to know each other all that well. If there hadn't been a war, things might have been different.'

Oh, they would have been different, Miranda thought. They would probably never have met. They'd be in different worlds, and it would all have been circumspect and uncomplicated.

'I'm sorry,' she found herself saying. 'I hope neither of you are too unhappy about it, but it's better to find out now rather than later.'

'Well yes, of course. It's not too difficult to end an engagement, but ending a marriage is a messy business.'

She smiled, and after a few minutes she said, 'You're staying in the army, Cedric?'

'Yes. For the time being, at any rate.'

'And what about later?'

'Oh, there'll be something. How about you?'

'I'm a suffragette.'

'Really? Votes for women, and all that?'

'Everybody tells us we'll never get them. I don't see why not.'

'Are you particularly militant?'

'Gracious, no. My sister is. She's over there. If you talk to her about the movement, you'll never get away!'

241

He laughed. He was remembering this girl, Peter Reed-Blyton's sister. She was pretty, nice sort of girl, but she'd seemed so young the last time he'd seen her, and there'd been Julie, with her worldly approach to life and her humour.

From further along the table, his mother viewed their conversation with a contented smile. It was all going very well, and meeting Miranda's mother's eyes they both smiled. It had been traumatic, but all was not lost.

Further along the table, a woman in a heavily beaded black gown smiled at Louise, and Louise smiled back. The woman seemed vaguely familiar, and yet she could have been anyone. People met up at the most unlikely places, and yet as once more she met the woman's doubtful smile she remembered – Algy Barrington's mother! – and she looked round quickly to reassure herself that Algy wasn't present.

Mrs Barrington had been so insistent that they took tea together, that she and Algy were destined to be great friends, or something closer, and now she hoped there was a chance of avoiding each other.

It was much later, when they stood chatting together, that Mrs Barrington looked at her again, but this time there was no bright smile on the older woman's face, only a sad, tearful one. Impulsively Louise walked towards her, and Mrs Barrington dissolved into tears.

'Oh my dear,' she said unhappily, 'how sad that we should meet like this, when I had such hopes of you and Algy being great friends.'

'Sad, Mrs Barrington?'

'Why yes, dear, poor dear Algy was killed on the Somme. I'm still in disbelief that I shan't see him again.'

'Oh Mrs Barrington, I'm so sorry, I didn't know.'

'He was such a nice dear boy. You thought so, didn't you, Louise? And he liked you tremendously. He mentioned you in his letters, asked if I'd seen you, hoped that after the war you'd really get to know each other better, and now he's gone.'

Faced with his mother's grief, Louise felt suddenly inadequate. She hadn't known Algy Barrington very well, and she hadn't really liked him very much, but she felt strangely superficial. She'd been proud of her vain, butterfly existence, believing that she was having one hell of a good time, even when people like Algy were dying, and seeing Martin Broughton looking across the room at them she turned away angrily. Was that how he saw her? An empty, frivolous girl, who thought of nothing beyond the empty amusements of the moment because there was nothing in her head to speak of more important things?

An elderly man in uniform joined them, and quickly she reached out to embrace Mrs Barrington, saying briefly, 'I'm so sorry. May I call to see you?'

'Oh please, yes, my dear. Please do.'

In another corner of the room, her brother was surrounded by girls, young unattached girls who smiled and giggled, captivated by his looks and his charm. Andrew was learning who they were as introductions were performed, and smiling mothers gazed on expectantly. It was the first of many banquets, but there would be others, and their hopes were high that friendships forged at this one might continue. There weren't enough men to go round, there needed to be more, and as yet the ending of the war was only a superficial thing. Real peace was a long way coming.

Louise's father sat slumped in the drawing room in the company of a group of other men, wishing the party was over and they could leave for home. His wife stood with other wives, admiring each other's gowns, issuing invitations to forthcoming events.

Seeing his sister standing alone Andrew excused himself, aware of the sad smile on her face.

'Why so dejected?' he said with a brief smile.

'I've just heard that Algy Barrington was killed on the Somme. That's his mother over there.'

'I knew about Algy.'

'You didn't tell me!'

'The last time we spoke of him you didn't seem to like him very much.'

'I know. Oh Andrew, I feel such a fool. I suddenly feel I don't know anything about anything. What have I ever done for the war?'

'Saved my father from making conversation with people he wasn't really interested in. Added a little sparkle to boring luncheons, a little glamour to dismal dinner parties.'

'Oh Andrew, it's been so superficial. Look at Imogen at that hospital, working herself half to death, and even Cora helped out with wounded soldiers. Miranda's doing what she can to get votes for women.'

'And perhaps failing miserably.'

'But what have *I* done?'

'Well, right now, my dear, I don't think it's much use trying to think of something, as you've already made up your mind. What are you going to do with your life now the war's over?'

'I don't know.'

'You could join the contingent who are looking for a husband. All these girls, potential debutantes for the next line-up, you could be the belle of the ball.'

'And you're being sarcastic. Our father's bored to death and our mother would prefer to be with Martin Broughton. She'll hate him having to talk to other women all evening.'

'Why does it bother you so much, Louise?'

'Because she's my mother, and he thinks I'm useless.'

'Has he said as much?'

'Only inferred it.'

'You think they're having an affair, don't you?'

'Don't *you*?'

'No. Broughton's ambitious, and he's also a decent sort of chap. Quite honestly, Louise, I like him.'

She stared at him angrily, then with a toss of

her head she said, 'I'd like this affair to be over. It's late, and look at father! He's bored out of his skin, and he'll grumble all the way home.'

Meanwhile, Cora didn't feel that she was making much progress with Peter Reed-Blyton. He was hard work. They'd talked pleasantries, but when their talk had strayed to the war he'd been quick to change the subject. What could she find to say that would amuse him, or even interest him?

'Will you stay in the army?' she asked him.

'I think so. It was to be my career, and Cedric's too, I think.'

'Oh yes, but then my father was a soldier too.'

'Yes, of course.'

'Your father's a politician. Could you go into politics?'

'I know very little about it. What are you going to do?'

'Mother says it's a pity we never got to finishing school in Switzerland. I'll be twenty-two next birthday, so I'm not going back to school to mingle with seventeen- and eighteen-year-olds. There'll be coming out balls, I suppose. We have those to look forward to.'

'Of course.'

She wasn't at all sure he wanted to hear about coming out balls. He was polite and distant. What would Louise have talked to him about? As if he guessed her thoughts he said, 'Isn't that Andrew Maxton's sister over there?'

'Yes, Louise. She was at school with me.'

'I know Andrew, but I've never really spoken

246

to his sister.'

'She's beautiful, isn't she, and very amusing.'

'Really.'

Did he want to meet Louise, as he had appeared to want to at Jean's wedding? Was he interested? Did he think her more mature? After all, from what she'd been hearing, Louise had had far more experience entertaining young men, and even older ones.

'Cedric seems to be getting along with Miranda. I do hope so. She's always liked him,' she said.

That remark brought a brief smile to his face, and she wished she hadn't said it. After all, what did men talk about when they were together? Which girl fancied them, and which girl they'd found entertaining? What would Peter say about her? Probably that she was a nice girl, and very little else.

Across the room, Miranda was talking to Cedric. She remembered him at that Red Cross Ball with that other girl – laughing, happy, two young joyous people having a wonderful time, and falling in love and now here she was, finding it difficult to find something to talk about that they were both interested in. They'd exhausted the war, his last few days in London, her involvement with the suffragette movement, which at least had given him a little cause for amusement. She thought that Louise, too, looked different from her usual smiling self. She seemed almost morose, and her brother was looking down at her almost anxiously. Following her gaze, Cedric said, 'Andrew Maxton was my commanding officer, a decent chap. Is that his sister?'

'Yes, Louise, we were at school together.'

Why did everybody notice Louise? Why wasn't she wearing white or cream, like every other girl? Why did she always look so beautiful?

'Have you enjoyed the banquet, Cedric? I think most people have,' she asked, in an effort to keep the conversation alive.

'Of course, very nice. Mother loves things like this. She'll be pleased it's gone so well.'

She was suddenly spared from saying anything else by the commotion going on across the hall, and Cedric said hurriedly, 'Hello, something's amiss,' and the next moment the door was flung open, a servant hurried in to speak to his hostess, and she in turn approached Lady Maxton. It was obvious that something was wrong, and immediately Andrew and Louise joined their mother as she hurriedly left the room.

'What is it?' they were demanding of each other.

Mrs Hambleton said, 'I'm afraid it's Lord Maxton. He's had a heart attack.'

Nineteen

Upset and apologetic, Lady Maxton spoke to her hosts before she went to meet her husband in hospital. Andrew went with her, so it was left to Martin Broughton to take Louise home. She sat with him in the car, and they drove in silence.

There had been so many times when she and Martin had had nothing to say to each other, but on this occasion she was grateful for his strength and for his supportive silence.

She left it to Martin to inform their servants what had happened, and he immediately asked if she would like sustenance, before disappearing to spread the terrible news.

When Martin joined Louise in the drawing room, he found her standing on the hearth, staring into the fire. Their eyes met across the room, and he said softly, 'This is terrible, Louise. Hasn't he been well during these last few days?'

'I haven't seen much of him. You know Father, he's always so distant, either sitting in his study or involved with some visitor or other.'

'Well, there's nothing we can do until your mother and Andrew report. Why don't we have a drink, or would you prefer tea?'

'Sherry perhaps.'

'I suggest tea. You've probably drunk enough of the other stuff for one evening.'

'Even at this time, Martin, you have to cast aspersions on my moral character.'

He smiled. 'Is that really what you thought I was doing?'

'Well, yes. Don't we always say or do the wrong thing to each other?'

'This time I really didn't intend to. Do sit down, Louise, and take off your wrap. It's quite warm in here, and there's nothing we can do until we hear about your father's condition.'

How slowly the time passed. Louise leafed through several magazines while Martin exhausted the morning newspaper, both of them disinclined to enter into any form of conversation.

It seemed incongruous that they should be sitting in silence, wearing evening dress, and waiting anxiously for whatever news her mother and Andrew might be able to bring them.

At last, Louise jumped to her feet, saying, 'I'm getting out of this dress. I feel so silly sitting here all dressed up for a party when the party's obviously over.'

He offered no comment, and she hurried up to her room, where she hunted impatiently through her wardrobe before selecting something more appropriate.

Meeeting the butler in the hall, he smiled sadly, saying, 'It's a sad business, Miss Louise. I hope we have news of the master very soon.'

Martin was sitting where she had left him, and as their eyes met it seemed that they were both afraid of the thoughts circulating in their heads.

Martin got up to add more logs to the fire, and Louise said quickly, 'Do you think my father's going to die?'

'I hope not. He'll have the best of care, I'm sure.'

'How long must we wait?' she asked.

The city road outside the house was quiet, with the sound of vehicles only occasionally, and she saw that it was almost three o'clock. The Hambleton's banquet would by this time surely be over.

Suppose her father died, she thought anxiously. How soon before her mother married Martin Broughton? And where would they live? Surely not here. Wouldn't this house belong to Andrew, who would be the next Baronet, and what would happen to her? She couldn't live with them. How could she bear to see them happy in some romantic paradise?

She dozed fitfully, and it was Martin, pulling back the drapes at the window to display a cold, grey dawn and rain splattering on the panes, that woke her.

'What time is it?' she gasped.

'Nearly seven o'clock,' he answered. 'We haven't long to wait, Louise. They're here.'

Her mother came into the room first, weary and fragile, and then Andrew came, meeting their anxious eyes with a shake of his head.

'He's still alive,' he said quickly. 'They told us

to come home, that there was nothing either of us could do, and they'll be in touch later this morning. He's still unconscious, and it's a very severe heart attack he's had.'

'But he's always been so well,' Louise said. 'You know, he never even had a cold. If *I* had, I was simply told to forget it and get on with things.'

'Well, apparently his heart hasn't been good for years. He never wanted anybody to know about it.'

'Is he going to die?'

'We don't know,' her mother said softly. 'I suggest you go to bed and try to get some sleep, Louise. We can't do anything, none of us, until the hospital get in touch later this morning. Thank you so much for staying with Louise, Martin. You've had no sleep and you have that very big meeting this morning.'

'I'm alright, Isobel. I probably dozed off during the night.'

'Can I get the servants to serve breakfast or something?'

'Not for me, Isobel, I'll get off home. Do let me know as soon as you hear anything about Henry, and try to get some sleep yourself, my dear.'

He took Isobel's hand and held it for a little while, then with a smile he said, 'Hope for the best, dear. Try not to be too pessimistic.'

Louise's eyes followed him as he walked across the room and into the hall. Hadn't he wanted to embrace her mother? Hadn't they felt

252

the need to stay in each other's arms until they were sure it was for the rest of their lives?

Her mother got stiffly to her feet and, looking at Andrew, she said, 'You've been a tower of strength, Andrew. We simply have to wait now. Goodnight, both of you, or perhaps I should say good morning.'

Louise looked at her brother anxiously, before saying, 'Do you think he's going to die Andrew? It's only a few hours since we were dressing for that banquet. It seems so odd.'

'I don't know, Louise. We'll have to wait. Why don't you go to bed? We can do nothing else until we've heard from the hospital.'

How could she possibly hope to sleep when her entire life could be changing? If her father died, she had no doubts that her mother would marry Martin Broughton, and she couldn't visualize a life with them, but where would she go and with whom? Andrew would marry, and he had his own life.

Louise thought about her schoolfriends. She had been the happy-go-lucky one, the girl with a light-hearted approach to life. No particular man to care for, at least not for years, or so she'd told herself, and them, in that silly confident other world.

The news from the hospital that morning was grave. Her father had had another heart attack mid-morning, and he died before noon. This was followed by the days of mourning leading up to his funeral, and as Louise stood with her mother and Andrew in the overwhelming contours of the cathedral, she was only aware of Martin standing next to her, but he had come for her mother, never for her.

The weeks that followed seemed empty and aimless, but one day Andrew surprised her over breakfast by saying, 'I'm going away for a few days. I've told Mother, but I don't suppose she remembers. She's away with the fairies at the moment.'

'She's away with Martin.'

'Martin's busy at the House. She's filling her life with all sorts of things.'

'You don't want to know anything about them, do you, Andrew? Where are you going, anyway? Are you going alone?'

'Yes. I've been four years at war, and I know precious little about England. Perhaps it's time I took a look around.'

'Around England! But where?'

'Oh, around. I've never been north of Stratford on Avon. Time to do it now before I have to start thinking about the future, *my* future.'

'I can't think where you'll go. I had a letter of condolence from Imogen. She talked about their horses arriving back from the war, about the farm and the sort of life she's living. It's all so different to our lives. I like Imogen, but I doubt if I'd like her lifestyle.'

'That's because you don't know about any lifestyle but yours.'

He smiled at her as he left the table, and several minutes later she was joined by her mother, who sat absently leafing through her mail.

'I thought you were out, Mother,' she ventured.

'No. I'm out later. Some meeting to do with the Party.'

'Martin's party?'

'Well, obviously.'

Her mother seemed unduly concerned with the letter she was reading, and Louise asked, 'Is it from somebody special, Mother?'

'From cousin Helene. She'd like me to go to stay with her in Switzerland, but I have too much to do here at the moment. Besides, we never really had much in common.'

'Where in Switzerland does she live?'

'Geneva. If you'd gone to finishing school, you'd no doubt have spent time with her.'

'Does she mention me?'

'Of course. She says you'll be getting ready for the Season. She doesn't seem to have realized that your father's death has affected us at all.'

'I don't remember her. What was she like?'

'Pretty, frivolous. I think you'd like her. In fact, there are times when you remind me of Helene.'

'Is she married?'

'For the second time, I think. Or is it the third time? I'm not sure.'

'You mean she's been divorced? Rather risky, wasn't it?'

'Her first husband was killed on the ski slopes, and I think the second one died in some accident or other. I'm sure she got married again, but we sort of lost track with Helene after two marriages.'

'I think I might like to visit her. If she's invited you, don't you think she might settle for me?'

Her mother looked at her expectantly. Of course, to get Louise out of her hair, if for only a little while, would be a good idea. Her father's death had put a stop momentarily to the balls and other festivities, so she was wandering around like a lost soul, and a respite in Switzerland might be just the thing to keep her entertained.

'Did Andrew tell you he was going away?' Louise asked.

'Yes, but I don't know where he's going.'

'Looking around England. I can't think why, when there's a lot more going on in London.'

'Oh, well, he must have something in mind.'

'Who do you think he'll marry? There were dozens of girls bobbing around, and one or two girls at the banquet he might have fancied, but he didn't seem interested in anybody in particular.'

'No, I didn't think so. And your two friends, Cora and Miranda?'

'They've only ever been interested in Peter and Cedric. Dictated by their mothers, I think. Did you never dictate one for me, Mother?'

'Not that I can think of. You were always such an independent sort of child. We knew there'd be somebody one day.'

Andrew stood on the hillside looking down on the beautiful stone house where Imogen had told him she lived. He had journeyed up by train after purchasing a return ticket. After all, he didn't know if he'd be welcome, since their last meeeting had been inconclusive and suppose she'd met somebody else? After all, this was Imogen's world, the lonely hills and the deep ravines and tumbling rivers that epitomized the Peak District.

He walked down the narrow country road until he came to a stile with a narrow path leading down to the house, and then he saw the rider, a woman riding a large black horse and jumping the fences with consummate ease.

He knew it was Imogen, even though she was wearing a riding hat, and he smiled, lengthening his stride, and then he saw that she was not alone.

A man riding a chestnut horse followed her, and then they were riding side by side, laughing together, and he hesitated. Of course, he could be a man she'd known for years, a local man who lived the way she lived and liked the things she liked. After all, what did they really know about each other except that there had been some sort of spark between them? Just a man and a woman, momentarily attracted, followed by the tortuous silence of war.

He had to go on. He'd told her they would meet again, and even if she'd forgotten, a promise was a promise.

The two riders paused to see the stranger descending the hill, then Imogen recognized him and galloped towards him, followed by her companion.

Their eyes met, and her eyes were warm, her smile welcoming, and she jumped down from her horse and he went forward to meet her. For just a brief moment they smiled at each other, then he reached out and took her in his arms. They stood without words, but they were both aware of a moment so special there was no *need* for words. Then the other rider was getting down from his horse, and he was smiling, before he came forward with hand outstretched to greet him.

He was a handsome man, but quite a bit older than Imogen. That was Andrew's first reaction, before Imogen said, 'This is Louise Maxton's brother Andrew, Daddy. Andrew, this is my father.'

The relief was incredible, and then they were walking together towards the house and Andrew was saying, 'I should have let you know I was coming. I really shouldn't have descended on you like this.'

Her father smiled. 'We're farmers, Andrew. We're used to unexpected guests, even animals! I'll take these two horses down to the stables, dear. You introduce Andrew to your mother.'

'Does Louise know you've come?' she asked him.

'Actually no. She knows I'm seeing a little more of England, but not exactly where.'

She laughed. 'How long can you stay?'

'Well, I bought a return ticket on the railway. I wasn't at all sure you'd want me to stay.'

'But of course I do. My parents will make you very welcome.'

And in the days that followed they discovered themselves, and it was a week later that Andrew telephoned his mother to say he was staying in Derbyshire with Imogen Clarkson's family.

'But why didn't you tell us?' his mother exclaimed.

'Because I had to be sure, Mother, for me and for Imogen.'

'Sure, Andrew?'

'Yes, Mother. I want to marry her. I love her, and the feeling is mutual.'

'But are you sure, dear? This is all so sudden! You've known each other very briefly. What about other girls you've met! Andrew, it's not like you to be so confident so soon. Wasn't there some trouble in the Clarkson family? They are friends of ours, dear. We don't want any problems or you marrying a girl they won't recognize.'

'Mother, I'm telling you I'm going to marry Imogen. Outside that fact, nothing is important.'

'But it's so soon after your father's death. Shouldn't we discuss it, Andrew? I'll talk to Martin, see what he thinks.'

'Mother, it has nothing whatsoever to do with Martin. He isn't family. I'm old enough and intelligent enough to make my own decisions and choose the girl I want to marry.'

'When are you coming home?'

'Sometime next week. I'm due back at headquarters.'

'Yes, there's that too, Andrew. Does she know you're an army man?'

'She knows, Mother.'

'And it doesn't matter?'

'Mother, this conversation is too important to have on the telephone. We'll speak again when I arrive home. Is Louise there?'

'No, she's having lunch with Cora and Miranda. I rather think those two girls are feeling excited about their futures.'

'Are they? Oh, well, Louise will no doubt enlighten them soon enough about mine. Goodbye, Mother, see you soon.'

Imogen Clarkson was not the girl Isobel would have chosen to marry her beloved son. What was she going to say to the Clarksons? And Janice Clarkson was one of her closest friends!

When she informed Martin Broughton of Andrew's decision, all he had to say was that Andrew was old enough to make up his mind about something as important as a wife, and it was nobody else's business.

Louise thought the situation entirely delightful. She'd always liked Imogen, and for the first time in her life she agreed that Martin Broughton had spoken some sense by disagreeing with her mother.

Indeed, when Andrew did come home, everybody seemed amazed at the speed surrounding the forthcoming nuptials. He told his mother they would spend considerable time at the country house in Hartford so that Imogen could have her beloved horse there. His mother was welcome to make the London house her home for as long as she wished to be there.

Louise was quick to accept Helene's invitation to spend time with her in Switzerland after Andrew's wedding.

Standing behind the bride and groom as Imogen's chief bridesmaid, Louise could only reflect that it had all happened so quickly. Her father's death, her brother's marriage, and then what? Her mother and Martin Broughton's.

Her mother looked young and elegant, and if she was older than Martin it didn't show. Why was there suddenly so much for everybody and not enough for her? And yet wasn't this what she'd always said she wanted? To be different, to be grown-up and sophisticated. So why did she feel like a girl struggling on the edge?

Her gown was her favourite azure blue, while Miranda and Cora, who were also bridesmaids, looked pretty in very pale blue. Wasn't it all going well for them too? Their mothers were smiling, well pleased that the men they had wanted for their daughters were now in attendance, and in two days, time she'd be leaving with Helene for Geneva.

Helene had promised her that she would love Switzerland. There would be skiing and dancing, handsome young men to escort her, and the sort of life she'd envisaged but never experienced. How long would she be able to stay there, and what would she come back to?

Isobel Maxton was relieved. There had been no friction between her new daughter-in-law's relatives and her parents. Indeed, they were a different generation from the one that had made such stringent rules. Times were changing, however slowly, but perhaps in a few years it would no longer really matter who you married, and where you were born.

Sitting in the congregation were the two aunts Louise had lived with for a short while, and looking at them she remembered Jimmy Kent. She could remember him now without feeling guilty that she had used him and hurt him, stupidly and uncaring, and she was glad he was married and hoped that he was happy.

Martin Broughton mingled with his constituents, most of them old friends, and he reflected on the wedding, which hadn't been the one Isobel had envisaged. Happily, she had been mistaken. The Clarksons appeared to have buried old hatchets, and the bride was both beautiful and charming. Martin was certain that Andrew had chosen wisely and well.

Across the room Imogen was in happy conversation with the three girls she had been at school with, all of them laughing, evidently on this day very much in love with life, even Louise. Martin and Louise's eyes met across the room – hers unsure, his also – two people who would have been friends, if there hadn't been too many doubts.

Smiling, Louise asked Miranda, 'Everything going well for you two then?'

Blushing, Miranda replied, 'What do you mean?'

'You know what I mean. How goes it with you and Cedric?'

'We're friends. We meet, and he takes me out to dinner.'

'Is that all?'

'Well, he's only recently broken off his engagement.'

'Does he ever mention her?'

'Never.'

'Well, that's a good sign. And how about you, Cora?'

'I'm good friends with Peter. We're happy together.'

Imogen smiled. 'Really, Louise, shouldn't we let them get on with things and wait to hear their news at some very early time?'

'You're going to Geneva, Mother says,' Cora said to Louise.

'Yes, to stay with Helene. I really don't know her all that well, but she's very nice, and she's promised we're doing to have a very good time.'

'Is that her, talking to your mother?'

'Yes, she's quite fashionable isn't she?'

'You will write and tell us all about it, won't you, Louise? You might meet some handsome Swiss gentleman, or some Austrian Count or other!'

Louise smiled. Oh yes, a count would be acceptable, even to a mother who often despaired of her, to Martin, who thought it was time she grew up, and to the dear old aunts, who thought she had let them down.

Ah well, time would tell. But what if there was another Jimmy Kent?

Twenty

Louise sat on the terrace overlooking the beautiful lake and reflected that it had been a year, a whole year, when she had learned to ski, danced the night away with some handsome aristocrat or other, learned to speak better French, and had become something of a fashionable icon.

She talked of returning to England because she didn't wish to become a problem, but always Helene urged her to stay on.

'You make me feel young again,' Helene would say. 'I was getting dull and stupid, there were no new men around, and now here we are, you setting the ballrooms alight and me earning a reputation as your mentor.'

She heard often from Imogen and her brother, but her mother seldom wrote to her, preferring to write to Helene with whatever news she had, and Louise felt increasingly frustrated that she was learning nothing about Martin Broughton.

Her father had been dead over a year now, long enough surely for them to announce something more serious than friendship?

Helene and her mother had been school-friends, and once she had asked Helene how deep their friendship had been over the years. Helene had smiled, perhaps a little cynically, before saying, 'We all liked Isobel, but we were all very sure just how far we might be allowed to go at her coming-out ball. Your grandmother already had warned us not to encroach on what she considered to be Isobel's future.'

'You mean my father?'

'Yes.'

'But he was so much older than mother, and surely there were other men? Younger, more important, more aristocratic.'

'Perhaps, but he was very rich, unburdened by death duties, and of an age to father children and then think of other things.'

'It sounds particularly uncaring.'

'I suppose it was, but we accepted it. We all knew how it had to be.'

'But you came here, Helene, you got away from it.'

'I came here when the man I wanted in England married somebody else, somebody with more money, somebody his parents thought more right for him.'

'That is terrible, Helene!'

'Oh, I don't know. My father never had any money, he was a gambler, and so my grandparents paid for my education because my father owed money all over London. I wore hand-me-downs from cousins I seldom saw, and although I went to the deb balls, I sat on the side lines

265

because most of the men couldn't afford to get too friendly with me.'

'But you married well here. Were you happy with him?'

'With Ernst, yes, reasonably so. He was fifteen years older than me, Count Ernst Von Karlsburgh. Not to be compared with one of England's belted Earls, of course, but it sounded well, and we lived well.'

'You never had children, Helene?'

'No. That didn't worry either of us. Ernst's title went to his brother's son. You've met him.'

'Yes, I thought he was nice, and his wife too.'

'Your mother said in her last letter that she was spending a few weeks in Scotland. She didn't say whether she would be with somebody or alone.'

'I'm sure she'll be with somebody.'

'And it doesn't make you happy?'

'I don't really care one way or the other.'

'No news in the letter you received this morning then?'

'It was from Cora Hambleton, another schoolfriend. She's about to announce her engagement to Peter Reed-Blyton, something she's always wanted, but not always considered possible.'

'But you're pleased for her?'

'I suppose so. I'm expecting another friend to announce her engagement to Cora's brother any day now. Again, something dreamed of, but not anticipated.'

'So you're likely to be bridesmaid again in the near future.'

'Oh gracious, I hope not, I used to shock them at school by saying I wanted to marry an old man with all sorts of medical things wrong with him. Somebody who would make me very, very rich, and there would be younger men dancing attention all the time.'

'And did they believe you?'

'I don't know. I only know it's not what they wanted.'

'What did your mother want for you?'

'She never put it into words, but I should imagine it was an earl with a stately home and loads of money. I'm afraid I've disappointed her sadly.'

'Oh, I don't know, there's plenty of time. You're still in your early twenties.'

'My mother was married and a mother when she was my age.'

'Perhaps one day it's all going to change.'

'I can't see it happening. My friends will have children who they'll bring up just like their mothers did with them. They'll dictate who *they* should marry and it'll all start again, another cycle, another certainty.'

'Perhaps another generation might rebel, Louise, have you thought of that? Perhaps the people who are nobody now will be somebody one day, envy and jealousy will rear their hungry heads, and none of us will really know if times are better or worse because of it. But it's not going to happen today, so perhaps we should be talking about where you are spending your evening and who with, and what you

267

intend to wear.'

'At some villa near the lake, with Count Wolfang Brughes, and I intend to wear the white dress with the scarlet poppies at the waist.'

'Wolfgang is very nice.'

'Yes, Helene, they're all very nice. I rather think my old aunts would have approved of most of them.'

The next morning, the manservant brought the post to the breakfast table, laying the envelopes on the plates in front of them. Louise recognized her mother's handwriting on the envelope waiting for Helene, while the letter addressed to her was from Imogen, and contained the joyous news that she was expecting a baby in time for Christmas. Louise was delighted for them, but at the same time she felt strangely isolated.

Helene picked up the letter from Louise's mother's envelope with a brief smile before saying, 'Longer than usual, Louise. Why doesn't she write to you as well?'

'She does when she feels like it.'

'Oh, well, there should be plenty of news in this missive.'

There would be news of Andrew's baby, and possibly news of where her mother and Martin were spending their time, but looking at Helene she read a certain cynicism in her smile that tempted her to say, 'Is it about Andrew and Imogen, Helene?'

'Some of it. Not very much though. No, darling, it's about Isobel and a certain Scottish Laird who has asked her to marry him!'

'Marry! My mother?'

'Yes. It seems a little too soon after your father's death, but wedding bells and christening bells seem to be the going thing.'

'But who is this Scotish Laird? I've never heard of him! What about Martin Broughton?'

'Not even mentioned, darling. Either he didn't come up to scratch or *she* didn't.'

'Doesn't she mention me at all?'

Helene scanned the pages until she came to the end, saying, 'She hopes you're enjoying life in Geneva, that I'm happy to have you, and suggests you return to England if I can't cope.'

'Cope with what?'

'You, darling. Your high living, which I'm sure she thinks you're finding altogether exhilarating.'

'But who *is* this man she's marrying?'

'Apparently she's known him several years: he knew your father. He's about the same age as your father was, so he's hardly likely to be sweeping her off her feet. Wasn't Martin Broughton younger than your mother?'

'Yes, quite a lot younger, Andrew said.'

'He's probably found a younger woman, and you have to admit, darling, that she's better off with an older man.'

'But it's so soon! There was nobody but Martin when I was there.'

'And that's what we've got to think about, darling. Can you really visualize living in Scotland? And if not, where will you live? The old house belongs to Andrew, but you need to be launched into English society as soon as possible, and your mother's the one to do it.'

'I couldn't possibly live with my mother and a man I don't know.'

'Well, you can't live alone. It just isn't done, my dear.'

'I could live with the aunts. They've forgiven me for past demeanours!'

Helene laughed. 'Of course, I can see you growing old with those two old dears, acting the part of dear old aunt to Andrew's children, and spending occasional weeks in the wilds of Scotland.'

'I suppose I shall have to go home. After all, you've put up with me long enough.'

'Not so, darling. I've loved having you, and what's to go home to? Oh no, you'll stay on until you *have* to go home, and then we'll go together to attend your mother's wedding. We'll wear the most exciting gowns. We could even shop in Paris for them! And all your old friends will be pea green with envy at the show we're putting on.'

She could laugh at Helene's idiosyncrasies now, but when she was alone she couldn't see the bright side. Who was this man her mother was marrying? Had she always been so terribly wrong about Martin? Maybe they had never had an affair. Maybe he was even glad that her mother'd moved on, or perhaps he was miserable that she had found somebody else.

She had hated the thought of her mother

marrying and expecting her to live with them when she felt she never could, but the alternative was even more disastrous.

She had never even been to Scotland, let alone thought of living there with a mother she'd never been close to and a man she didn't know. Life with Helene was fun, but it couldn't go on indefinitely, there had to be some other life. But where would she find it, and with whom?

Similar thoughts were occupying Imogen's mind as she discussed the situation over breakfast with Andrew.

'How well do you know Lord McEmeray, Andrew. How long has your mother known him?'

'I have no idea, darling,' he replied, his face oddly grave and perplexed. 'I was never sure there was anything concrete with Martin, but she tells me her fiancé was a friend of Father's many years ago, that they lost touch, and that it was only recently at some political meeting they made contact again.'

'Is your mother really into politics? I only thought she was interested because of Martin.'

'My sister thought they were having an affair, but I wasn't sure I agreed with her. My mother and Louise have never really got along. I don't know why, unless it's because Louise was not the conventional sort of debutante, destined to dance to Mother's music.'

'I like Louise. She's my friend.'

'Of course, but I'm not sure what is going to happen now. Will there be room for her in mother's new life? There's certainly a home for her at the London house if she should wish to remain there, but who would she live there with?'

In Geneva the next morning Louise watched Helene eyeing her morning mail with something like dismay. Looking up, Helene said, 'How absolutely dreadful! My mother-in-law's decided to pay us a visit, and I shall hate every minute of it.'

'When is she coming?'

In four days' time, on Friday, and she's bringing with her a mountain of luggage and three or four servants, like she always does.'

'You don't like her, do you?'

'Darling, she's difficult. She's Austrian and comes here to see that the money my husband bequeathed me is being used sensibly and astutely instead of being squandered on fripperies, with which she disagrees.'

'Fripperies? Such as?'

'The wrong sort of clothes, the wrong sort of people, and ridiculous pastimes.'

'And people like me?'

'Perhaps, darling. She'll ask what you are doing with your life, and why are you spending it with me, who she's always considered a disaster in her son's life.

'If she thinks that, why does she bother to visit you?'

'To reassure herself that she's right about me. You won't like her, Louise. She'll do nothing to make your stay here a happy one.'

'Then perhaps it *is* time I went home. Helene, you've been marvellous, I've loved being here, and you've made me feel so much better about so many things I was uncertain about.'

'Not entirely, darling. You're still unsure about your mother, and about where you're going. Perhaps you *should* go home to sort your life out. Maybe you will love living in Scotland! Stalking deer with your stepfather, dancing Scottish reels with all those delectable young highlanders in tartan kilts, and learning to understand a dialect I never could.'

'I'll go to the London house. Mother will be there until she marries. I'll certainly never live with her in Scotland.'

'Then I suggest you look around, my dear. Go to the coming out balls, meet the sort of men your mother visualized for you, and be nice to their mothers, Louise. That's the advice *I* was always given. Now I have to practise being nice to Katrina.'

'Your mother-in law.'

'Yes. The name is far too pretty for her. I always thought so.'

Louise was not to know that her future was a favourite subject among her friends and associates in London. It was discussed at balls and race meetings, at social gatherings wherever they took place, and Martin Broughton was well aware that he, too, was the subject of much controversy.

Lady Maxton was now out of the picture, and he found himself surrounded by aspiring young debutantes and a great many other ambitious women. He was a man going places, a Minister, and one no doubt who would find himself in the House of Lords as a reward for his services to parliament. But, more than that, he was a handsome, mature man who had left the insecurities of youth long behind.

Isobel Maxton viewed the machinations of the women surrounding him with cynicism. He had been her friend, liked her, admired her, and in many ways had felt sorry for her, but she knew now that he had never loved her. She didn't want a friend. Given time she wanted a husband, and the right *sort* of husband. A Scottish peer with riches, a manse in the highlands and a home in London also, was a good proposition. She wasn't entirely sure that he was her sort, but then Henry never had been. Theirs had been an arranged marriage that had been, in all respects, similar to the marriage her parents had had. She had played her part to perfection and she had a wonderful son, even though her daughter seemed destined to give her problems.

Louise was a rebel. She'd constantly asked Martin to talk to Louise, to make her see that she was causing problems, but Martin had said, in the end, that it was none of his business. Andrew, too, had told her to leave matters alone, that when the time came Louise would find her own niche in life. But she despaired that Cora and Miranda had both found fiancés. She only had to listen to their mothers enthusing about the forthcoming nuptials to make her feel her own daughter would disappoint her sorely. Her Scottish husband would find a lot to dislike in his flighty English step-daughter, and with that in mind she seldom talked to him about Louise. Let him discover in time that she was a problem that would be reluctant to go away. Because of that, she had been happy for Louise to stay with Helene, and she viewed her return to London with a good many doubts.

Their first meal alone together was hardly a joyous reunion. They talked about Helene and her mother-in-law, about the young men who had taken her dancing and skiing, and in the end it was Louise who asked, 'Did I ever meet the man you're engaged to, Mother?'

'Perhaps, dear, I don't know. Both your father and I knew him well. He has the most beautiful castle in the Highlands. Did you never go to Scotland? I can't remember that you did.'

'No, Mother, I've never been there.'

'He's extremely nice. I shall like living up there.'

'You said you could never live anywhere but London, Mother.'

'Did I? Well, we're all entitled to change our minds, and that was probably when your father was well and I expected to be living here for ever. It's such good news about the baby, and Imogen looks so well.'

'I was never very sure that you liked her, Mother.'

'Well, neither was I. I never for a moment thought Andrew would marry a girl from Derbyshire, when there were so many girls around here on offer.'

'That's it, isn't it, Mother? On offer. That was not what Andrew wanted. *I* don't want it either.'

'What *do* you want, Louise?'

'Some man who wants me for me, not because I'm Lord Maxton's sister or because my stepfather's a Scottish peer.'

'And how will you know for certain?'

'Perhaps I never will. He could be a somebody, or a nobody. Maybe there won't be anybody at all, but it certainly won't be a man who's made a bid for me.'

In the days that followed she met her old schoolfriends quite often, either for lunch or shopping for their trousseaus, and her head spun with their certainty that the dreams they had cherished for so long had become reality.

'What about you?' Miranda asked. 'Surely you found somebody in Switzerland? After all, you were there over a year. Mother says she remembers Helene very well. She was always popular with the boys, and very flighty.'

'Men like Helene, but she's not anxious to remarry. She's popular, rich and beautiful, so why look for some man she doesn't need?'

'Surely she doesn't like going to functions on her own? She needs an escort,' Cora said adamantly.

'She isn't short of escorts. Neither of us were.'

'Well, tell us who you met! Were they handsome, rich? Did you fall in love?'

'They were handsome, rich and available, and

no I didn't fall in love. Isn't love often over-rated? Oh, not for you, perhaps, but you know me.'

Meeting her friends unsettled Louise, and Imogen was so ecstatic about the birth of her baby that she felt she had nothing useful to contribute to their conversation.

She was relieved that neither Miranda or Cora had invited her to be a bridesmaid, their excuses being that she'd been away for so long and they hadn't known when she was expected to return to London.

Her mother informed her that her fiancé intended to journey down to London for the weddings, and later in the year she would spend time with him in Scotland. In many ways she felt superfluous in their lives, and strangely she missed her father. He had never been the sort of father she could have taken her troubles to, he'd been sarcastic and distant, but there had been times when she'd appreciated his dry humour and cynical approach to life.

She felt that she was living in limbo, spending her time in exclusive shops looking at clothes she didn't need, and making conversation with women she didn't really know. There seemed to be so many mothers of charming sons who had already run the gauntlet of debutante balls where Louise had not been in attendance. Now they asked if she was in London to stay, and they hoped she would take tea with them one day, or attend some forthcoming function.

When she informed her mother of these encounters, all her mother said was, 'Really, Louise, you should take advantage of these invitations. After all, you do need to meet some decent young man who would escort you around London or elsewhere.'

Louise had the distinct feeling that her mother was glad that she would soon be leaving her difficult daughter behind for a life more in keeping with serenity and the aspirations of her youth.

Twenty-One

Imogen handed her baby back to his nanny, saying, 'He's so good, Rosie, he doesn't give any of us much trouble.'

'No, indeed not, ma'am. He's the best baby I've ever cared for.'

Standing looking through the window Louise turned to watch Rosie leaving the room before saying, 'Have you decided when the christening's going to be?'

'We've decided to get your mother's wedding over first.'

'What have you decided to call him?'

'Charles, after my father, and Henry, after yours. Charles Henry Andrew, we thought.'

'What shall we all call him though? Not Andrew, it would be too confusing.'

'Charles, I think.'

'Nice. We've never had a Charles in the family. I know very little about mother's wedding. I'm sure Andrew knows much more.'

'I know that she wants the wedding to be very low key. Scotland, I think, because she doesn't want it to be a social event.'

'But who will want to travel to Scotland, and where will we stay before the wedding? What about the baby?'

'Andrew and I have decided we'll drive up. We'll spend the first few days in Derbyshire so that we can leave Charles with my parents and pick him up on the way back. You can travel with us if you like, Louise, though I'm not sure what your mother has decided to do about the journey.'

'So there'll just be the family, no guests?'

'Martin Broughton has been invited, and I believe he intends to be there. Andrew is to give her away. You'll be her only attendant, and honestly, Louise, I don't really know very much else at the moment.'

'We do seem to have had a surfeit of weddings after Miranda and Cora's. Gracious, but they didn't exactly have low-key affairs. All of London turned out for them!'

'And you were very glad that neither asked you to be a bridesmaid.'

'I know. They thought I'd still be in Geneva with Helene. Do you think they're happy?'

'Satisfied, perhaps.'

'That's a funny thing to say.'

'I know. They got what they wanted, and we both know how long they wanted it.'

'I never expected you to capture my brother, Imogen, but I'm glad that you did.'

'Capture?'

'Not the best word, perhaps. I was never very good with words. But you know what I mean.'

'Louise, it worries Andrew that you're not better friends with your mother. Why is that?'

'I don't really know. I resented her taking me to live with the aunts; I thought it was because I'd interfere too much with her friendship with Martin Broughton. It seemed to me I was never the daughter she wanted, and I know that Martin didn't like me. I thought that was because she often discussed my shortcomings with him.'

'Did you think they'd marry?'

'Yes I did. They spent time together, he was always the man she consulted about everything. I thought she was in love with him. I'm sure Andrew thought so too.'

'Yes, perhaps he did.'

'Then why is she marrying this man in Scotland who none of us know? I couldn't have lived with her if she'd married Martin Broughton, but I can't visualize living in Scotland with this new man either.'

'You know you can live in London. After all, it's where you grew up. It's been your home for a long time.'

'But it isn't my home now, Imogen. It's your home. And how can I live there on my own, surrounded by familiar things and old servants like the proverbial old maid aunt?'

Imogen laughed. 'You'll never be that, Louise.'

'No, I'll probably end up by scandalizing all of London by entertaining dubious men in your house, and my nephew Charlie will be advised to have nothing to do with me.'

'And that will be the Louise I remember. I wonder who Martin will take to your mother's wedding?'

'You mean there *is* somebody?'

'He was with a woman at a dinner party we went to recently in London, I believe she was one of his constituents.'

'Who was she?'

'I don't know. She was young, pretty, fashionable, and she appeared to be enjoying his company.'

'Then he's probably taking her to Scotland.'

'Like with your mother. I think Martin Broughton keeps his personal feelings very personal indeed.'

'Oh, well, I don't really care who he goes around with. He's out of my life now that mother's found herself another suitor.'

Imogen looked at her thoughtfully. There was a strange restlessness about Louise these days that was far removed from the happy-go-lucky girl she remembered from their schooldays. Louise had always been the girl to laugh at life, expecting it to be fun, but not this new Louise, who was often cynical and confused. She evidently found herself at some sort of crossroads in her life, and the roads ahead were burdened with insecurities.

As if she was aware of what she was thinking, Louise said, 'Why don't we take the horses out, Imogen? I don't really enjoy riding in the London Park, but I love it here and I know you do too.'

'Does that mean that you'd like to stay over this evening instead of going back to London?'

'Oh Imogen, I don't really know *what* I want, I'm all at sixes and sevens. Perhaps I should get back to London, but I never know where Mother is these days. One time she'd have been with Martin, but now surely not.'

'It bothered you that she was with Martin, didn't it?'

'Yes. Now I don't really know why, because he's not the man she's marrying.'

Once she was back in London, there was a servant to open the door for her, a servant to serve her tea, and yet the house felt empty. Her mother was out, but a small fire burned in the grate of her favourite sitting room, so Louise went to sit there, leafing through a magazine, wondering how long it would be before her mother returned to the house.

She heard voices, her mother's laughter and then Martin's voice, and in the next moment her mother was tripping lightly into the room, followed by Martin who acknowledged her presence with a brief smile.

'You're back, Louise. You decided not to stay with Imogen,' her mother said lightly.

'Yes, there's so much I need to know about the wedding.'

'What is there to know, dear? It's in Scotland. We're to stay for a couple of days with the Mc-Emeray family at their house not too far away from where Fergus and I will be living. It really is the most beautiful castle, Louise, you'll love it.'

Louise looked at Martin, sitting composed and silent. How much was he hating this chatter about the castle in Scotland and her mother's new life? Her mother was being insensitive, but then perhaps he didn't really care.

'You and I will travel up by train, Louise. Will you be joining us, Martin?'

'No, I shall be travelling up later. Possibly the day before your wedding.'

'And will Angela be accompanying you, Martin?'

'Angela?'

'Well yes, she was with you at that dinner party a while ago. I'm sure I invited her.'

'Hardly necessary, Isobel. Angela and I are not an item, in any case, she is in Australia with her mother.'

'Really? I didn't know they had people there.'

'They don't. Will you and Fergus be staying on in your fairytale castle, returning to London or travelling elsewhere?'

'We do intend to go abroad sometime later, but we shall remain in Scotland for the present.'

'And Louise?'

'There's plenty for her to do in Scotland if she

decides to stay on. I'm sure she's something more adventurous in mind though. I wouldn't have thought that roaming the glens was my daughter's idea of high living.'

'You must have thought so at one time mother,' Louise said coldly. 'You were perfectly happy to leave me in the countryside with the aunts.'

'I wouldn't want a repetition of that adventure in Scotland, dear. I'm hoping you've put all that behind you.'

'So you'll be travelling back to London with me, Louise,' Martin said.

'Really, Martin, that is very sweet of you, but I'm sure Louise isn't expecting you to look after her.'

'I'm not, Mother. I'm perfectly capable of looking after myself,' Louise said, jumping to her feet.

At the door she turned to ask, 'What clothes do I need to take for two days in Scotland, Mother? Perhaps I should take a look at what I've got.'

'Yes, that's a good idea, dear. We'll have tea, Martin. It's so long since we chatted together.'

Across the room, Louise looked into Martin's eyes, and she was unsure what to make of the gravity she saw in his expression. She wasn't going to stay on in Scotland, and Martin would not want to travel back with her. She'd travel back with Imogen and Andrew. But then why should she? She was a grown woman! She was capable of travelling back on her own. Why should Martin Broughton feel responsible for her?

The day that they were to travel to Scotland finally arrived, and they ate dinner on the train before retiring to their first class sleeping apartments.

Louise reflected that conversation over their meal had not been easy. Her mother's thoughts had been miles away, and Louise could only fixate on how little she knew of the man her mother was journeying to Scotland to marry. She had longed to ask questions, but she had had the feeling that her mother would not appreciate them.

She had asked one question, and that was to inquire when Martin was expected to arrive in Scotland. She was told that he would be there the next day, and that the McEmerays intended to hold a large dinner party for all their guests. 'I hope you've brought an appropriate gown, Louise', her mother had said. 'Nothing too frivolous. Not for a *Scottish* party.'

The McEmerays received them most charmingly on their arrival, and on that first evening Louise met her mother's intended for the first time, and he reminded her forcefully of her father.

His conversation seemed to be mainly on work that needed to be done at the castle, and Louise wondered how her mother could compare him with Martin – Martin, who was handsome and knowledgeable about so many things, while Fergus seemed totally absorbed with ordinary things.

Conversation eventually got around to the dinner party on the following evening and who had been invited. Louise was left to wonder how Andrew and Imogen, as well as Martin Broughton, would view her mother's changing lifestyle.

She should have known that both Andrew and Martin would be both gracious and charming with their hosts, and indeed the next evening was a success, and after the last guest had left, Imogen said softly to Louise, 'I enjoyed it, didn't you? It was different, but everybody seemed very nice and welcoming.'

Louise agreed, and Imogen said, 'Ready for tomorrow, dear?'

'I think so.'

The wedding day dawned. It was to be held in a tiny church near the castle, but it seemed the villagers had come from far and wide to see the Laird marry his English bride.

Louise had had little choice in the choosing of her own gown, since her mother had decided she should wear magenta, hardly a colour she was fond of, but her mother thought it would look well against the pale blue one she had chosen for herself. She knew her mother would look beautiful, as always, and as she followed her down the short aisle she was aware of the looks of admiration they were subjected to.

Later, as they were surrounded by well-wishers, she asked herself if Martin minded, when only such a short time ago he and her mother had seemed inseparable.

Beside the array of kilts and lace ruffles, he and Andrew seemed strangely dignified and austere, but she was only aware of Martin's smiling face as he bent down to congratulate the bridal pair.

How much did her mother mind? Why was she marrying this man Louise hadn't known existed until that letter had arrived in Switzerland? It wasn't for the money, surely. Martin was a rich man, and her mother hadn't needed to marry for money, anyway, but then Andrew was beside her, saying, 'Well, it all seems to have gone rather well, Louise.'

'Do you think she's happy?'

'Why shouldn't she be? Isn't it what she wanted?'

'I don't know. Once there was Martin, and now he's watching her marry somebody else. How much does he mind?'

'He seems to be complacent enough to me. You know, I never really thought they were a pair. Maybe Mother would have liked them to be, but I'm not so sure about Martin.'

'Maybe he's cold and cynical, not the marrying kind.'

'And you've dreamed up a picture of him that could have been entirely distorted.'

'And *you're* too clever by half.'

He laughed. 'Well, perhaps one of these days we'll find out we've both been wrong. Perhaps when Martin decides to tie the knot.'

After the feasting, Andrew decided he and Imogen should depart. It was some way to drive into Derbyshire, and Isobel seemed most anxious that Louise should go with them.

'I really don't see why, Mother,' Louise argued. 'I do have my return ticket for the sleeper, and I was quite happy in it on the way up here.'

'But you could see Imogen's parents, and Charles. Besides, taking the sleeper would mean Martin having to look after you, and I don't really know what he has in mind.'

Martin smiled. 'I'll tell you what I have in mind, Isobel,' he said. 'To catch the same sleeper and arrive early in London. I shall be quite happy to escort Louise, if she's agreeable.'

Isobel had always known when her mother was unhappy with things. The slight shrug of indifference to say she didn't really mind, but that she'd been unprepared for Martin's firmness. And later, as she stood in the courtyard to say her farewell, she sensed her mother's displeasure again. She kissed her mother on both cheeks saying softly, 'I do hope you and Fergus will be very happy, Mother. I'm not sure when I shall see you again. Perhaps you'll be coming to London?'

'Oh, I've had a surfeit of London for the time being, dear. You really should think of looking round for an apartment, Louise. That house is far too large, and in any case it's *Andrew's* house now.'

She was saved from answering by Martin's voice saying, 'Ready, Louise?' and after shaking Fergus's hand they hurried towards the waiting car, and she turned to see her mother staring after them, her expression wistfully yearning.

Louise waved to her, but she didn't respond. Her expression was not for her daughter, it was for the man walking beside her.

Louise had never thought she would ever be dining with Martin Broughton in the restaurant car of an express train, taking her home from Scotland after her mother's wedding to a man she barely knew.

He was being gallant. Treating her to polite conversation, and then, as she responded nervously to his wider knowledge and his discussions of his work and his travels, she found herself comparing his conversation to that she had often listened to from men who were obsessed with themselves and with a world she had little knowledge of.

'I hope I'm not boring you, Louise,' he said gently. 'We don't seem to have talked very much, and I wasn't very sure what would interest you. Have you come to terms with your mother's marriage?'

She looked at him doubtfully before saying, 'I really don't know, Martin. I don't really know my mother very well.'

He smiled. 'No, I never felt that you did.'

'I always thought she would marry you.'

'I know you did, and you were not very happy about that either.'

'I want my mother to be happy, but I've resented that she's always seemed so close to Andrew but not me. My friends were close to

289

their mothers, so why wasn't I?'

'Perhaps, in time, you will be.'

'I don't think so. Do you mind that she's married Fergus?'

'No, of course not. I wish them all the happiness in the world.'

'But you spent so much time together!'

'Time wasn't enough, Louise.'

'For you or for her?'

'For both of us, perhaps.'

'But it's all been so fast. I didn't know he existed, did you?'

'I'd met him several times. He was a friend of your father's, you know, and I'm sure it will work out for both of them.'

The time went quickly, and it was Martin glancing quickly at his watch which made her suddenly realize that most of the other diners had already left their tables, and she said quickly, 'I hadn't realized it was so late. I hope you haven't been too bored.'

He laughed. 'I never expected you to bore me, Louise. Maybe I was the one boring you.'

'Oh no, not at all.'

'Then perhaps we should think of retiring. I had a very early start this morning, and I have a meeting tomorrow that promises to be rather exacting.'

'Yes, of course. You should have said, Martin.'

'Perhaps we'll talk again one day when life is more normal.'

'Normal?'

'Why yes. When you've stopped asking ques-

290

tions about things that once troubled you, when we can meet and greet each other like old friends, something we haven't been able to do very often.'

She looked into his eyes and they were kind, his smile singularly sweet, and as they left the table and walked towards the door she felt like asking *when* would they meet, when would they talk, how many other girls would he talk to and how much did any of them matter?

At the door to her compartment she looked up at him and smiled. He took her hand and said gently, 'I'll meet you for breakfast, Louise, and see that you arrive home safely to a whole new world.'

Now she was alone, conscious of the train speeding through the night, for the first time afraid of the new world he visualized. Hadn't she always been the confident one, laughing at other people's insecurities, pretending that for her they didn't exist? She should be missing her mother, asking for the love she thought she had had as a child, but that love had never followed her into girlhood and she had never missed her father.

Sitting on the edge of her narrow bed with her hands clenched in her lap, all she was aware of was that she wanted Martin in her life.

She knew now that she had never hated Martin Broughton. She'd resented him, been jealous of her mother, had wished he was old and ugly instead of charming and handsome, and now he was free to be there for some woman he could fall in love with.

She thought about all those nights when she'd hated the fact that her mother and Martin had visited the theatre, danced together, or just talked together. She'd pretended to her friends that she was a happy carefree girl with no problems, sophisticated beyond her years, and her mother had been unable to understand her.

That was why her mother had complained so bitterly to Martin about her, why she'd made him dislike her, why everything could have been so different.

Sleep didn't come easily that strange turbulent night, and it was Martin knocking on her train compartment door which suddenly roused her the following morning.

She opened the door a fraction to find him smiling at her and saying, 'Gracious, are you only just awake?'

'I'm sorry, Martin, I slept very badly, so I must have overslept.'

'It doesn't matter. I'll meet you for breakfast. There's no need to hurry.'

But there was need to hurry. After today he'd be out of her life, and every second, every minute counted, so she hurried with her toilet, and as he rose to greet her he said, 'You *have* hurried, Louise! Now what are you going to have for breakfast? The house will seem very large and empty when you arrive home.'

Of course it would be empty. Too many servants dancing attention, too many empty rooms speaking of the people who had left them, too many memories. She couldn't go on living there, on borrowed time in a borrowed house, and she was suddenly aware of Martin's eyes looking at her with a strange sympathy.

'Don't worry,' he said gently. 'It's early days yet. You'll come to terms with it all in time. You're young and pretty, you'll have so many suitors falling over themselves to get your attention, you know you will.'

While he complacently went on with his breakfast she longed to scream at him that she didn't want any suitors, that she wanted something she'd lost and and there was no going back.

The morning was hectic, and when they arrived in London the platform was crowded. Indeed, the entire station was hardly a venue for conversation, but Martin found a porter and succeeded in shepherding them to a waiting taxi rank. Soon they were driving through the busy city streets towards her home and every second was taking them nearer to the end.

She found the words to thank him for his kindness in looking after her, to which he favoured her with his brief smile and an assurance that he had enjoyed her company, and then they were outside her house and he was getting out of the taxi to escort her to the door.

He smiled down at her, taking her hand and saying, 'I'm not very sure if and when we shall meet again, Louise, but we didn't start off very well. Perhaps the next time we can be friends.'

He was aware of her tear-filled eyes and

trembling lips, then without a word she knocked sharply on the door, which was opened almost immediately by a man servant. Without a backward glance she ran into the house and Martin, meeting the servant's surprised eyes, turned away – uncertain and bemused – to where the taxi waited for him.

Twenty-Two

This had been her home, this mansion where her father had talked politics and her mother had enchanted numerous guests with her beauty and graciousness. Now her brother and his wife would rarely be in residence, because they both preferred the country, and so she was here alone, thanks to her brother's largesse and her own dependency.

She'd known long before she left school that all was not well in her life. She'd blamed it on her mother's friendship with Martin, telling herself that it was wrong, that they were being unfair to her father, but it hadn't really been so. She'd resented the fact that her mother was beautiful, loved by a younger handsome man, and she'd been jealous. But why had her mother been so anxious to bore Martin with her daughter's every childish misdemeanour, and why had she insisted she stay with the aunts instead of bringing her home?

Surely her mother hadn't been jealous of *her*? Not when her mother had so much, and Louise herself was only just finding her way into a new adult world, a world that was insecure and dangerous.

Hadn't she always been the sophisticated one, amused by Cora and Miranda and their obsession with men they wanted to marry, and feeling vaguely sorry for Imogen, returning to obscure country life? And now they were all convinced that what they had aspired to had materialized, and here *she* was alone and lonely and totally obsessed with a man she had thought she disliked and who obviously didn't think much of her.

She was in love with Martin Broughton: with his maturity, his looks, everything about him. Was he still in love with her mother? Did he still think she was a wild, stupid child who was capable of experiencing love with the first boy she'd met?

Of course, they'd meet again some day. He with some older, more sensible, woman he could respect, and she, flitting from one man to another in an attempt to appear popular.

Why should she worry? She was rich. She could fill her days with fashion shows and extravagant shopping, and her nights with balls and dining out, and she needn't worry about men. There were many men who would be only too anxious to find a baronet's daughter with money and the right background. The thing was, she was too sophisticated for her own good. She would be aware of their intentions from the start, and there would be no love, no romance, only hypocrisy.

Disconsolately she wandered downstairs, and a servant asked if she would like tea served in the drawing room.

Her mother had made quite a thing about tea in the drawing room. She had dispensed China tea and hot buttered scones with charm and elegance, and her guests had always left with the feeling that they had spent a truly worthwhile afternoon. Many were the times they had welcomed Martin with his charming smile and humour, while she had looked on, entirely cynical and, now she could admit it, jealous.

What would Martin be doing tonight when his meetings were over? Dining out with some woman who had taken her mother's place? Perhaps telling her about the wedding he'd attended, the journey home with a girl he hadn't really liked and his relief that it was all over?

The telephone was ringing shrilly, and she picked it up to hear Cora's voice saying, 'You're back, Louise! I wasn't sure if you'd be staying in Scotland. How did the wedding go?'

'Very well. We got back this morning.'

'We! Are Andrew and Imogen there with you?'

'No. They drove to Derbyshire to see Imogen's parents and collect Charles.'

'So how did you get back? By train?'

'Yes, of course.'

'All by yourself?'

'Actually, no. Martin travelled with me.'

For a brief moment there was silence before Cora said, 'You always called him Mr Broughton. He is very attractive, isn't he? Did you suddenly find him so?'

'It's not something I thought about, Cora. I have to leave you now, Cora, I have visitors. I'll be in touch later.'

There were no visitors, but the conversation had exasperated her. Of course Martin Broughton had always seemed attractive, painfully so when her mother had been involved, but now she wanted no questions about him, no sly innuendos that she might be finding him *too* attractive.

That silly schoolgirl Louise had been the one who had boasted about older men with their experience, their money and even their shorter lifespans. Now Louise resented those brittle words that had amused and shocked her friends, but had never really been meant.

She didn't have very long to wait before Miranda telephoned, and she guessed immediately that the two women had already spoken to each other.

'I was so hoping you'd be home,' Miranda said. 'I'm anxious to hear all about the wedding. Was it very nice? I'm sure it was.'

'Yes, everything went very well.'

'When did you get back?'

'This morning.'

'Did Andrew and Imogen travel with you?'

'No, I came back with Martin Broughton.'

'Really? Wasn't he there with the woman he's been seen about with?'

'He wasn't with anybody.'

'Well, Mother said she didn't think there was anything in it. After all, there must be dozens of women attracted to him.'

'Miranda, I'm so sorry, but I really do have to go, I have visitors. I'll be in touch when we've more time to chat.'

'Oh, of course, dear. We must meet up soon. Cedric's so involved with the army right now, and I don't see him nearly as often as I should, but that's the army for you, isn't it? No young man in the offing for you then?'

'Nobody remotely interesting. Goodbye, Miranda.'

Of course she'd meet her friends. They'd be enthusiastic about married life and its satisfactions, while she'd be predictably scathing about normality and the littleness of love.

It was later in the afternoon that Imogen telephoned. 'The house must seem awfully big and empty, Louise,' she said. 'Perhaps you should think of staying with us for a while. I'm sure it seems difficult without your mother.'

'Actually, it doesn't, Imogen. Mother and I never saw much of each other socially.'

'Andrew wasn't very happy about that.'

'I know, but it does mean she won't be missing me.'

'You got along with Martin?'

'Yes, he was very charming and chivalrous

and we arrived home without hating each other, something I would at one time have betted against!'

Imogen laughed. 'Well, don't be too lonely, Louise. Remember you can always come here. How is your day going?'

'You mean my day or my life?'

'Your day, dear. I'm not asking any questions about your life.'

'My day's been boring. I've unpacked my suitcase and put away my clothes. I've had two telephone calls, one from Cora the other from Miranda, and I told them both a lie.'

'A lie?'

'Yes, I said I had visitors when I hadn't.

'Why didn't you want to speak with them?'

'Oh, you know what they're like. The wedding, Martin...'

'Martin?'

'Yes, the woman he's been seen with lately, the women who are falling over themselves to take Mother's place, and his attractions, of which I'm well aware.'

'I've never heard you speak of his attractions before.'

'I've said too much, Imogen. I'm going. See you very soon. Give my love to Charlie.'

What to do with the rest of her day? Martin would already have forgotten their time on the train together. he would be involved with his meetings, with politics in general, with the women only too anxious to ingratiate themselves with him in the hope of better things, and they, too, would be interested in her mother's wedding, and no doubt relieved that she was no longer a threat to their hoped-for prospects.

The servants served her with a late lunch and over it she debated whether she should walk in the park with the dog, visit the shops or answer the letter that was waiting for her from Helene.

In the end she decided to exercise the dog, but the walk was uneventful. She met nobody of note, and even the dog seemed faintly uninterested. It was hardly surprising, since Buster had been her father's black Labrador, and could boast eleven years. On arrival home he went straight to his basket and eyed her, she felt, with some resentment.

Now she read Helene's letter, only to discover that she was visiting friends in Rome with the express purpose of avoiding her mother-in-law for the foreseeable future. She smiled, picturing Helene's face, but her letter ended with her thoughts on Louise's mother's wedding, and ended with the words, 'It's your turn next, darling. Some divine man, who is all you want him to be.'

Martin's afternoon meeting with his constituents was over. It had been the usual sort of meeting, laced with promises and complaints, and now they were standing around in groups, chatting, drinking tea, and it seemed every woman was interested in the wedding he had attended the day before. After all, most of the women had thought he would be the one capturing the heart of Isobel Maxton.

Without exception, they had believed Martin and Isobel had been destined to be together, but most of them had resented the fact that she was a beautiful woman married to an older man and too involved with their MP. Then suddenly she was a widow, and if they had had expectations they were forlorn ones. The fact that Isobel had decided to marry a Scottish Peer and move out of their lives had revived those expectations and a handful of them were making it clear that they welcomed the situation.

The meeting had gone on too long. He would like to make his excuses and leave, but to what? The usual conversation with like-minded men at his club or the solitude of his house?

Once there had been Isobel, with her humour, her charm and her problems – too many problems, largely of her own interpretation.

He thought about Louise. All day, in spite of the questions and answers he'd been subjected to, he'd thought about her, about her tears, the anxieties of a woman too young and beautiful to have any.

At last he made his excuses, and one woman asked plaintively, 'Aren't you feeling rather lonely at the moment, Martin? Perhaps you'd care to join Brian and myself for dinner.'

He smiled. 'Actually, Margaret, I have an engagement this evening. Perhaps some other time.'

Another Isobel, he thought. Bored, with a husband she had little in common with now, and for both of them he would have been a distraction.

He was relieved to reach his car without further delays, and as he drove away he inadvertently headed in the direction of the Maxtons' house. Why had he done that? For years he'd been Isobel's friend, had listened to her problems, her husband's problems, and had sat down to meals with them. Now there was Louise. He was remembering her tear-stained face, a girl troubled by circumstances she'd been oblivious to, and yet he was also remembering their journey from Scotland the day before.

She had been incredibly normal, humorous and intelligent, and there had been the potential for real friendship and sympathy between them. Why had he never seen it before, and why had her mother been so anxious to keep it from him?

He arrived at the house and parked the car, unsure whether to go in. He should drive away, forget his involvement with the Maxton family, which had gone on too long. He and Louise had resolved their differences. Now, whenever they met, they could greet each other without rancour, as old friends.

Convinced he was doing the right thing, he restarted the engine but made the mistake of looking up at the house, only to see Louise standing staring down at him.

He had to go in there now. She had seen him, and there was no excuse to drive away. Resignedly he got out of the car and, acknowledging her presence with a brief smile, walked towards the house.

It was Louise herself who opened the door to him, staring at him with an expression he didn't understand, and he said hurriedly, 'My meeting finished early, So I thought I should call to see if everything is alright. You seemed rather dejected when I left you this morning.'

'Yes, I'm sorry. Please come in, Martin. Can I offer you a drink or would you prefer to stay for a meal?'

'Force of habit, Louise?'

'Something you did for so long. Only, things are different now, aren't they?'

'Different?'

'Of course. You don't need me to tell you how different, I'm sure. You must see how big and empty the house is. I'm very conscious of it.'

'I'm sure you are, but isn't it the start of a whole new life for you, Louise? At your age all of life is before you – friends, some man, hopefully the right one – and if you need any advice from me you know where to find me.'

'Do I?'

'Well, I'm not moving house, and you are one of my constituents.'

'Is that how you regarded my mother? I don't think so.'

'Then how should I regard you?'

'Martin, I don't know. I know you didn't like me, so has that changed?'

'Why did you ever think I disliked you? I never gave you that impression, surely. You were simply Isobel's daughter, you were a schoolgirl seldom seen. All I knew about you was that you gave your mother problems which she discussed with me.'

'The problems I gave her were largely imaginary. We didn't actually meet very often. When I was home she was out doing all sorts of things, and if I'm lonely now, I was even more so then because I used to expect more.'

'Louise, if you want a friend, I will try to be that friend. I'm not even sure if you'll take advice from me, but it will be there if you want it.'

'And to some woman who fancies you, and who you care about, I could be that pesky kid who never leaves you alone and doesn't know how to take advice.'

'If I can start from today, can't you?'

'We can start by dining together. Or do you have another meeting to go to? Mother accompanied you to so many of them.'

'I wouldn't expect you to do that.'

'I know, I'm too frivolous. I don't live in the real world.'

'Then perhaps that's the first step, to make sure that you do.'

'The new Louise, the proper conventional Louise! Will anybody recognize me?'

Twenty-Three

July 1939 – End of Term

To the two women strolling across the lawns towards the river it might have been a similar morning twenty-five years ago. That morning there had been four of them celebrating their last day at school, yet wary and disappointed about the uncertainties of the life they were returning to.

They walked largely in silence, their thoughts adult, very afraid of a world filled with dangers that were new and potent, but yet echoed those they had been faced with on that July day years before.

There were village children playing on the river bank, just as there had been then, but they walked on towards the bridge, coming at last to the grassy crag they had known then.

They stared across the river, and it was Miranda who said quietly, 'It's exactly the same, isn't it? It could have been yesterday.'

'Except that there's only you and me,' Cora said plaintively. 'It's only the place that's stayed the same, Miranda. Our lives are very different.'

'Has any of it worked out like we thought it would?'

'For us, yes, we got what we wanted. The other two didn't know *what* they wanted.'

'Oh, I don't know. Imogen didn't have plans but she did get a man she fell in love with, and Louise didn't really surprise, us, did she?'

'Surprise us?'

'Well, yes! Didn't she always try to shock us?'

'Oh, yes. We all thought it was her mother who Martin Broughton was in love with, and now he's married to Louise. That surprised everybody!'

'And he's been knighted for services rendered, they're living in Singapore, and they have two sons. No daughters to send here. What about our girls? We knew what we wanted. Do you think that they do?'

They stayed silent, staring into space yet seeing nothing, until Cora said, 'Were we really wise to ask for so much so soon? Have you regretted any of it?'

'Have *you*?'

'Oh no, of course not.'

'Be honest, Cora. I know it hasn't always been sweetness and light for you. Peter can be distant. He likes his own way, and you let him have it.'

'It's easier that way. I've got the girls, and I've had what we promised ourselves: security, money, a lovely home. Men don't think like us, anyway.'

'It wouldn't have been enough for Louise.'

'Well, Martin's at least fifteen years older than she is. Would we have wanted that?'

'Would it have mattered if you'd been in love

with him?'

'Perhaps not.'

'Imogen's boy has gone into his father's regiment, so when the war comes he'll be in it immediately. I thought Stephanie liked him. I was hoping so.'

'There you go again, Miranda, just like mother did with me. Some boy, set your sights on him, hope for the best. Are you telling me it's always been the perfect solution for you and Cedric?'

'You know it hasn't. You know there've been other women.'

'And one in particular.'

'Sophie Beaumont. All London knows about her.'

'But you've simply carried on as though she doesn't exist. Did he never ask for a divorce? Has he never said he would like to marry her?'

'No, and I never mention her. We don't talk about it, Cora. I've got all the material things in life, and up to a point we get along. He loves the girls, and he wouldn't do anything to bring change into their lives. Why muddy waters that are calm?'

'Surely it must trouble you, Miranda. Particularly as everybody knows about it.'

'It did at one time. Now it doesn't. Cedric and I are seen together, we attend functions amicably, and strangely enough I don't even think about it very much.'

'Well, your girl and mine will be saying goodbye to the school tomorrow. Stephanie doesn't say much about the future. Does Rachel?'

'Not in her letters. It was different for us. Our mothers interfered too much, perhaps, and I don't want to be seen as a domineering mother, planning my daughters' futures for them. Alison will be here for another four years, and so will your youngest daughter.'

'I know. It's Stephanie I worry about, mostly. I do want her to find the right sort of man, and you know what it will be like when the war comes. All sorts of different men coming into their lives, even foreigners.'

Cora laughed. 'We should't worry, Miranda. They'll sort themselves out I'm sure. Perhaps we should think of wending our way back to the school. We've got afternoon tea and the concert this evening, then tomorrow we'll be taking all our girls home for the summer holidays, and two of them won't be coming back here. What sort of future will our older girls have?'

Neither of them really knew. They wanted the same sort of things for their daughters that *they'd* aspired to, but would the girls want it? Cora wished her husband would concern himself more, but he was cynically amused by her anxieties and constantly told her their daughters would find their own niches in life. What about Miranda's daughter? How much or how little did she know about her father's involvement with another woman?

As they strolled back towards the school, the problems in both their lives seemed as close as the problems that had existed in the summer years before. They would have been more troubled if they had heard the conversation taking place in the school hall while their daughters waited for afternoon tea to be served.

Rachel Reed-Blyton said feelingly, 'I suppose they've walked across to the river. Mother always said it was a favourite place of theirs. You know what they'll be doing, don't you?'

'No, what?'

'Making plans for us. No coming-out balls because of the war, no finishing school, no unsuitable boys, just like it was for them. So, what are we going to do?'

'I know what I'm going to do,' Stephanie said adamantly. 'I'm joining the services. Probably the ATS so that I can get a good commission. After all, my father's an army man.'

'Your mother'll never permit it!'

'I'll talk to Dad. He'll be all for it I'm sure.'

'And you think you might meet up with Charlie Maxton? You fancy him, don't you?'

'Right now I do, but who knows who else I'll meet? What do you want to do?'

'I could take to nursing wounded heroes. Wasn't that how Lady Maxton met her husband?'

Rachel giggled. 'I'd hate to be a nurse. No the ATS is for me, but for God's sake don't say anything to Mother. She'll do everything she can to stop it.'

'You need to talk to your father first then.'

'I know. He's terribly entangled with that Sophie woman right now though. Even when he's on leave we don't see much of him.'

'Don't you mind?'

'I should, shouldn't I? But it's gone on so long, and Mother doesn't seem overly concerned. After all, even after all this time Dad seems quite happy to carry on the way they are.'

'I don't want a marriage like that.'

'Nor I, but life alters many things.'

'That's a strange, philosophical thing to say.'

'I know. I do feel that our mothers were not nearly as sophisicated at this age as we are, and I don't know why. Do you think it's because our grandmothers interfered too much? It's not going to happen to *me*.'

'We *are* only seventeeen.'

Similar conversations were going on all around them. When their mothers eventually joined them such conversations were forgotten, but only for the time being. They could rekindle them when the time was right.

Imogen rode her horse back to the stables on what she considered a perfect summer's day, but in her heart she felt only anxiety and sorrow that war was once more looming, with all its misery and stupidity.

Tomorrow she would bring Steven home for his summer holiday, and she already knew the eager questions he would be asking. 'Was there really going to be a war, would it last long enough for him to be in it, would his older brother have to go soon?' She would try telling him that any war was an abomination, but Steven was a boy and boys saw the adventure, never the catastrophes.

She left her horse in the hands of the groom and walked towards the house, savouring the green lawns and avenue of beech trees, the sunlight shining on the beautiful old stone house, and she paused to look at the unfamiliar car driving through the gates.

She was not expecting visitors, since she saw most of her friends when in London. All the same, she hurried down the hill towards the house, and by this time the car had come to rest. She gazed with astonishment at the figure of Louise climbing out of the driver's seat.

She had thought Louise was still in Singapore, since they had heard nothing of her returning to England. Now Louise was coming to greet her, embracing her warmly and saying, 'I might have known you'd be out with the horse. It's such a lovely day.'

'Louise, what are you doing here? When did you get here? Isn't Martin with you?'

'No, he's still in Singapore, but he'll be here within these next few days. I came early so that I could pick David up from his school.'

'Will you be staying with us?'

'Perhaps tonight if that's possible. After that we're staying with Martin's mother.'

'But you'll be going back to Singapore?'

'Actually, no. Martin's been recalled. Apart from that we know nothing at all.'

'So how long will you be staying with Martin's mother?'

'Until we get a house sorted out. We'll have to

look around for something we both like. That's if Martin's staying here, but it rather looks that way.'

'I suppose it must be this wretched talk of war. There will be one, won't there, in spite of Hitler's promises.'

'Promises we can't rely on. Yes, I'm sure there will be one. Martin's sure of it too.'

'But you're glad to be home, Louise?'

'Oh yes. I loved Singapore, but I'm dying to see the boys, and however much we love being overseas, this is home, isn't it?'

'Yes. I'm not sure when Andrew'll be home, he's with his regiment somewhere, but he'll be pleased to see you.'

'Have you see anything of Mother? Does she ever visit?'

'She came with us to Sandhurst for Charlie's passing-out display, both she and her husband, but she seems quite happy in Scotland. She hardly ever comes to London. Do you hear from her?'

'A birthday card, and another at Christmas. She insisted that we didn't exchange presents, that she had everything she needed and so did I.'

'Wasn't that a little bit unsettling, dear?'

'Not really. I never really expected mother to be warm and close.'

'Did she ever understand about Martin? That you fell in love with him, that you married him?'

'Imogen, I don't know. All those years I believed I didn't like him, that we didn't like each other, then when I realized I loved him I never quite knew how my mother would take it. Maybe she loved Martin, even when she married somebody else, but if she did I can understand how his marriage to me would affect her.'

Imogen decided to say nothing further. Andrew had seen his mother's chagrin, her insistence that her daughter's marriage couldn't last, that it was all a terrible mistake, and then her unspoken bitterness when the children arrived and the marriage seemed happy and fulfilled.

That evening they spent chatting about old times, their schooldays, their marriages, and Louise said, 'I suppose Cora and Miranda keep in touch. I must let them know I'm back in London.'

'I don't see much of them, but yes, we do keep in touch.'

'And are they happy in those marriages that were planned for them?'

'If they are not, it's doubtful if we would ever know. I don't know Peter awfully well, he always seems such a remote sort of man, but the two girls are lovely. I'm not very sure about Cedric either.'

'I rather liked Cedric. Why are you unsure about him?'

'Well, there are rumours flying around that he's over-friendly with some woman called Sophie Beaumont. I've seen them together, but I don't really know her.'

'And does Miranda know, do you think?'

'If she does, she gives nothing away. I think so many times about the four girls we were then. Miranda and Cora knowing what they wanted, me just wanting to get home to the farm and my horse, while you ... what did you want really, Louise?'

Louise sat looking thoughtfully through the window where the sun was setting behind the hills in a warm rosy glow, and eventually she smiled, saying, 'I hadn't a clue what I wanted. I talked a lot of nonsense about the future. I had a lot of growing up to do.'

'And when were you grown up enough to want Martin?'

'My mother was eighteen when she married father and he was forty-three. I always thought he was too old for her, they were wrong for each other, but father was difficult, taciturn and seemingly old, while Martin was charming and, even when I thought I hated him, he made all the men I met seem infantile, too young. Then when I did really get to know him I fell in love with him.

'He found me work to do – helping in the constituency, working for some charity or other – anything to keep me occupied to show me that there were people in the world needing help, that there would be something in my life more useful than sitting around waiting for the next amusement.

'He actually introduced me to a very nice man who worked for the Party. He was intelligent, good-looking and extremely nice, he was also only a year older than me and he sort of fell for me.'

'And...?'

'I didn't fall for him. I fell for Martin, and I told him so.'

'And he said?'

'Oh, you know, the usual stricture. That he was nearly old enough to be my father, he was set in his ways, I must realize the whole situation was ridiculous, we should see less of one another, and I should concentrate on some man nearer my own age or risk alienating my family.'

'Your family?'

'Well, Mother, and it *has* certainly alienated her. We didn't see anything of each other for two years. I was unhappy, miserable, and so I went to stay with Helena. I didn't know anything about it but apparently there was a much publicized affair to be held in Brussels, where a great many countries including England would be represented, and suddenly she was advising me that we should spend a few days in Brussels. On our last evening we were invited by a Belgium friend of hers to the Opera House, where most of the visiting dignitaries were expecting to attend. The opera was *La Traviata*, and Martin was with some other people in the next box.

'We met during the interval, and again at the end, and then in somebody's home we were invited to. He was predictably intent on keeping me at arm's length, and we talked about trivialities. I learned that we were invited to yet another function that day and I said that by all means Helene should go, but since I had a headache and felt rather tired I would take a taxi and go to our hotel. Helene looked predictably uncertain, and poor Martin was unavoidably coerced into taking me himself.

'I hated that drive across Brussels. It was sheeting with rain, and Martin sat next to me like the proverbial icicle, unwilling to melt. Even when I came back to London and took up the old jobs again he kept me at arm's length. It seemed to me that after all those long years of growing up, only Martin meant anything to me.'

'And Martin realized it too, but when?'

'There was a charitable organization going out to South Africa to assist with so much poverty there and I put my name down to join it. I would have to stay on there for several years. I thought it was the only way to get him out of my system. He thought of a thousand and one reasons why I shouldn't go, but in the end the only real reason was that he loved me, that if I insisted on going then he would follow me out there.

'Even then, he didn't immediately ask me to marry him. He made love to me, we had the most wonderful, exciting love affair imaginable, and then I was pregnant and he *did* marry me.'

'So David wasn't really premature at all?'

'No, just wonderful. Perhaps people were not too surprised at the wedding. We'd been together a lot, and if they did think the age difference was a bit too much, we were so obviously in love, and if we'd wanted children it was good that we didn't waste much time. I tried not to think about Mother. David doesn't really know his grandmother, and he simply stares at her birthday card and puts it to one side.'

'Perhaps one day she'll want to see him, see you all.'

'I doubt it, Imogen. It doesn't matter. She's got Andrew.'

'You're her daughter, Louise. David's her grandson, just like my two boys.'

'Not quite, darling. Martin's his father, and we'll never know how much he really figured in Mother's life.'

'Andrew says he was her friend, a shoulder to cry on, a charming gallant escort when your father couldn't be bothered. Surely you, too, see it like that?'

'If that's all he was, why is she so resentful?'

'Can't you ask Martin? He's your husband.'

'It isn't a question I could ask or expect him to answer. If I did I would see the shutters come down, and a sort of anger that I should feel the need to ask such a question.'

'So you're really happy?'

'Yes, I really am. He's warm and funny, and I feel I'm living in an adult world with a mature man who loves me. I've grown up, Imogen. Can you really remember what we were like, those four girls frolicking together on that last day in school in 1914? You were the nicest of the bunch. Cora and Miranda were away with the fairies, and I was silly and immature, pretending